BLOOD SINGERS

A BLOOD WORLD NOVEL

BLOOD
BOOK ONE

TAMARA ROSE BLODGETT

The girls that keep me Sane on Shelfari (and otherwise): Beth and Dianne I love you guys~

BLOOD THOUGHTS

*Once they had eliminated the impossible, whatever remained,
however improbable, must be the truth.*

~Sherlock Holmes

PROLOGUE

*J*ulia pressed her nose to the glass, the trees a sea of green as they rushed outside her window, her momma and daddy's voices a low and pleasant drone from the front seat.

She hated the belt, it pressed across her neck in an uncomfortable place, itchy and suffocating.

"Momma," Julia whined plaintively.

Her mother's chocolate eyes appeared over the front seat, such a contrast to the auburn hair held in her customary pony tail.

"What is it?"

Julia worked her small finger under the belt and said, "I hate, HATE this stupid strap! I want to take it off!" Julia crossed her arms, huffing.

Momma sighed, unlatching her belt as she turned in the front seat to adjust the neck restraint portion of Julia's seatbelt. As Momma got nearer Julia smelled the special perfume that she wore. At once Momma's scent assaulted her where it intimately combined with the perfume she always wore.

Daddy said from the front, "Amber, sit back down. The belt's latched, she's just going to have to deal with it for another ten minutes."

Julia's eyes narrowed to slits. Daddy was so stubborn. *His* belt didn't bite into *his* neck! 'Cuz he was a Big Man! Ugh... Julia fumed.

Momma smiled and began to turn and Julia saw Daddy's face in profile, watching to make sure she sat down safely.

He only took his eyes off the road for a moment.

It was enough.

Julia saw twin beads of light bear down on their car as an impossibly large grill came to eat them, the chrome winking in the late afternoon light.

Daddy made a correction to the right but that threw Momma on top of him, imprisoning their bodies in a macabre dance, the steering wheel sandwiching them together.

As if in slow motion Julia saw her mother's face as Amber looked at her father.

The knowledge of their impending death appeared on their faces like an unspoken promise.

Julia screamed as the truck slammed into the car and the belt that she hated so much whipped against her neck and slammed her against the back seat with such force that the breath left her small body.

She watched her parents crushed together in a final embrace.

The metal colliding was an earthquake in her ears and something wet and warm hit her face. She opened her eyes and her parents were... everywhere, their blood like a blanket that coated her face and hair.

Her brain howled, refusing to accept what was happening. Her vision clouded. Her neck and head throbbed and her lungs were a burning inferno with the need to scream.

The last thing she remembered was her mother's hair entwined in the steering wheel like so much spun copper.

CHAPTER 1

TEN YEARS LATER

*J*ulia stuffed her wool cap down more firmly on her head and waded through the icy puddles on the way to her 1977 Chevy Blazer. Fall had edged into early winter and the dampness of the rain had solidified into a dangerous sheet of ice.

Julia had known better and instead of wearing the latest Ugg fashion boots she'd slogged on her XtraTufs. They had an unparalleled ugliness but did the job. She might keep her ass in the air instead of pegged on an ice puddle by wearing her trusty boots. She threw her backpack over one shoulder and balanced a steaming cup of coffee in the other hand. She'd lied through her teeth about the contents to Aunt Lily, who seemed to think caffeine was the devil's drink. Julia smiled at that. She thought she was done growing and besides, coffee was a mainstay of Alaskan existence. She shuffled to the driver's side and gripped the handle. Then her feet lost some of their purchase and she slid to the right, her coffee sloshing out of the slit on the travel mug.

"Shit!" Julia said, as a couple of hot drops landed on her wrist, scalding her.

Grappling with the handle she jerked the door open and threw her palm on the driver's seat, steadying herself until she could heave her backpack inside.

But her breath stilled in her lungs when she saw what waited for her.

A single rose, its tremulous form in a beautiful, ethereal tangerine color lay inches from where her reddened and chapped hand had slapped down.

She'd almost destroyed it while saving her sliding butt from falling.

A smile stole over her face and she carefully put her travel mug in the cup holder between the seats and picked up the flower.

No note.

But she knew who had laid it there.

Her fiancé, Jason. Actually, it was a secret. Lily would have ten different kinds of cows if she knew how serious they were.

She looked around, her breath coming in white puffs in the crisp air. The snow having not committed itself to falling yet, the promise still hung there in the air. It would be like him, Julia thought, to pop up and grab her from behind, twirling her around just as she discovered his present.

But he wasn't there.

Huh, she turned the keys and jacked up the heat all the way. Five minutes and she'd hit the road, head to Homer High. She was spoiled. Usually Jason picked her up but today she had to head over to the DMV and get a stupid emissions test. It was amazing they even allowed her to drive her gas-guzzling truck. She sighed. Soon, she'd be with Jason.

school

JULIA TORE off her multi-colored itchy hat as she waltzed into the school. The familiar smell of kids, books, lunch and all the other school fragrances wafting across the air, the chill of late fall left outside the doors.

She fluffed her champagne-colored hair, hoping to eradicate the hat head she'd tagged herself with on the way over.

"Hey, bestie!" Cynthia cried.

Julia laughed, like she hadn't just spent all day and a night last weekend with Cyn? She acted like they'd been separated for months.

"Hey Cyn," Julia said slowing, letting her catch up.

As usual, Cyn was dressed to the nines. High heels, ridiculously tight-ass pants and the latest, off-the-shoulder top with a crazy zebra pattern. It made Julia dizzy looking at it.

"What?" Cynthia looked at Julia's face.

"Your top, it's like some kind of optical illusion or something."

"I know, right? It's hot-hot-hot," she snapped her fingers after each word for emphasis. Julia rolled her eyes, there was no cure for her Fashion Awareness.

Julia considered herself Fashion Challenged. Yessiree. Irrefutably. Getting everything to match and be comfortable was of utmost importance.

Of course, once Julia mentioned Cyn's shirt, then she was honor bound to give Julia the once-over. Scanned from the top of her head she had almost escaped the wrath when Cynthia's gaze landed like a lead weight on her boots.

"Argh!" she shrieked in horror. "You wore your Tufs to school again! And don't give me any of that horse shit about how we're seniors and absolved of everything," she rolled her eyes dramatically, "fashion is the exception. And those," she waggled her fingers at Julia's offending footwear, "are for...for..."

"Gardening only," Jason interjected smoothly, his arm sliding around Julia's waist. He'd heard the XtraTufs speech before.

"Don't you defend her either!" Cynthia lambasted him and Jason, all mock innocence said, "Who me?" his hand to his chest.

Cynthia's eyes narrowed to slits. "You're no help, Jason Caldwell, she could wear a shapeless sack over her whole body and you'd still think she was gorgeous."

"Guilty," he said, his forehead dipping to peck Julia's head, still fuzzy from the hat.

Julia leaned back against his chest, her head tucking comfortably underneath his chin and sighed. This is where she'd wanted to be from the moment she opened her eyes. Against him, soaking up his warmth. Letting it seep into her bones and chase the coldness of the morning away.

Cyn snapped her fingers in front of Julia's face, "snap out of it Jules!"

Jason laughed, Julia was known to mentally wander. It was becoming an annoying theme lately.

"What? Cranky witch!" Julia teased, taking a swipe at Cyn with her woolen hat.

She ducked smoothly, accustomed to Julia's abuse. "Okay... so, did you get that English paper done we started on Friday?"

Julia dug around in her backpack until she found a crumpled piece of paper at the bottom and turning, she slapped it against her locker, smoothing it with her other hand. Jason's big hand was a warm presence on her shoulder, kneading it softly.

"Are you kidding? Terrell will never accept that mess," Cynthia said, throwing out one hip and putting a hand on the jutting point.

Julia shrugged a shoulder. "It's a rough draft. Besides,

keeping the standard low like I do assures me gravy when I turn something in."

Julia smiled at her awesome logic. School just didn't appeal. It was something she survived until she could graduate. It was Jason that was going to University of Alaska Anchorage. He was set with a full ride.

Mr. Basketball. Julia turned to look at him and wondered for the millionth time why he'd want her. He was so gorgeous and she was so... her. It didn't matter that Cyn thought she was pretty. Whatever. Cyn was her BFF, that's what they do, cheerlead.

Julia still didn't have A Plan. She knew she couldn't wait to get out of Aunt Lily's place and begin a life with Jason.

Cynthia gave an elaborate roll of her eyes and caved, saying, "You can try all your down home weasel-like charm on Terrell while Jason and I turn in real papers. Unwrinkled papers." She cocked her brows up to her hairline and looping her arm through Julia's, she dragged her to block one.

The Dreaded Language Arts. Everyone knew there was nothing artful about it. Jason laughed as they trudged to class, Julia's arms linked with theirs.

CHAPTER 2

AFTER JASON

*J*ulia's chin touched her chest, lank strands of hair swirling around, her arms jerked up and chained above her head. Her hands had lost feeling hours ago. A cloak of numbness stole over her body and her mind screamed, her body aching for food.

But she'd be damned if she'd take it from her captors.

The Murderers.

The creature came to her, his teeth gleaming in the low light of where they kept her.

She looked at him, her eyelids at half-mast, as piercing silvery irises bored into her gaze. Julia felt the weight of their desire fill her mind, pressing without mercy against the fragility that was there.

Forcing his will.

"You must eat, Julia. You will eat," he said in a fierce whisper.

"Why don't you... Go. To. Hell!" she rasped, as loud as she could. Weakened by lack of food, her voice held all the emotion that she couldn't scream, buried in the air grown pregnant with contained frustration and violence.

Violence against her.

"Let me convince her," the one named Pierce said, his stare covering her body like decaying liquid.

The leader, William, turned and stood in one fluid movement. "I have seen your methods with other Blood Singers. We will not use that here, with this one."

Pierce smirked. "You grow attached. She is a vehicle for our needs, nothing more. She is human."

William took Pierce by the collar of the shirt he wore and dragged their faces together until they nearly met. "She is much more than that. What if she is The One? Look at the sign upon her head." He shook Pierce in disgust and pushed him away. Pierce reared back and opened his mouth and something burst from the flesh as he hissed his displeasure.

Fangs.

Julia swallowed. She felt like she was in a nightmare she couldn't escape from. She protected herself by dwelling in her memory bank. It was full. There, Julia felt rich. It was there that this new reality couldn't impede.

William and Pierce looked at her quickly. "She pulls away inside herself again! Fool! I almost had her!"

It was as if Julia could see through a glass, though darkly. Black water covered her vision and the horrible creatures that had torn her away from a future of love and contentment, to a new one of terror and uncertainty, rushed toward her and she let the water cover her consciousness. They were as dim orbs of pale flesh as they sprinted to her side.

She fell back in the well of her mind, the liquid forming a barrier between them and her memories.

For now, the memories won.

* * *

senior year, springtime

CYN BENT her head over the textbook and then looking up, scowled at Julia. "This is simple, you're over thinking the stuff."

Julia was beyond frustrated. She'd flunked lame-ass Algebra II when she was a junior and was on the eve of graduation, still struggling though the concepts. Cyn at her elbow, ramrodding it down her throat wasn't helping the learning curve.

Julia's brows jacked down over her whiskey-colored eyes. "I don't get it! They put the alphabet in math and now it's a big jumble of nothing!" she wailed.

"How in the righteous world did you pass One?"

Julia gave her a sheepish look.

"You're kidding me, right? You cribbed off of Jason?"

"Like when am I gonna use this worthless crap?!" Julia said, throwing her pencil down.

"You're not! That's not the point, Jules. The point is Getting The Grade. We're American, we're not supposed to be the intellectual global force. We just get the degree, then go on to college and get *that* degree," she shrugged her shoulders, *simple, right?*

Julia crossed her arms underneath her breasts. "You don't see what's wrong with that picture?"

"Doesn't matter what I think. I just work the system."

"Huh, we're nothing but a bunch of sheep, manipulating a broken system."

"Speaking of manipulating..." Cyn said, a contemplative expression crowding her features.

"Ah-no. I am not going to dress up," Julia said.

"Listen, we're almost done with this math cram..."

"It's a cram all right," Julia said.

"Anyway," Cyn said, drawing the word out dramatically, "this is your last final before graduation. Prom is coming. Let's get you hot and sexy for your man-toy."

Maybe Julia shouldn't have told Cyn about the secret engagement. But she told Jason if she didn't tell someone she'd burst. Now it was an endless barrage of teasing.

"Jason's not a 'toy', Cyn."

She scrunched her face. "Okay... ooh, touchy. Calm yourself."

Julia blew a stray hair away from her forehead. She had to give in to Cyn or she'd be after her ass until she chose a dress.

"Okay!" Julia threw up her hands. "I'll go."

"That's not good enough. Tell me what I need to hear. You could go and watch me pick out a dress and worm out of everything." She gave Julia steady green eyes.

Damn, she had her there.

"Okay, I'll try something on and choose a dress for prom. Happy?"

"Repeat after me: It will not be a sack," she said in her droll way.

Julia fumed. Did she really think she'd pick out some shapeless sheath?

"I do," she said.

"Hey! I didn't say anything..."

Cyn made a circling motion with her index finger alongside her head. "Saw your wheels turning."

Huh.

She repeated the sack thing and Cynthia smiled.

Onward and upward.

Jason

JASON POKED the stick into the fire, mercilessly stabbing the coals, trying to decide if he should put another piece of driftwood on or not. He looked at Jules, talking animatedly with

Cyn and Kev and smiled. The hell with it, he'd put on another chunk. She'd wander over here eventually and be colder than a brick of ice.

Couldn't have his girl cold. That was against guy-code. Keep your chick warm, fed and most of all, protected. He let his gaze linger on her. He couldn't believe she'd be his soon. They'd graduate, then get married. His parents would be steamin'-pissed but they'd get over it. It was always what *they* wanted anyway. He'd been the good boy. He'd done basketball until his body still felt like it was on the court when he laid down on his bed each night. He'd sucked up the grades, played his ass off and helped his girl limp through Math and Science. He smiled, thinking of how much Jules hated the Math-Science grind. He took her profile in, blonde hair that wanted to be red, that damned wool cap covering some of it. Her legs encased in jeans that dragged along the sand and her bright red puffy coat. It was her face above the collar of her jacket that Jason's eyes stroked with love.

Her face. He knew Julia was The One the moment she moved to Homer when she was almost nine. Sullen and alone, living with her aunt, she'd been new with no friends. He'd been a gangly and awkward nine. He'd started as her champion then and never looked back.

Now and forever.

As if sensing his thoughts, Julia turned to look straight at him and a smile broke, her amber eyes like glittering jewels in a face caressed by firelight. Her face asked a question and he gave a slight shake of his head, *it's nothing*, his look said. She turned away, the ghost of a smile still playing on her lips, then she burst into laughter at some dumb thing Kevin said.

He looked away from her and added two more chunks to the fire. It burned brightly and became hot.

* * *

Cyn

CYNTHIA WATCHED the two of them jammed together like sardines and smiled. She was happy for Julia and Jason. They'd been two peas in a pod since fourth grade and Jules'd had it tough, she deserved the happiness. They made a cool couple. Jason was six-foot two and towered over Jules at only five-four but she never seemed short. Cynthia had never met anyone more alive, more independent. It was amazing her Aunt Lily had picked up the torch after Jules' parents passed. Cynthia had to admit that Lily rankled her ass sometimes too. She was so strict on Jules, like she'd ever do anything? Hell, she was a secret prude. She hadn't even done the deed with Jason. Dating three years and nada.

There's willpower for ya!

She looked up through her mascaraed eyelashes at Kevin, her steady and at-hand date for prom and sighed. He was absolutely hot. She wasn't letting him get away. Cynthia had all the titillating details for Jules later. She'd act bored and then listen raptly while she dished on her love life. A slight frown bunched her eyebrows together. She'd have to ride Jules' ass about going to Soldotna and picking out a prom dress. She was insisting on Vegas for the wedding (she was sure to get out of getting a dress). Cynthia did a mental eye-roll. But Jules wasn't getting out of prom. Cynthia had tried to talk Jules out of marriage for shit's sake. I mean, what, she'd been eighteen for six months? What's the rush? Cynthia thought it had something to do with both her parents being killed when she was young. It had really scarred her. She wanted something to hang on to, something tangible and real.

Cynthia wasn't sure getting married at eighteen was the answer. But even she had to admit, she couldn't do wrong with Jason. He worshiped Julia. She looked at the two of them together as she snuggled in next to Kevin and watched Jason touch Jules, cupping her face like a fragile egg as they began to kiss.

"Looks like they've got the right idea, Cyn," Kevin said, waggling his eyebrows.

Cynthia gave him a mock punch. "You just want to get lucky!"

"There *is* that," Kevin replied, only half-joking.

"Ah-huh, that's what I was talking about."

He dipped his head and gave her a peck on the lips and she turned on the rough driftwood log where they were perched, the warmth of the fire beating against her back and drew him against her. His mouth found hers and they twined themselves against each other. The sky lingered above them as black velvet with stars sprinkled about.

* * *

dress-up

JULIA THOUGHT she'd slit her wrists if she had to try one more dress on. She paced the room in a huff. She should have never said yes. Cyn had her dress-napped the instant they came into the boutique. Remember, Fashion Aware. Of course, everything looked good on Cyn. With her tall, lanky frame, she could get away with anything. She'd chosen a shell pink, full length gauzy thing that made her look like a princess.

Or, a queen, judging by the way she was beating the hell out of Julia with her scepter.

"Come on Jules, I'm thinking one more?"

"NO! I promised I'd try on dresses. For you! Now look, what is this... number fifteen?"

Cyn had the grace to look ashamed, flashing both hands twice.

"Twenty!" Julia all but shrieked.

"Right. Well... you're totally hard to find something for! I mean, who has your coloring anyway?"

Julia huffed, her eyes taking in the pile of gowns growing in the corners like obscene shrouds. "Okay... one more. Then we pick *whatever* from the pile!" Julia said, her palm striking out at the material like it was alive.

"Okay. But if you're only gonna try on one more dress, it's going to be green."

Julia groaned. She hated green.

Cyn brought out her hands in supplication. "I know you hate green but just trust me, K?

* * *

Cyn

CYNTHIA INSISTED on she and Jules going together to prom so they could make their grand entrance and blow the dudes away. She'd also taken the initiative and ragged Julia's ass until she caved and let her do the make-up and hair for both of them. She wasn't letting her bestie into prom with anything resembling hippie chic. Julia was going to look put together and polished if it was the last thing Cynthia did.

Cynthia dug around in her huge purse until she found her makeup bag and dragged it out, throwing it on Julia's vanity with a resounding smack.

Julia eyed it warily. Pointing to it she asked, "what's all that crap in there?"

"Make-you-beautiful-stuff."

The corners of Julia's mouth turned up. "That's a technical term, right?"

"Hell yeah!" Cynthia enthused with a wink.

Julia sighed, she knew she'd look like a French whore by the time Cyn was done with her but she'd released the reins and Cyn was firmly in charge of Prom Fashion. She had an errant thought wondering about what Jason was up to. Definitely not this.

"Woman-up, Jules! I'm not taking a skin graft or something. Seriously, you act like you've never worn makeup before."

There was a significant silence.

"Okay, that was sorta lame. You, the makeup queen."

Julia slouched and Cyn poked her in the back. "Posture, princess."

Then she set to work. Foundation, powder, eyeliner... false eyelashes.

False eyelashes!

"No way! I am not putting that crap on my own eyelashes." Julia stared at Cynthia in a huff.

"How about just a few on the outer edge? It'll make your eyes look bigger."

"They're big enough," Julia thought, if they were any bigger she'd be a toad.

"They're ginger-colored! You can hardly see them," she wheedled.

Julia shook her head. "No. Just... put the brown mascara on and be done with it."

Cynthia sighed, defeated. She made it a point to spend a ton of time on each eye, finally swiveling Julia around in her chair to look at her reflection.

Julia stared.

And stared some more.

A slow smile spread on Cynthia's face. "See, Jules? You're a goddess, who was to know!"

Julia couldn't believe the transformation. The mossy

green of the dress set off her hair, making the red in it look like molten champagne. Her eyes sparkled like gold topaz, gems in a pale face with shimmering lips in a pouty apricot. She opened her mouth. Closed it. Opened it again.

"You can tell me now," she said, smug.

Julia turned from her reflection and scowled at Cyn.

Cynthia waited.

Well-hell. "You're the greatest."

Cynthia grinned. "I know, doll-face."

Julia rolled her eyes. What was Jason going to think of her in this get-up? With the make-up and…. everything? Julia rolled her glossed lip into her teeth and nibbled anxiously.

Jason waited impatiently for Julia to arrive. He knew he should have nixed the lame Plan of the Girls. Them going together! Retarded. He'd let Kevin convince him it was easier not to fight Cynthia.

"Listen man, just let them. I don't want to deal with Cyn when she gets a head-o-steam about girl shit, you feel me?" Kevin had said.

"What's so flaming-ass important that I can't pick Jules up?"

"I told ya, they're putting the masks and garb on."

"What?" Jason asked, confused. He was already feeling gay in a tux, the bow around his neck was a slowly encroaching noose. He tugged at it again.

"Hey! Don't dick with that, it screws up the gig."

"What's a gig?" Jason asked, messin' around with the stupid noose.

"It's… damn-man! Leave it alone!" Kevin said, slapping his hand away impatiently. He took either side of the corners of the bow tie and aligned them with Jason's Adam's apple.

There, Kevin thought. He wondered if his ass-hat friend could leave it alone for the next two hours.

Probably not.

19

"It's a military term... it means to keep all your accessories in line with the middle of your body," Kevin said in a matter-of-fact way.

"That's great, Kev. I'll sleep better knowing your ramrod dad gave you a few pointers."

"Hey jag-up, Dad served our country and has a few pearls of wisdom once in awhile."

"Along with some colorful vocabulary."

"No shit, right?" Kevin said, totally missing the irony.

Jason smiled and shook his head as they hopped into Kev's car.

They made their way to the last dance they'd ever attend.

* * *

Jason

KEVIN CAUGHT sight of Julia and elbowed Jason.

They looked at the girls as they entered the gymnasium where fake acrylic stars danced above their heads like wayward diamonds.

Jason couldn't take his eyes off of her. The breath left his body in one, exhaustive rush.

Jules was drop-dead gorgeous.

Jason knew that people said that all the time about chicks, sometimes dudes even. But Julia floated inside the auditorium on a cloud of emerald vapor, her dress the color of green kissed by autumn... and stunned him into silence.

Her hair looked almost red, its normal gold color boosted by the pine of the dress, her eyes a sparkling gold. They took up half her face.

He still couldn't look away.

She walked toward him slowly and he noticed the dress showcased how curvy she was. She wasn't a twig and she wasn't heavy. Jason took in a shaky breath, his eyes on her hourglass figure as she moved toward him.

He noticed all the other guys were staring at her too and frowned.

Julia reached him just as he put his hands out for her and his face smoothed.

He pulled her closer and leaned down until his jaw brushed her temple. "You're beautiful," he whispered against her fragrant skin.

Julia knew she looked beautiful.

She didn't need a mirror to tell her.

Jason's eyes told her.

They moved out to the dance floor, hands knotted together, gazes locked.

Julia waited in her bed with bated breath. Jason had dropped her off from prom and promised to sneak in her bedroom window later.

Much later.

Aunt Lily had the irritating habit of checking in on her.

Julia clutched her cell in one hand so she could text Jason the instant she did.

She laid on her side for, she swore, ten hours. Finally, Lily opened the door a crack and, seeing that Julia appeared asleep, closed it softly behind her.

Julia let a long breath out, texting Jason.

He must have been waiting outside her house like a good stalker-boyfriend and she let him in as he stumbled from outside the window.

"Damn! I won't miss that anymore. No more nut-cruncher windowsill for me!"

Julia cocked and eyebrow. "We wouldn't want your, ah, nuts crunched. No, that wouldn't do," Julia said in a low, teasing voice.

"Come here," Jason said, thinking about how he'd kiss that

smirk off her face. She was killing him. Standing there in her pajama bottoms and a cami. Her hair was still loose and curled from prom, the makeup still on.

"Aren't you supposed to take all that crap off your face?"

She scrunched her nose in that way he loved and said, "Nah, pillowcase will get rid of it."

"Really?" Jason asked, grinning. He walked over to her, admiring her in her post-prom glory.

"The dance turned out okay, Jules," he said softly, bending to kiss the hollow between those sexy bones that intersected her neck.

She nodded, a little breathless as his breath moved over her pulse. She wound her arms around his neck and his lips traveled up to her jaw then made its way to her forehead. He began peppering her face with butterfly kisses, his lashes grazing her skin above his lips. Her breathing became shallower and Jason picked her up and carried her to the bed.

They lay together, head to hip, the heat of their bodies one hot line. He moved against her, his hands on her ribs, kneading her flesh as she wound a leg around his hip, their mouths moving against each other.

His hands traveled and Julia pulled away.

"Jason," she whispered.

"What?" he said, never breaking from his sensual assault on her. She could hardly breathe, she just wanted... she wanted to finish what they started. But she wanted forever more.

She thought of her parents. Long gone. A thread that tied the fabric of her being together.

He paused and pulled back to look at her face, a sliver of moonlight a pale slash across her eyes.

He saw the expression there and pressed his forehead against hers.

"I know," he moaned.

"I'm sorry," Julia whispered. "It's not that I don't trust you."

"I know," he repeated against the skin of her forehead.

A lone tear escaped her eye and Jason caught it, staring into those eyes. Those eyes that he'd looked into for a decade.

"I want to be married. It's what my parents would have wanted," she said and Jason felt her tremble against him. He silently promised to make her first time extra special. It'd be perfect if it killed him.

"You still miss them," he asked as a statement, tightening his hold on her.

"Every day," she replied through eyes that had glossed with a sheen of tears.

He smiled. Jason wanted her so damn bad. It wasn't just sex, he could have tapped any mindless alley cat in the school.

She was his and he was hers. Jason knew Jules was the one he wanted from the moment he saw her.

He leaned down and kissed the crescent-shaped scar on her forehead, the only thing that marred her perfect skin.

He could wait. He could wait forever if it meant being with her.

They lay together in each other's arms until dawn shattered the darkness into a million pieces of golden orange, rose and scarlet, flinging the colors about the room like so much broken glass.

CHAPTER 3

PRESENT DAY

*L*iquid lapped Julia and the water parted, ice replacing the subtle undulation of comfort she'd been under.

She came to the surface of her consciousness in a nauseating wave. She became aware that she was drowning.

Drowning in hunger and weakness. She didn't have the strength to move. Loud voices assailed her. They floated around her, stabbing at her consciousness until she finally understood where she was.

If she'd had the strength, she would have wept.

The creatures that had stolen her life away were arguing about her again.

"I am phoning him. Gabriel must be made aware of what is happening here!"

Julia cracked open her eyes, wide and grainy, her mouth felt like the Sahara Desert. She was so thirsty her bones ached with it. How long had she been out?

"She is killing herself," the one named William said. His fists were clenched and anxiety tightened his already stark features.

"Call him. Ask him what we must do. If she is as important as you hypothesize, it is necessary, no?" Pierce queried reasonably.

She lay perfectly still but they heard a change in her breathing and turned their silvered eyes to her.

She had just enough energy to lift her forearm and cover her eyes. She would not look at them.

"Just kill me," she said listlessly. Without Jason, why go on? She couldn't bear to think of all of it right now. The shards of that nightmare would not be a memory she would look at any time soon.

If ever.

She didn't hear them approach but an icy hand clamped around her forearm gently and moved it off of eyes that ran with tears. Julia was surprised she had enough tears to shed. Her mind was so beleaguered with grief she could hardly breathe. Why didn't they just kill her now?

After all, that's what they were good at.

Killing.

William tapped his cell to hibernate and pocketed it inside the jacket he wore. He breathed out in an elaborate exhale. They took a chance implementing this protocol. If they did not follow it to the letter, they would lose her.

This girl. The Blood Singer from the Book of Blood.

The Rare One.

He gave Pierce a full look as they walked together toward the girl.

Julia watched them come, one dark and one light. Angels. They looked like angels.

Angels of death.

Her arms long ago released, she lay there, unable to move a muscle. Only her eyes rolled in their sockets, tracking their approach.

William crouched down, feeling the hollow on the underside of her wrist, where a thready pulse beat. "She is close, it is a near thing."

Pierce nodded. "It must be you. You are the one with Singer heritage coursing through your veins. Maybe you can bring her back."

William had hoped that she would come around these past months. But they could tarry here no longer. The Were drew near, circling like sharks in water saturated by blood. This coven grew restless with her presence, Blood Singers were a stick to stir the cauldron of trouble. He had already waited too long. She was weak, compromised.

Julia looked up at him with eyes of liquid gold and he breathed through his mouth, hoping the scent of her would not impede what he must do.

It was a risk he must accept.

Julia saw William look at her intently and kept her eyes open with effort. Something was building, it thrummed deep in her bones like a call. Julia whimpered. She hated to be weak but knew what they were capable of. She watched as his eyes drank in the sight of her. Then his fangs elongated, escaping his mouth. She opened her own to scream and nothing came out.

His eyes tightened at her expression as he tore into the flesh of his own wrist. Black blood began oozing out of his damaged forearm and flowed down, dripping onto her neck. The droplets splattered like hot candle wax on her skin.

"Drink," William said, lowering his wrist down to her mouth.

She shook her head, with her ebbing strength she clamped her lips together.

William's eyes flicked behind her and he grunted, frustrated.

"Hold her," he said with a voice filled with regret.

Large hands clamped onto either side of her head and she was helpless to move in the jaws of their hold.

Just helpless, Julia seethed with frustration.

The poison of his body poured into her mouth in a steady stream and she fought, trying to move her head, but steel bands of flesh held her in position.

He pressed his forearm onto her mouth and with his other hand he pinched her nostrils together and she sucked the blood down into her throat as she began to clench her teeth around his arm.

He didn't react like she thought he would. He dragged her against himself, Pierce releasing her in surprise. Her mouth on his arm, clamping down. Julia bit down with everything she had.

His eyes dilated, the silver disappearing to be replaced by deep crimson. He pressed her against him, his fangs completely extended.

"William! Control yourself!" Pierce yelled, coming for him.

Julia hung on for dear life as she watched those black eyes look at her with such longing and loneliness. As he reared to strike a fist crashed into the side of his temple.

Her mouth was torn off his forearm, her body sliding off his lap onto the floor.

Julia lay in a small heap on her side as a fire burnt inside her. It became a delicious roar within. She was being consumed by heat. It burned and itched. She melted into the intense warmth, her consciousness narrowing.

As her mind dimmed, she saw the other creature check on William, his black eyes shut.

The creature named Pierce looked in her direction and he was sideways.

Julia knew what else he was.

Vampire.

She fell into a deep abyss of grayness, her mind shielding her from what she couldn't handle.

She floated swiftly down her memory pipeline, grateful for the escape it gave her.

* * *

last day

JASON HAD his fingers entwined in Julia's, their last day of school finally here, his plane tickets bought for Vegas. They were gonna do it. She looked up at him and smiled. He looked into the light gold depths and almost stumbled. She always had that affect on him. He'd been drawn to her from the beginning. A small furrow stood between her brows. Julia's hand came to her temple, rubbing.

He pulled her over to the side of the hall, the sea of bodies and backpacks jostling past, an excited buzz thrumming in the halls. He slid his palm underneath her honey-colored hair and wrapped the back of it on her neck, gently kneading the soft skin.

"Is it the headaches again?" he asked. Jules had been having these bone crusher headaches. Jason thought it was the stress at home, trying to plan a secret elopement could take its toll on a girl. He smirked.

"Huh, you really care!" she said, giving him a mock-scowl, putting her hands on her hips.

Her luscious hips, he thought.

"No!" Ah... I was just thinking all your super secret spy moves you're pullin' around Lily are getting kinda old?" He cocked an eyebrow.

She nodded, true... but. "Actually," Julia looked down at her hands that had found their way to Jason's hips and she couldn't look away, a blush came over her face.

Jason put a gentle finger under her chin and raised it until their eyes met. Chocolate meeting gold. "What is it?"

She shoved her erotic impulses away and concentrated on his question instead, the blush still staining her cheeks.

Jason saw the high color marking her cheekbones a delicate pink and wondered what she'd been thinking about. He opened his mouth to repeat the question and she interrupted, "It's the dreams, I'm having them again."

"Oh," Jason said, pulling her in against his body. He hadn't liked the dreams. He wasn't going to tell her, but he'd begun having some of his own. And they were goddamn doozies.

"Get a room!" Kevin yelled, walking by, arm slung around Cynthia. Jason gave Kevin the finger and Julia grabbed it in the air.

"Don't," she hissed, giving him another scowl.

Jason threw up the other hand and flipped him another bird.

"You're impossible!" Julia said sternly. Then she smiled.

She began laughing and convulsed into a stream of irrepressible giggles.

"That's so helpful, Jules. You're so *on it.*"

Julia looked at Jason and he was standing there, in full view of the world, giving Kevin the double-finger send off.

Oh my god, Julia clutched her sides, howling.

Julia was bent over until she noticed a pair of hot pink boots come into her line of sight.

She grabbed Cyn's sweater and hauled herself up.

"Hey asswipe, you're not sensing any adults around?" Kevin asked.

Jason dropped his hands as one of their teachers made his way toward them in a huff of righteous Adult Indignation.

Terrell.

Great. Instead of calming down, it had the opposite effect and Julia continued laughing, tears streaming down her face.

Terrell lurched up to the group. Taking a look at the Wade girl, doubled over in fits of hysterical giggling, he dismissed her. It was the basketball boys that he had his attention trained on. He didn't care if the Caldwell boy had got an A in his class, there was something fishy about them. Especially that never-apply-herself-girlfriend of his.

He got right up in Caldwell's grill, momentarily nonplussed that the kid had him by four inches. "Listen here, Caldwell. I don't give a good lick about how great you think you are, or that it's your last day here, this isn't the court. You don't own the school, the halls, nothing. Act like an adult and maybe, just maybe, you'll become one someday."

Terrell had sobered Julia up and she didn't like how Terrell was talking to Jason. Big surprise, she didn't like Terrell that much. She and Cyn had their arms crossed and Kevin stood looming over Terrell.

He didn't seem intimidated and Julia suddenly remembered a term that Lily used, "little man's syndrome." *Maybe he had a dose of that*, she thought.

"We clear?" Terrell asked. But he wasn't really asking. He was commanding. He wanted a certain kind of response.

Please don't get nailed on the last day, Julia thought, seeing Jason's fists clench and loosen. She watched him notch down his anger at Terrell and her shoulders relaxed. Looked like things were gonna settle down.

Then Terrell looked at her. Really looked at her, starting at her head and ending at her feet, sweeping over her private parts with a lingering look.

Gross!

"Hey perv!" Cyn squeaked. "Why don't you go die somewhere?"

But it was Jason that knotted his fist in the teacher's collar and dragged him close. "Don't you look at her," he said in a low voice, violence swirling beneath the surface.

Kevin was prying his fingers off of Terrell. "Don't... he deserves it but don't. He's pushin' ya."

Their eyes met and Jason released Terrell, pulling Julia behind him protectively.

He looked smug. "I knew you'd mess up. This is all I needed to get you where I want you."

Jason was confused, he'd seen the perv look at Julia and some of the other girls but what did it have to do with today? Why had he been so overt with Julia? His eyes narrowed on the teacher.

Jason planted his legs apart, hands on his hips, looking around once to make sure Julia was behind him and safe. This guy had lost it.

Kevin hit him in the arm and Jason's face whipped back to Terrell as Cyn gasped. Jason became focused on the gun that was naked in Terrell's hand.

What-the-hell was this? Jason thought, backing away, Julia a warm presence at his back.

Julia wasn't laughing now as kids in the hall, who had just been thinking how much trouble Jason was going to be in, scattered like beetles out of a jar, screaming as they ran down the hall.

Julia's headache slammed into her uncontrollably, spearing into her temple at a fever pitch. But it was the frenzied gaze of the teacher that she couldn't look away from. His beady hazel eyes shifted between the three kids, seeking.

Finally, he caught a glimpse of Julia behind Jason and said, "It's you. If you were not here, then I could... stop having this pain. The pain would stop.." he said, brandishing his gun in the air, kids slamming themselves on the hallway floor.

Julia felt something integral slip into place, the pain slipping away and becoming a burning mass.

"Hey whack-job!" Kevin said, going for the gun at the same time that Jason did. It wasn't choreographed and as their bodies moved, a gap opened and Terrell pointed the barrel.

At Julia.

All that focus, a warm liquid pain that she buried for the moment came to her in a sliding push. With nothing but raw emotion, she looked at the black hole of the gun and mentally shoved as the hammer pulled back.

It clicked.

Time slowed down, Jason batting the gun away even as the bullet rushed toward Julia, Cyn screaming in the background and Kevin landing on Terrell, their bodies crashing to the floor.

Julia moved as the bullet entered the curtain of her hair instead of the fragile bones of her face, its course veering at the last moment and she fell sideways away from the trajectory. Hitting Cyn, they both stumbled into the lockers.

"Julia!" Jason hollered, sprinting to her side, kicking the gun away as he came. His eyes frantically took in her body, checking for damage.

She was unscathed.

Miraculously.

As sirens wailed in the background Jason turned around, leaving Julia in Cyn's arms and grabbed a fistful of hair on the top of Terrell's head. Using it like the dull side of a hammer he picked his head up and slammed it into the floor.

Again and again.

Cops came and pulled him off but the damage was done. Terrell lay in a pool of his own blood, spreading into the soles of all who had gathered.

CHAPTER 4

"*J*ulia," a voice whispered to her as if through a tunnel. She came awake in stages, still feeling like she was in the school hallway, watching Jason beat Terrell's head into the floor until it split open like an egg.

She opened an eye and looked into silvered ones, reflective.

Julia flinched.

Her captors.

The vampires.

Once a myth, now she believed through hard evidence and even harder experience.

Even as his eyes clenched from her reaction his expression showed cautious relief and he stroked a wisp of hair away from her temple.

Julia found her voice, "Don't touch me."

His hand paused, then finished the movement. He stood and Julia looked around, taking in the room for the first time. She'd never allowed herself to care about her surroundings. The one named Pierce loomed into view and she shrank back.

"We will not harm you," he began.

"Right... you guys are so *harmless*," Julia said in a voice husky with disuse.

William and Pierce looked at each other. Finally, William said, "We did... *I did* what I had to. To pull you out of your dreamscapes. If I had not done that," he shrugged impossibly broad shoulders, "you would have buried your psyche there forever, until there was no feeding you, hydrating you..."

"Until you ceased to exist," Pierce finished for him.

Julia tried to sit up and succeeded, barely. She felt better, actually. Who were they to play God anyway? Maybe she didn't want to exist? Had they thought about that?

They watched her warily. She swung her legs off the bed she'd been lying on. She tentatively put her feet on the rough wooden surface and stood. The blood rushed to her head and her vision swam in streamers of dull colors before her eyes.

She commanded her legs to hold her even as they folded.

A blur of gray reached her and she was swooped up in the arms of the hateful vampire, William.

"You're too weak to walk," he said in a voice that reverberated through her breastbone, melodic and low. It affected her. She didn't know why but his nearness frightened her and she saw the reflection of it etched on his face. It pained him... that she was afraid.

"Let me down," she whispered.

"Pierce, get Susan again."

In her periphery she saw a blur of color and heard a far off door open then shut.

They stared at each other, the Blood Singer and the vampire.

"Why am I here?" Julia asked, resisting the deep pull that

emanated from her body to his. She didn't know what it was but it was organic.

Needy.

She felt liquid fingers sink into her, through her skin, deep in her marrow, clinging to her consciousness like cobwebs.

She closed her eyes and breathed deeply. When she opened them, William gave her his steady regard. "You are safe within this coven."

"I am not safe with you. I will never be safe again."

William flinched. Knowing that she could not separate their acquisition of her with the violence that had surrounded it. She was lumping the groups together, the Were and Vampire. Now was not the time to correct her misapprehension. Not when the Were's rancid breath was upon their doorstep. When the whole coven was on the chasm of blood lust from her months here. The fragrance of her rarity permeated every nook and cranny that the haven provided. Even the most immune amongst them, of Blood Singer descent themselves, were itching with need. The time was ripe to make haste to his home kiss. The coven where he had always been.

Just thinking of the city and what lay underneath it made his sluggish heart beat faster, primal adrenaline surging through his limbs.

Julia responded to his physicality, taking a sharp inhale, her body tingling in reaction to his thoughts.

"It's the blood share... it will pass," he said, intuiting her body's response.

"Put me down," she repeated.

William gently put her on her feet, his hand gripping her bony elbow, which had become like a twig since they had taken her.

Julia longed to tear it away from him but knew that she

35

could hardly stand. She fumed where she stood; trying not to think about the blood she'd drunk from her husband's murderers.

The memory encroached on her mind ruthlessly and she shut it down like all the others she didn't want to see. Biting the inside of her cheek. Blood welled inside her mouth like sour copper and she made a slight noise. William looked at her sharply, sucking in his breath and began to breathe through his mouth.

Julia smiled genuinely for the first time since her ordeal began as a terrible idea took shape in her mind.

She knew how to escape.

Just as she would press her advantage a large woman burst through the door and Julia's heart skipped a beat, racing inside her rib cage. She swayed and William pulled her gently against him.

She didn't resist, there was no use. But she would soon permanently resist.

Oh, so permanently.

* * *

caregiver

SUSAN LOOKED at the Blood Singer that the runners had acquired some months past and it was the first time that the girl hadn't been half-unconscious. Countless bowls of soup, water poured down her throat, sponge baths and dressings she'd shared with the girl.

But she looked at Susan as a stranger. For she was. The trauma surrounding the acquisition had been so over-whelming the girl had yet to recover. When she was finally dying, William had been beside himself to save her and been given the green light.

Blood share.

He had done it, even with the potential for scrambling the wires of his quarry, he had done it.

Now she stood, now she looked as if she might survive.

Even Susan could see beneath the dishevelment and scrawny physique to the healthy girl she had been. She would be well again, Susan vowed.

She had to be.

Julia was the Rare One. Susan's eyes flicked to the pale, moon-shaped scar on the girl's head.

Susan approached her and took her gently from William's arms, his hands trailing reluctantly from her body. Susan glanced at William, the feral vestiges about him still.

"You'd do well to leave us for a time," she said significantly and William nodded. Heaven knew he was having to stretch his limits with her fresh blood a darkly blooming fragrance in the room, suffocating his reasoning.

His directives.

William walked away, the pull of his blood in Julia's body beating in time with his heart. It felt like warm taffy as he moved through the door, swimming upstream. His hand landed on the doorknob.

Julia watched the vampire turn the knob, stiffen and quickly slip through.

Susan breathed a sigh of relief when the vampire left. Julia tried to pull away but Susan gripped her upper arm, her fingers encircling the whole of it.

Julia glared at her. "Take your hands off me."

Susan smiled. "Listen to me," she began, her eyes boring into Julia's. "I am not like them. But you know that, don't you?"

Julia didn't answer. She was not going to cooperate with any of this.

"I am human..."

"Yeah, whatever. You work for them. That's all the info I need."

"Who do you think got soup down your throat? Bathed you? Put clothes on you?"

Julia looked at her in horror. She touched her when she was unconscious. Julia studied her closely. There was something... almost familiar about her.

Memories assaulted her in a torrent. Being in a tub and floating. This woman washing her... ugh. Julia thought of the intimacy all that entailed and wanted to throw up. She remembered the food that she'd been spoon fed woodenly. She'd wanted to die.

She still did.

Susan looked at her, watching the emotions and thought processes flood her face, filling it with recognition and understanding.

She nodded. "You remember."

"Yes," Julia replied through clenched teeth.

"Not a very grateful sort, are you?"

Julia tore her thin arm free, her legs trembling. "I didn't ask for anyone to care for me," she said in a fierce voice, the first, hot tears falling. "You should have let me die. That's all I want. I want to die."

Susan was moved with compassion. This waif with such bottled up emotion and aggression had lost too much. They would have to start from nothing with her.

Ground zero.

Susan crossed her arms and stared at Julia, who glared back, raising a hand to move her tangled hair behind her ear.

"Well, my dear, you're not going to die. On the contrary, my job is to get you living and healthy for transport."

Despite her commitment to be contrary, Julia heard herself ask, "Transport... where?" her lip quivered, on the brink of crying harder.

"Seattle. You were acquired by that coven."

Julia's vision wavered, tripling. She began to fall and Susan screamed, "William!"

Suddenly she was held in arms of warm steel. Julia's heart slowed and her body calmed, her body's chemistry lulled by his closeness. Just before she crossed the threshold into unconsciousness her mind told her what she feared most.

Blood share, her body a traitor to her mind.

Somehow, she was connected to her captor. Whether she wanted to be or not.

Julia faded, the tailspin of knowledge following her down into the spiral of her dreams of before.

CHAPTER 5

CONSEQUENCE

Truman looked from one to the other of them and sighed. "Listen kids..." he ripped a hand through his already disheveled hair. "I believe you tried to do the right thing, but Caldwell..." he spread his palms away from his body.

Jason dropped his eyes, his hands gripped in Julia's. He hadn't meant to kill Terrell. But... when he saw him shoot at Julia, something profound and primitive had kicked in. All he could think of was eliminating the threat.

Eliminating Terrell.

So he did. Terrell was gonna kill her. A red veil had descended, clouding his vision, clouding his mind. It hadn't lifted until the cops had pulled him off Terrell.

Four of them.

At least they'd let him wash off. Wash Terrell off him. He'd had blood splatter and gore wrist-deep. His stomach churned a little with the memory.

Now he and Julia were in the police station, making noise about self-defense. The cop might look like a rumpled dishrag but his eyes were sharp, sharp like the bald eagles that flew outside the windows. Those eyes tracked him like the majestic bird, equal parts wise and aware, missing nothing.

"You're of age, son. It doesn't matter that you were still technically a student. We know you're over eighteen. Hell... you're almost nineteen, aren't ya?" When Jason nodded, he continued, "So is your girl here." His gaze went to Julia and Jason tensed. The cop took that in, wondering about the extreme protectiveness of the kid, it struck him as noteworthy. If he could be called a kid. He looked like a man to Truman, all height and muscle mass. A jock.

The girl was the opposite. She had a sullen and fiery cast to her but she was a tiny thing, different coloring, all champagne and... those eyes, he thought, repressing a shudder. They were like a cat's, spun gold. They followed him with an intensity that was unsettling. He cleared his throat. "As you know, the teacher was the one that brandished and fired a weapon. You may be able to get off with counseling. But, your reaction wasn't typical and there will be some accountability for that."

Jason nodded and Julia stifled a sigh. She'd never get the image of their teacher's brains on the floor out of her mind. The bigger question would always be: why? Why did he try to shoot her?

As if reading her mind, Detective Truman asked, "Is there some reason Terrell would commit violence against you, Julia?"

Her face showed her confusion, Truman thought. She didn't know either. He'd do some digging and see what was what. Try to make sense of the senseless.

His eyes flicked to Jason. "Your parents have made your bail. And," he waggled a finger, "I wouldn't skip town, pal."

Jason almost laughed. Like he'd leave Julia.

Ever.

He squeezed her hand and she squeezed back. He stood to leave, pulling her with him.

His last thought as he left the building was that their elopement plans were screwed. With a grim face, he pulled Julia behind him, his parent's car parked in front of the broad concrete steps of the precinct.

The storm on his dad's face told him what the next few days would be like. The barometric pressure was dropping as it moved in.

* * *

Jason

IT WAS a tense drive on the way to Julia's house, his parents were glancing back at them in the rear view mirror surreptitiously. He wanted to comfort Julia more than he wanted to worry about a lecture from them. Forget that he'd almost been killed himself, that he'd protected Julia... maybe more kids. It was all about image. And he had tarnished theirs. He was so pissed he could spit. It'd be so great once he and Julia were safely in Anchorage, married and beginning their life together. His parents could piss up a rope. He'd accomplished everything they wanted, they needed to get off his dick about it.

Julia interrupted his thoughts with a small noise and he looked down at her, a small bundle in the cradle of his arms. He was instantly alarmed.

Delayed shock.

Great timing, they were just pulling up to her front door, her Aunt Lily waiting on the top step, wrapping a thin cardigan around herself, her hands fisting the material in a death-clench. She skipped down the stairs, making a war path for their car.

Before Jason could properly shield Julia, Lily had torn open the door, putting her hands on Julia.

"Don't, Lily," Jason said, meeting her tense and angry eyes.

"You don't tell me what to do. I almost lost my niece today. The one that you were taking care of." She said that last like an accusation and it made Jason's heart clench in his chest. He *had* taken care of her. The best he could. He didn't need this right now.

Julia didn't need it.

He looked down at Julia, her skin clammy and pale, her breathing rapid.

"What's wrong with her?" Lily asked in a panic.

"She's in shock," Harold Caldwell said.

Jason sighed. "Please move, I'll carry her into the house and get her in a supine position."

Thankfully, she backed away and Jason unfolded his body outside the car, swiveling Julia as he went, swinging her up into his arms.

"Jason," she said, her eyes fluttering open. They widened and she said, "They're coming... the wolves and... the blood... blood..."

"What is she saying?" Shelia Caldwell asked.

Jason shook his head, puzzled. "I don't think it's anything. She's in shock, getting her lying down is key here, Mom." Jason's eyes left the loose group of adults and he strode to the house, toeing open the unlatched front door. He pegged the first sofa he saw and brought a still and pale Julia to it, laying her down gently. He swiped a hair from her forehead and kissed it. She felt cool. He wasn't leaving until she was okay. *She was far from okay*, he thought as he looked at her.

"Stay away from here, Jason," Lily yelled, huffing into the room.

"I don't think this is helping things..." Shelia said, her hands fluttering helplessly in front of her.

43

Lily gave her a withering look of such contempt that Shelia took a step back. "Don't tell me what is helpful or what is not. What would you even know about suffering... challenges, anything? Eh?" Seeing Shelia's helpless expression she said, "That's what I thought. Go home to your fancy house and your comforts and leave me and my niece alone."

Harold Caldwell looked down his nose at Lily Wade. She was beneath him. He had suffered the relationship between Julia and Jason, knowing it was a high school sweetheart thing. Jason would see that she was all wrong for him and dump her when he was attending college. This incident might prove to be the perfect break for the relationship.

It put Harold in good spirits. Magnanimous spirits.

"We understand, Lily. Of course we'll leave you here to comfort Julia." He smiled the first genuine smile of the day since hearing the wretched and humiliating news of his son's involvement in the shooting. He began to back out of the house when he caught sight of Jason moving back toward the couch. He pursed his lips into a thin line.

"Jason," he commanded in a low tone.

Jason didn't even turn. "What?" His eyes on Julia's pale face, her lips tinged blue.

"Let's go."

"No," Jason said, his eyes steady on Harold's.

Lily's head snapped up. She wasn't having this big guy in her house. This kid that Julia was gone over.

This family! How dare they try to bulldoze their way in her house, force their involvement. She picked up the nearest phone, her finger hovering above the number nine. "Don't make me call the police," she threatened Jason in a low voice.

Jason couldn't believe this was happening. The hell with this! He walked right back over to the couch and scooped Julia up in his arms, her soft moaning twisting something inside his chest.

44

Without mercy.

"Put her down, Jason!" his dad yelled. Their eyes met again.

"No. I don't give two shits and an eff what you guys do. I'm an adult and everyone needs to back right the hell off."

He'd never talked to his dad that way. It was long-past due.

Lily stabbed the numbers in the phone and Shelia tore it out of her hand and jammed it into the receiver. "Please," her voice trembled, "let's discuss this."

Lily looked at them like they'd gone insane.

"Listen here, Jason. I posted your bail. I am responsible for you until that hearing, where you'll be found innocent. Until then, don't jeopardize this with your he-man stunts. Leave that girl where she belongs. NOW." Harold planted his hands on his hips and stared at Jason.

A loud ticking from the clock on the wall reverberated around the room, the moment swelling unbearably around them, the tension a living breathing thing.

Jason wanted to scream so badly his eyes burned with frustrated unshed tears. He turned away from them, blinking fiercely, feeling like he was betraying her.

Betraying Julia.

He laid her back down on the couch, her eyelashes like soot against chalky cheeks and turned before he wrapped her up against him again. Saying nothing, he stalked out of the house, shouldering past his dad and almost knocking him over.

He looked up as the cold air hit him, the clouds roiling above him, the look of their charcoal anger exactly matching his.

CHAPTER 6

EXISTING

*J*ulia sullenly took another spoonful of soup. After a week of suffering through liquids, she'd finally been upgraded to soup with meat. Susan was the cook too. Versatile gal.

If Julia was honest with herself, she had to admit that Susan was a saint. But she was not here to make friends. Every day she thought of how she could get away, each day she wanted away from William, and to a lesser degree, Pierce.

At least she finally had answers. William was deliriously complacent with her presence here. He thought he had it handled. Well, he had another thing coming. Julia was waiting for the best opportunity she could manage to leave permanently.

William had expounded on her importance, making her desire to leave even more acute.

Blood Singers were rare. They were critically needed in the human population. The vampires looked at the humans like cattle. Blood Singers were just a fraction of the human population; one tenth of one percent, to be exact.

Julia had listened to his speech silently. William and Pierce were "runners." Their express purpose was the acquisition of Blood Singers. The Blood Singers balanced the vampires "food load." The properties their blood afforded made the human population's blood of a high enough quality to sustain their existence.

Whatever, Julia thought, remembering his words.

"So you see... how essential you are?" William spread his palms out on either side of his body, his coal-black hair shimmering with blue low lights in the subdued glow of the dining hall. His silver eyes bored into hers and a sudden memory of them shifting to a red so deep it was nearly black as he'd almost struck her flesh caused her heart to speed slightly. She rode it out. He could probably hear her blood course through her veins. That's all she needed. Julia would never be able to help herself if he was anticipating all her moves, especially as weakened as she'd become.

"Why take me? It sounds like you need us out in the... populace," she restated, genuinely puzzled.

"We're reconnaissance," he said simply. "We seek the Rare Ones."

"Okay," Julia threw up her hands, her soup forgotten. He frowned when she pushed the bowl away. "I give. Who are the Rare Ones?"

William stared at her and she held his gaze. "You are a Rare One, Julia."

She shrugged. So? Who was he kidding? How was it different than what he had essentially told her? Basically, the Blood Singers of the human race were the purebred cattle of homo sapiens.

Wonderful.

He took in her expression. "Maybe you have not asked the right question. It is quite simple, actually."

Julia thought about it. It slowly came to her. "Why do you have that name for us... Blood Singer?"

He smiled at her like she was a prized pupil and looked

achingly human for that one moment. Then his face fell into the handsome but otherworldly lines she was becoming accustomed to. "Do you not feel it?" He placed his fist to his chest, where his heart must beat.

Or did it?

They stared at each other and Julia felt a pull to him. She fought it, it was simply like ignoring one voice amongst many. She tried that, tuning out that one strand, like a distant bell that sounded. She silenced it with an effort.

His hand slowly fell from his breastbone. "That is the call of the blood. I have shared mine with you. It now calls to yours."

"Why?" Julia asked, deeply creeped out.

"Because I have shared blood with you."

"No, you forced your blood inside of me!" she raised her voice at him, crossing her arms, high color seeping across her cheekbones.

William's eyes narrowed slightly. "True. So that you might live, I gave you my blood. I have Blood Singer ancestry." Julia cocked an eyebrow, the conversation becoming more confusing by the moment. What he said next made her forget her curiosity like falling off a precipice. "How do you think we found you? Found... Jason?"

His name fell like a stone in the room, the horrible memory threatening around the edges of her consciousness. She clenched her eyes against the images assaulting her.

He continued as if the oxygen had not been forcibly torn from the room. Julia felt like an elephant had sat on her lungs. "Your blood calls to us. It sings to us. We follow it like a melody on the wind. All roads lead to the Blood Singer."

Julia opened her eyes. A startling revelation was blossoming in her mind. "Jason was... he was a Blood Singer?" she asked on a breathless whisper.

William nodded.

Julia jumped off the bench and flung herself at William, beating against him with her fists. Her hair flailing wildly about her. It was like beating a brick wall. Stony and cold. "You killed him! You had no right!" she wailed. "You killed him..." she sobbed as he grabbed her wrists. "Why didn't you kill me instead?" Julia asked on a sorrowful moan as she sagged against him, fainting from exhaustion.

William picked her up in his arms, the burden of her weight no more than a feather. His pain at watching hers was unmatched with anything he had ever known.

He carried Julia back to her room, his soul as heavy as a ton of lead.

* * *

Julia

WILLIAM HAD BEEN FAIRLY quiet since the scene in the dining hall the week before and Julia was glad. She thought the ache for him would never end. But thankfully day by day it lessened. She didn't want to be tied to the blood drinker. Because that was what he was.

All he was.

He and Pierce lingered in the hall, speaking in covert whispers as she dabbed at the corners of her mouth, bread half-eaten in front of her.

The dreams had started again and with them, her long-lost friend, Headache. She sighed, rubbing her temples.

William and Pierce were suddenly beside her. "Are you ill, Julia?"

She glared up at the pair. A prudent girl with half a brain would have been scared of the vampires; deadly and menacing. But she didn't care about her welfare anymore, her future. She wasn't interested in being taken anywhere with them.

"No, I'm fine." She looked at them impassively.

Pierce stared a moment more ,then turned to William. "Perhaps her awakening has begun."

Julia thought she was about done with the revelations.

"Possibly..." William said thoughtfully.

"What?" Julia asked, standing, her arms crossed over her body, she hugged herself to stay warm. She looked up at the pair, such a contrast to each other. They were huge men... *vampires*, Julia self-corrected. She gulped back a sudden stab of fear.

"Rare Ones go through a..." William struggled for just the right word.

"Transition?" Pierce supplied.

Julia's brows jacked down over her eyes and she said, "Haven't you two kidnapped Blood Singers before?"

William's expression darkened at her terminology. But Julia remained steadfast. It was what it was.

"We have acquired some of Rare One lineage but never a pureblood. Never once," Pierce said.

"Adolescence!" William said triumphantly, remembering the word.

What-the-hell? Were they stupid? "Look guys," they turned their simultaneous attention unnervingly on her. She stepped back, then realizing it made her look weak, she reclaimed it. "I am clearly a woman. Full-grown guys," she ran a hand down the front of her body and the vampires tracked it. She was immediately embarrassed but bottled it up before they noticed. She rushed on before they could comment. "What I'm saying is, I went through adolescence years ago. I am done with all that," Julia said waving away their weird ideas with a hand.

Pierce shook his head and William said, "No. The Rare One comes-of-age much later than one that is just a Blood Singer. The purer you are, the greater the manifestation of your latent talents."

Julia's eyes shifted back and forth between the two of them. "What talents?" she asked slowly.

William paused, then dropped the bomb, "Paranormal talents."

Julia's hand whipped out and gripped the table that stood behind her. The hell with appearing weak, she backed up until her thighs pressed against the bench.

Insane Vampires. It wasn't just enough that there were such things as vampires. These ones were crazy ass loons.

It just kept getting better and better.

Julia despaired.

"Are you having headaches?" Pierce pressed.

"Precognitive dreams?" William asked silkily.

Julia's head snapped up and locked with William's gaze, gold meeting silver. She shook her head in denial. She would not be their stupid Blood Singer messiah or whatever-the-hell they were looking for. She redoubled her determination to escape.

Soon.

CHAPTER 7

GRADUATION

*J*t was cool, the air holding none of the heat that would be found in other parts of America. Here at latitude fifty-nine, late May meant maybe sixty degrees. Maybe.

Today it was a cool fifty-eight. Intermittent clouds floated overhead and the breeze from the Homer Spit had made its way to the high school, slowed but not beaten.

Julia looked away from the Valedictorian who was expounding on the benefits of altruistic endeavors.

It was all bullshit, said through the bullhorn of what she could gain by making a good impression on whoever was listening. Julia swung her leg restlessly until Jason stilled it with a hand on her knee. His eyes swung to hers. "It'll be okay, just today, then we're free."

The girl droned on, the guys got a fine sheen of sweat over their brows, all that satiny polyester was causing the greenhouse effect.

Finally, the staff herded them through the line and they shook hands, stood for pictures and ate the celebratory cake courtesy of Costco. It was anticlimactic anyway.

It only served to underscore that uneasy feeling Julia had. Like she was waiting. Ever since the Terrell incident.

Death, she corrected herself.

She had felt a portent. A feeling of impending doom. It felt like a ticking time bomb. Her sleep was leaving her these days and nightmares were taking up residence in its absence.

She was exhausted and Jason was worried.

If that weren't enough, there was the impending trial. If a jury of Jason's peers found him not guilty in the death of Terrell, then he was free. Unfortunately, because of the nature of how he had... killed Terrell, he had a mandatory six weeks of anger management classes. And of course, he was angry about the classes.

Total irony.

The Caldwells had not really forgiven Jason for making them look "bad" by killing Terrell. Even Truman defended Jason, saying he'd saved lives. Of course, what the Caldwells weren't telling Truman was that her life was not that important to them. It hurt, but Julia had to stay focused on her future.

With Jason.

When the lame reception was over they drove to Julia's house so she could change. Then it was out to the beach with Kevin and Cyn.

Julia opened the door, Jason behind her. He'd been so quiet in the car. She knew something was on his mind.

Seeing that Lily wasn't home from work yet she walked to her room. Tearing open her closet door, she chucked out her beach jeans, T-shirt and the faded, battered Salty Dawg Saloon hoodie. It was her most beat up one but she loved it. She'd bribed a tourist one summer to go in there and get one for her. It was a Homer landmark, a cabin from 1897 that had grown into a rough and tumble tavern.

She pressed the hoodie against her face, inhaling the

fragrant soap Lily used and a pang of homesickness struck her. *She was really going*, she thought, a little forlorn. Just six short weeks.

Jason came up behind Julia and wrapped his arms around her, the graduation gowns wrapping and mingling together around their legs. "It's not like she's gonna die. You can come back and visit her, Jules."

Julia nodded silently. She understood that. She did.

But there would be no one, no family to see her get married, no one to appreciate her husband. Just Lily. And Lily was bitter. She had gotten saddled with her brother's kid and that had been a stain on her heart, spreading across that muscle that throbbed in her body with increasing speed. Until all of it was covered in resentment.

Jason kissed her temple, his lips hovering above her skin like butterfly's wings, fragile but present. She leaned back against him. He turned her and slowly lifted the gown off, the rasping of the satin catching on the fine strands of hair that had escaped the clasp she'd secured it in. He tossed it aside and tore his gown off, tossing it onto the floor at his feet.

Gathering her in his arms he kissed her, pressing his lips to hers with heat.

Jason's lips moved over hers with pressure and longing, combining in a succulent pull. Julia's mouth opened and her arms slid around his broad shoulders, the muscles bunching as he pressed her closer. She gave a little moan and he moved them backward, where they fell softly on her bed. He broke the kiss when they landed, his elbows braced on either side of her body.

"I can't wait to make you mine, Julia," he said, dipping to kiss her temple again. His lips slid from that point, making a blazing trail down her jaw, then a sideways path to her mouth.

He lingered there, scooping her long hair from where it was pinned underneath her, fanning it out behind her. Jason slid her further on the bed, falling to the side of her. He cupped her face and pecked her lips again. Searching her face, he saw the lingering anxiety there. "Lily'll come around, you'll see."

"She may not. But, even though she took me in and saved me from the system, it wasn't her choice."

Speak of the devil.

Julia heard Lily buzz into the house and start clanking around in the kitchen. Supper preparation. Julia wasn't that interested. Eating hadn't been a big priority since Terrell. She'd never been an emotional eater. When stuff got intense, food lost its appeal.

"Come on," Jason kissed her again, then kissed her once more on that tender spot between her earlobe and her collarbone. She smiled, a little breathless. She knew some guys would have been trying to attack the obvious, but not Jason. He really loved her. He wanted her but he wanted her for the right reasons.

Jason was the man for her.

But in the end she didn't get him after all.

* * *

later

RIGHT AWAY JULIA knew she should have worn a puffy over the top of her hoodie. She sighed, stepping out of Jason's big truck, the lift kit making the whole thing a hike to get in and out of.

She gave a scoot and a hop and got out before Jason could meet her on the other side.

He came around and closed the door for her. "You should have waited for me, I'd get you down," his lips turned up.

"I bet you would, pervert!" Julia teased as Cyn and Kevin walked up.

Kevin smirked, "I hear pervert. Must be Caldwell here."

"Thanks for the support, Kev," Jason said sarcastically.

He grinned, shrugging. "Welcome."

Cyn smiled at Julia, taking in the XtraTufs and hoodie uniform. Cynthia had on her Ugg boots. Stylish to most, ugly to her.

"Well, I see you are consistent," Cyn said in her droll way.

"Don't start, I didn't want to suffer through any more Unwanted Clothing."

Cyn rolled her eyes. "I did see you barely making it through the ceremony. Couldn't you have faked it?"

"Hell no! I didn't like any of the teachers and after the Terrell thing..." she trailed off then immediately felt terrible. They'd all been there too and here she was bringing it up.

"Sorry guys," Julia mumbled, bowing her head a little and letting her long hair form a curtain to hide her expression.

That had been beyond stupid, she could kick her own ass. Miss Sensitive.

Jason put a finger underneath her chin, tilting it so their eyes met. "Don't be sorry, Jules. All of us were there. It was me that killed him," he said in a low voice. "Ask me if I feel bad?"

She swallowed, her mouth dry. "Do you feel bad?"

He shook his head, solemn. "No."

"Hell, Jules," Kevin spread his arms away from his body, wearing a T-shirt that read, *Zombie Bait*, "you were in that psycho's cross hairs. Caldwell had to do it."

Cynthia looked at Julia and understood. They'd been friends for years, she didn't want to feel responsible for any accidents, especially after her parents.

Especially that. She reached out and put a chunk of hair behind Jules' ear. "Don't sweat that creeper, Jules. This wasn't your fault. Your fault that he died. Just because someone dies when you're around, doesn't mean you have to take the death on as your fault. That's crap and you know it." Cyn dipped down a little until she was eye level with Jules. "Are ya hearin' me?"

"Yeah," Julia whispered. She was so lucky to have these guys, unshed tears burnt the back of her eyelids. Tears were for sissies. She sucked it up, hugging Cyn with one arm and flung the other around Jason, her hand in the middle of his back. It was where she could reach him. He cuddled her as they did an awkward shamble to the bonfire that Kevin had built, the heat washing over her like a wave of comfort and serenity.

Too brief.

Her peace was too brief.

CHAPTER 8

SEATTLE

*P*ierce and William had deemed her ready. Ready for travel, ready for the final leg of their journey.

They were headed to William's home coven in Seattle.

Julia was ready too. She only had the smallest amount of guilt. After all, if Julia was truthful with herself then she'd have to wallow in it. The memory. Explore it. Reconcile that it was not William and Pierce who'd killed Jason. That they'd been too late to stop it from happening.

She would not let sentiment cloud her plan.

The memory began to play out like the nightmare it was. Julia felt the heat begin at her toes and roar up her body like she was a lone tree in a forest on fire. Her heart was beating rapidly, her palms sweating, and her breath coming in great whoops. She had to calm down.

Now. Before she had a full blown panic attack. That always got the full attention of the vampires.

She didn't want that.

Ever again.

Julia slowed her breathing, shoving the horrible memory

down in the well of her subconscious. It would come again, it always did, in the silent and unguarded moments of her wakefulness. It would surge forward like the tide to shore. She waited until her hands had only a fine tremble then picked up her bag.

Turning, she looked one more time at her temporary home. She sighed, closing the door behind her. Julia suddenly realized what day it was.

Over a year since her precious Jason had been ripped from her life. Torn from her soul, leaving it within her body, shredded.

She moved down the hall, seeing the two runners who waited so still against the exit.

Waiting for her. Their prize.

But not for long, Julia thought, covering her smile with an effort.

She moved forward and they fell into step beside her, leaving the house behind them forever.

* * *

IMAGINE the logistics of traveling with vampires. If it hadn't been her reality, Julia would have thought it was funny as hell.

But it wasn't funny.

They had driven up the highway to the Anchorage Airport, gotten on the plane (the red-eye flight taking on new meaning) and flown the lonely journey to Seattle.

She had a small window of time in which to escape them. They were already in the city where the coven was located. How to shake them before they arrived? Especially when William's blood was still in her body. Diluted but there, like a pulse. It would be a navigation tool.

Julia caressed her bag, the hair dye and change of clothes she had planned hidden inside. She smiled. It might work, but only if Pierce was the one that was nearby. If it was William, all hope was lost. She had another lapse of guilt, thinking back to her conversation with William on the plane.

William looked at her and Julia became interested in her hands. "You seem tense," he said as a statement. Pierce looked up at them sharply, then away.

At least they hadn't insisted on sandwiching her in between the two of them, that would have been awful. Julia purposely loosened her tense hands and laid them flat on her thighs. That was all she needed, William detecting something.

She met his eyes, the palest gray, striking against all that black hair. He gave a little smile and she realized she'd been staring. Her palms dampened and she resisted the urge to rub them on her pants. "I am," she answered honestly, knowing it would ring of the truth. "I mean, I've been with you for a year and now, I have to be with a bunch..." she looked around the tight confines of the airplane, "of you," she finished in a whisper.

William's eyes narrowed and Julia didn't squirm, she wasn't one to just keel over because someone had an emotional moment. She could hack it. "We have gone over this many times, Julia. They will welcome you. You shall be safe, protected. No more running, no more mystery."

She nodded. Julia knew what he'd said. She even felt that he believed it. But she'd been there that day on the beach, she'd seen what it was. How they were with each other, her.

The Were.

She shuddered, thinking of something else.

Anything else.

He reached out and placed his hand over hers and Julia let him. She'd learned early on that her resistance brought a barrage of questions and concern. It was better to pretend.

It'd make escape easier.

Turning her hand over, he rubbed a thumb over the pulse in her wrist, beating frantically like a trapped bird. His pupils dilated and he licked his bottom lip as her breath came shorter, his eyes darkening, the gray beginning to disappear like imagined smoke.

"William," Pierce said in a low voice. William looked across the aisle at him, his brow furrowed. Pierce looked pointedly at the contact between them and William removed his hand from hers, the lack of his touch leaving her disturbingly empty. What was wrong with her? It must be because of her nervousness with the execution of the plan. She had a stabbing pain for Jason in that moment. He'd have known what to do. But no more. Now it was up to her.

Julia had to be her own savior.

William waited until he seemed to get control of himself then said, "You will see. My home coven will be a place of respite."

Fat chance, *Julia thought.*

Before she'd been too weak to think of escaping. Now, all that time that she had been bereft over the loss of Jason and the others, was now at the forefront of her mind. Pressing her forward. Into the unknown.

She was in charge of her own destiny. Not the vampires. Not the werewolves.

She. Julia.

Only her.

* * *

escape

THEY EXITED before the other passengers, *only first class for vamps*, she thought sourly. Julia had never flown first class. Actually, she'd only been on a plane for a single trip. To fly from her home state, where her parents had been executed on the highway. She gulped at the memory. She gave herself a mental push forward as the chaos of the airport swirled around them, the vampires tracking the people around them.

The cattle.

She turned to William, willing her pulse to slow. "I need to change and use the restroom," she lied smoothly, her pulse sluggish. Why it was cooperating now, when in the plane it had been fluttering uncontrollably while he'd been touching her? Julia didn't know, didn't care. She was *that* close to freedom. She wasn't blowing it for anything.

Pierce waited and William ran his hand through his inky hair, making it spike. Turning that smoldering intensity to Julia he said, "Alright, but Pierce will need to stand guard outside of the bathroom until I can get our comrades here to escort you to the car."

Comrades. Translation: vampires.

Julia lifted an eyebrow. Smart of him. He was going to leave her with good old Pierce while he got a few more of the vampire crew up here so the precious Blood Singer couldn't get away.

Real circumspect guys. They thought they were so smart. Well, the element of surprise was the only thing she had and she was using it.

"Where am I gonna go?" Julia pointed out.

His eyes narrowed on her and Julia held her breath. He seemed to really deliberate until Pierce broke the swollen moment. "Just go. I will stand guard and you will return with the additional runners." He rolled his broad shoulders into a dismissive shrug.

William palmed his chin. "Fine." He turned to Pierce. "Be sharp, be vigilant, even now they may be about."

Julia looked around, expecting gnomes, trolls or both to pop up around her.

"The werewolves," Pierce clarified in a low voice.

True, there was them.

Pierce took her elbow and she walked to the restroom with him. When she glanced over her shoulder, William's form was a speck down the choked corridor.

* * *

JULIA THREW the bag on the bathroom floor stall, kicked off her flip flops, and dragged out the skirt, boots and shirt she'd cropped the night before. It would bare some skin but she'd take the jacket she had in her arm. She grabbed the box of black hair dye she'd taken from underneath the sink vanity. She rushed to the sink and began to chop off her long, ginger-colored hair to her shoulders.

Another girl beside her leaned back and said, "Ah, what are you doing?" she asked, snapping gum, watching as the hair piled at Julia's feet in a heap of spun honey.

Julia met her eyes in the reflection of the mirror. She asked, "What does it look like?"

The girl's eyes narrowed. "Butchering your hair like a dumbass," she said logically.

Julia smiled, she couldn't help it. Yeah she was. But it was necessary.

The girl took a hard look at Julia, then, shaking her head, she walked away. Giving her a last look that clearly said, *crazy bitch*.

Yeah, that was her alright. She guessed the plastic scissors didn't help with that. Can't get the real ones on the plane. She stopped up the sink and mixed the black dye. Lathering it in her hair she watched as her almost blond hair with a hint of red became a mass of black. It utterly changed how she looked.

The boots made her five-seven instead of five-four. She was taller, wearing different clothes and had black hair that was eighteen inches shorter than when she entered the bathroom.

She had the money she'd had on her the day that she was taken. Julia opened her palm and looked at the lonely thirty dollars and five dimes.

And one penny.

She made a fist with her hand and stuffed the change back in the pocket of her skirt. She grabbed her toiletry bag like a purse and made her departure when there was a pair of women exiting the bathroom.

Julia dipped her head and walked out, the hair still wet underneath, clinging to the nape of her neck like cold fingers.

* * *

JULIA KEPT her head down and her legs moving, her heart racing far beyond the effort she was expending. She had her toiletry bag clenched under her arm and kept moving.

She was exiting security just as William and the runners were passing through. Julia could hear his voice and she didn't turn. But she swore she felt a hesitation in his speech, a scorching gaze that she did not see but felt pass over her.

And then she was outside in the drizzle, the clouds making shapes across a full moon, twenty cabs in sight.

Julia hailed the first one. Closing the door behind her she said, "Get me to the closest bus depot."

The cabby turned around to look at her. "To where?" he asked, his voice accented, a turban on his head. Julia tried not to stare.

"Away," she said cryptically.

"Humph!" he huffed, slamming the flag that started the meter at two bucks.

They pulled away from the curb and Julia hazarded a look behind her.

Her mind recoiled in terror as she saw William and Pierce. And beside them, two runners.

Vampires.

Their noses were in the air. Scenting it.

Scenting for her.

CHAPTER 9

VEGAS

*J*ulia and Jason were kinda arguing. He thought Elvis was classic and she thought he was... well, kinda creepy.

"Listen Jules, everyone who comes to Vegas has to get married in front of Elvis, I'm just sayin'." He spread his hands out at his side like, *you see my logic.*

Actually, she didn't. She looked up at the oversized pudgy Elvis rendering. His clown red mouth, his tassels and studs on a grotesquely distended belly in an unflattering white was not something she wanted in attendance. Even if they *were* in cheesy Vegas. Even if they had stolen away to get married.

Jason huffed, planting his hands on his hips. "Okay, I see you don't see that as a sign: Elvis is the Symbol of Vegas." His eyebrows raised and Cyn giggled.

"I think he looks pretty gay, Jason," Kevin agreed, smoothly siding with Julia.

"Thanks for the love, ya ass," Jason said.

Kev barked out a laugh. "Anytime, pal."

Beaten, Jason looked over the small pamphlet of chapels, finding a few more on the list. His eyes shifted to Julia's, hazel with flecks of green in the brown. "The only thing you don't want is him?" he jerked his thumb toward Icky Elvis.

Cynthia rolled her eyes. "Yeah, Jason. No chunky monkey in white polyester. It's a no-go."

He glared at her and Julia said, "Yeah, that."

Jason sighed. He and Kevin put their heads together as Cyn came over to Julia, giving her a look from head to toe. "Glad I could get you out of those fugly boots, Jules."

Julia smiled, Cyn had outdone herself. Julia didn't look great in white but as Cyn had explained it, "you've earned white, virgin princess, but let's work with the weirdness that is your complexion." Julia had rolled her eyes, letting Cyn transform her.

Julia caught sight of herself in what could only be described as a fun house mirror, her long dress, grazing the floor, spiky ivory heels peeked out from underneath the hem, a platform gracing the bottom. Cyn had pinned her hair in an elegant up 'do, leaving a few wisps hanging down.

A row of creamy pearls with a champagne-colored wash encircled the base of her throat. Her mother's.

A lump gathered in her throat and she looked away from the reflection of her sweetheart neckline, satin and lace colliding in a fine webbing that cradled her breasts.

The absence of her parents on this important occasion was best left to future reflection.

Like never.

Jason had dressed in a deep navy suit, his tie a subtle crimson. A slash of color against the whiteness of the shirt.

Julia thought it looked a little like blood against the backdrop of white and shivered as a subtle feeling of foreboding stole over her. It was shattered when Jason flashed his smile, stabbing the pamphlet with his finger. "Found it, babe!"

Julia leaned forward and he drew her in next to his body, looking at where he pointed.

"Gnome Chapel."

She cocked her brows. "Really, Jason?" He smiled nodding.

"That's just switching out one creepy audience member for another," Cynthia said with revulsion.

"Nah, baby," Kevin said, pulling her tight against him and pressing a kiss to her temple, almost crushing the bouquet of lavender flowers she held.

"Hey! Watch the flowers, graceless." She giggled.

Kevin grabbed the bouquet, jerking it up over his head, slamming his lips against hers, his free arm coming around her back and pressing her harder against him.

Julia agreed, gnomes were creepy too. She looked up at the bigger than life-sized Elvis statue and sighed. Choices, choices.

Anything was better than Elvis.

* * *

now

JULIA LEANED her head back against the scummy seat of the cab, fingering the fine chain at her neck, the sterling sliding with her restless stroking, the ring at the end.

Tears threatened as Julia thought of the symbol of eternal love. Jason had insisted on buying the bands. He had purchased indestructible tungsten bands. A metal made of carbide, gun metal gray, polished to a mirror-like shine. He had said it couldn't be scratched, dented or bent.

Like their love.

Perfect, he'd said, squeezing her as he had slipped it on her finger, their clergy in the Chapel of the Gnomes had been smiling at them, his mouth full of missing teeth.

Vegas, a class act.

She didn't want a big diamond. She just wanted him. He'd said that later, after they got settled, he'd get her something to go with the plainness of the band.

He would never have the opportunity.

The cabbie stopped a scant five minutes after they'd left the terminal.

"I let you off here. Eight dollars," he said without verbs.

Julia frowned. Don't speak English, fine by her, but be civil. She handed him a twenty and he gave her the change.

She slid out of the taxi and found herself on a cement sidewalk surrounded by a wall of people. She didn't make eye contact with anyone but went to the first bus she saw and showed the driver her five bucks, six dimes and one penny.

"How far?" she asked.

He searched her face. "How far do ya need to go?" he asked, a kindness in his eyes.

She paused, aware of a line forming behind her. "As far as this will get me," Julia said, leaving it in his hands.

He nodded. "Let's play it by ear, okay miss?"

She nodded, so grateful for the unexpected kindness she felt her eyes glisten again. She had turned into an absolute crybaby. All it took was him saying that one phrase Aunt Lily had used, Julia's home that was so far away came to the forefront of her consciousness without mercy. She swiped at the wetness on her cheeks and gave him a watery smile as she moved to the back of the bus.

She sunk down in the seat, putting her knees up on the seat in front of her and looked out the window. As she gazed through the filthy glass the bus pulled away in a plume of noxious exhaust, leaving the depot for parts unknown.

Julia shut her eyes, remembering.

Jason kicked open the door and it slammed against the wall. Julia shrieked laughter as he crossed the threshold, her dress

69

swirling around their bodies. He slapped it closed behind them and dumped her on the bed.

She almost bit her tongue she was laughing so hard, but managed not to by a slim margin.

They'd had fake ID's and had quite a bit to drink and Jason was stubbornly hanging onto the notion that they could wait one more night until they were in their new apartment in Anchorage.

"I don't want our first time to be in a seedy motel in Vegas, Jules," he'd said, dragging his lips down her neck in a path to her collarbone, then pressing them against her mouth again. The pearls getting in the way of his mouth, he moved them aside with a finger and lavished her with his attention.

Julia didn't care that it was seedy. She pulled him down into the cradle of her body.

Her husband.

It had a surreal quality, she tried to grab onto the newness of it but it slid through the fingers of her mind like smoke.

He smiled down at her, his tie askew, his muscular arms pressing her to him.

He nuzzled her neck, "No," he whispered. "We wait until we are in our home." Jason wanted everything to be perfect for her, she was worth it. No booze to interrupt the clarity, their own digs. Yeah.

Julia sighed with frustration. "I had awesome lingerie!"

He raised an eyebrow. "Cyn?"

Julia caved. "Yeah, it was her idea." She smiled sheepishly.

"But you still bought it?"

She nodded, blushing. Just thinking about the skank-ensemble Cyn had given the nod to made her flushed with embarrassment.

"Wow, it must be hot, judging by that look," he searched her face, running a tender finger over her cheekbone, on fire with her thoughts.

"We have the rest of our lives. Let me hold you next to me all night. That'll be a first, along with a ton of other stuff."

They grinned at each other.

Julia thought she could live with that one thing. Patience, she thought.

But they didn't have the rest of their lives.

It was her biggest regret. She'd never been with Jason.

Even once.

* * *

JULIA WOKE WITH A START, darkness all around her. She was completely disoriented and swallowed the scream that rose in her throat as someone leaned over her, gently shaking her shoulder.

It was just the bus driver. Her memories came flooding back.

Escape.

No money.

Going nowhere.

"We're here," he said softly.

Julia rubbed her eyes. "What time is it?" she croaked out, her voice rusty after sleeping so hard.

He looked at the humungous watch on his wrist and said, "Straight up five o'clock." He looked at her, straightening. "My shift's done and we've traveled my whole route. Twice. This is the end of the road."

Julia looked up at the sign that read, *Valley Bus Transport. Welcome to Kent.*

"Where is this?"

He looked around. "It's Kent," he pointed to the sign. "Outside Seattle."

Julia had familiarized herself with the Seattle region and understood immediately the driver had just kept her safe and warm in the bus while she slept part of the night away, driving in a big circle.

She stood, looking at him. "Thank you."

He nodded. "You got a place to go?"

She shook her head.

"I can give you a ride to a woman's shelter."

Woman's shelter? Is that what he thought she needed? He watched her expressions wash over her face and slowly nodded. "Yeah, I think you're running. I think you're running from a man."

No, not a man, she thought. But it was close enough.

He didn't want to know what she was running from.

"It's a deal," she said, deciding to take her chances with the human.

It was better than the alternative.

She walked out of the bus with him.

Still running.

CHAPTER 10

WILLIAM

illiam took in the filth from the air, his acute senses filtering the smells that did not concern him.

There were many, but amongst those, there was a faint taste on the air.

Julia's.

He swiveled his head in Pierce's direction, his nostrils flaring as they transitioned between scenting to anger. Pierce had been a dolt, letting her slip by. His anger rode him hard, his body tenser, more than was even typical for him.

Every moment she was alone left her vulnerable to attack. Judging by the pungency of her aroma, his blood still in her to the vaguest degree, he judged she was within a fifty mile radius east of their current position.

He opened the door to the SUV, leaving the bus depot behind them without a backward glance.

"East," William commanded to the runner who had met them. His eyes meeting Pierce's in the rear view mirror, settling against the passenger seat.

They sped off, the blackness of the SUV melting into the night.

* * *

Julia

JULIA WASN'T the hugging kind of girl but she gave a big one to the man who had let her sleep for hours on his bus.

Alfred.

He gave her an awkward pat on her head and told her to take care of herself.

She turned as she heard the engine roar in his pickup truck and then dim as he pulled away. Julia looked at where she stood. The moon was full, the brightness cast making Julia feel strangely vulnerable under the yellowish glow of the streetlight, on display. She clutched her toiletry bag tighter, moving forward toward the door.

Julia walked inside, passing under a sign at the threshold of the building which read, *Freedom Affirmed*. Once through, there was a receptionist on duty, her hair was in a severe bun, glasses perched on the end of her nose. It was her eyes, full of knowledge from hard experience that finally relaxed Julia.

Eyes that seasoned eased her.

"Hello dear," the receptionist said in a pleasant voice, her bird like eyes taking in Julia's appearance, missing nothing. The dyed hair, the crazy get up, the lack of luggage. Julia guessed she was pretty much fitting whatever stereotype there was.

"Hi."

The woman raised an eyebrow, as she came around the desk to greet Julia. "I'm Shirley," she stuck her bony hand out and Julia took it, giving it a gentle shake and then dropping hers. Shirley's eyes searched hers and finally she said, "I guess you need a place to stay for the night?"

Julia nodded. Only one night? Crap, she'd have to figure it out day by day.

Shirley, apparently seeing how dejected she was continued, "We offer transitional services. We will help you find a job, another residence..." she spread her arms to each side.

Julia sighed. She was terrified of William and Pierce finding her. It wasn't rational. After all, once she got on the bus, her trail disappeared.

Or that's what she told herself.

But Julia had been with the vampires for almost a year and they made normal human senses something to which there was no comparison. Julia shuddered, remembering how easy everything was for them. William was a runner, chosen specifically for tracking.

He was engineered to find her.

Julia shuddered and Shirley gave her a look of sympathy, misinterpreting it completely. She took Julia's arm and they walked together to her room.

shelter

JULIA WAS AS SETTLED in as she was going to be. She looked around the room. Actually, it was a shared room, hardly more than a closet. The bathroom served two rooms for four women. The girl she shared with was at her new job, poised to leave the next morning. Julia looked longingly at the bathroom. She was dying for a shower.

She went through the clothes that Shirley had provided. There was enough for a week's worth. A plain, black duffel had been provided, courtesy of a sponsor of the shelter.

The clothes were simple but comfortable and fit well. A miracle. She was heavier than she'd been when the vampires had thought they'd lose her from malnourishment. But as Julia caught sight of herself in the harsh reflection of the florescent lighting that rode the top of the vanity mirror she blanched. Even to her she looked hideous. Large bruise type circles held court underneath her large, golden eyes. Her hair was a startling black, the ends hacked unevenly about her shoulders. It was her ribs, each one countable, her collarbone standing at attention which let her know how desperate she still looked.

How had she looked before? Julia didn't want to know.

Turning away she cranked on the hot water for the shower, the needles slamming into her hands that were still cold from the outside. The tingling of the warmth waking her skin up as she pulled the stopper and the spray rained down, beating the porcelain tub below. Julia stepped in, parting her lips, letting the water fill her mouth and run down her chin. The warmth and privacy made her want to cry with relief.

She hadn't realized how obtrusive her lack of privacy had been when Susan had been her caretaker or how oppressive William and Pierce's presence was. She was so grateful she could hardly stand herself.

Julia almost shrieked when she glanced down while rinsing the shampoo out of her hair and saw the tub filled with black.

What-the-hell?

She quickly toweled off and ran to the mirror. She swiped her forearm across the middle and there she stood, her wet hair like dark gold, a black wash hanging on but mostly gone.

Shit. There went her great disguise. Julia sighed. Figures she would grab the wash-out-gradually dye. She turned away in disgust. Jerking the nightclothes on, which consisted of panties and an oversized shirt, she slammed her body into the bed in a huff. She was certain she would fall right to sleep.

But she didn't. Instead, thoughts of Jason filled her head like they always did before sleep took her.

* * *

then: fire & ice

THEY FLEW DOWN on the small plane from the Anchorage Airport. Julia was stoked, they'd touch down in Homer soon. The only small glitch was Jason wanted to meet up with Kevin and Cyn one more time at their spot on the beach. Kevin was likely burning the hell out of the driftwood as they flew.

She wanted Jason all to herself.

He laughed as she cuddled closer, his finger tracing and alternatively swirling the wedding band she wore as he said, "It's a sendoff, Jules. Don't get your hot panties in a twist."

Julia rolled her eyes. "They are super cute panties, buster. Not that you'd know!" she said, giving him a playful elbow. He retaliated, tickling her without mercy. She shrieked in the confines of the plane, some of the other passengers giving the pair stern looks.

They offloaded and ran to their car parked in the lot, the mountains a backdrop behind Jason's car, the stubborn snow clinging to some of the nooks and crannies at the top.

Julia sucked in a lungful of the freshest air in the world, happier than she'd ever been. Vegas had been an assault on all her senses. Filthy, noisy, dirty, everything that wasn't home.

Jason opened the door for her and she piled in, roaring off to the spit. Cyn and Kevin were waiting and she could see the fire from the beginning of the spit, the flames rushing up to kiss the darkening sky.

An omen.

Julia's mind protected her from touching the memory which lay next. The one she couldn't bear to think of.

The one that was stealing her breath, robbing her of life, making her heart pause in her throat.

Julia finally fell into a fitful sleep as the vampires closed in around her.

* * *

vampire

THE FOUR OF them surrounded the human cattle, eyes glittering darkly at their prey. They could not afford to be circumspect, all four would need to be well-fed when they finally came upon Julia. William signaled to Pierce and they flanked the victim.

A pleasure to dispatch, William thought. Remembering how they'd come upon him, abusing the woman that Robert now eased into thrall as they moved toward the human scum. William licked the tips of his fangs as they tore through the tender flesh of his mouth.

Pierce's evicted his mouth as the smell of blood wafted to their nostrils.

"Listen scary dudes," the man said, defensively, "that bitch wanted it. I was only givin' her what she was beggin' for... you get my meaning," he said, grabbing his crotch in an obscene gesture of his self-perceived attractiveness.

"Yes," Pierce mused, "the abuse of her face tells us of her joy."

William hissed, moving toward him with sure footing, stalking closer, he jerked the foul human next to him until his rancid breath filled the intimate space. "The innocent do not defend their actions... "

"Thou dost protest too much," Pierce intoned, the ghost of a smile riding his lips as he moved toward their prey.

The other runner, Andrew, allowed his talons to tear through the tips of his fingers and used them like the small daggers they were, piercing the tender flesh of the man's back, his gurgled response matching the widening of his eyes. "What are you?" he whispered, his eyes bulging and distended as Andrew held him skewered like a shish kabob.

"Death," William answered, his fangs lengthening. He reared, preparing to strike.

He struck true, as did Pierce, Andrew's talons evacuating the holes caused by them.

Robert left the female in thrall, dazed and uncomprehending. In a blur of speed, he was at the human's side where he dropped to his knees beside the male. Working to the inside of his thigh, he tapped the vein with a vicious push of his fangs, piercing even the thick denim the human wore. He rolled his eyes up and met those of his comrade, Andrew, who shared the foul meal. The blood delicious, its host lowly.

The vampires fed. Two miles from where Julia laid sleeping.

But not peacefully, never that.

CHAPTER 11

*J*ulia *never* thought about the day Jason died. She did everything within her power not to.

That's probably why her subconscious took over.

She was too exhausted to fight it anymore. She was not in the vampires' clutches, she'd had a shower and even a little food. It made sense to sleep.

She needed to sleep.

Julia felt her body slide off into that strange midway point between true wakefulness and that of deep slumber. Her mind floated, circling the last things she had thought about. As she slipped into REM, her body jerked like it was falling, landing about where she'd left off in wakefulness.

Julia knew where she was going and began to struggle toward consciousness again, as if at the bottom of a lake, swimming to the surface.

But sleep was victorious, sucking her back underneath the waters of her dreams.

* * *

then

SHE AND JASON were almost to the spit when he got the text from Kevin.

Jason turned to Julia. "That's not their fire babe."

She arched her brow, looking at the blaze far down on the terminus of the spit, a glowing beacon. "Who else would start that monster?"

He laughed. "They want to go to that spot by the woods. More private," Jason waggled his brows, he couldn't wait to surprise Jules with their new place and all that came with it.

Right. Translation: let's make out. But now they were married, she was going to do more than that and without an audience thank you very much.

She sighed, some wedding night. She folded her arms across her chest, brooding.

"Listen, hun. It'll be fun, it won't get light until, when? One a.m.?"

The land of the midnight sun, Julia thought with more than a little hint of sarcasm. He wrapped his hand around her neck, massaging the stiffness of the travel away, catching little glances when he could, driving with one hand.

Julia guessed she'd forgive them. He was giving up his apartment, after all. Tonight was their last night before heading up to Anchorage. Just thinking about facing Aunt Lily tomorrow filled her with dread. Even knowing she would be relieved to see Julia go didn't make it better.

Jason looked at her with concern, then swung his attention to the road ahead of them. He took the turn for the small stretch of beach where they liked to hang. Only the four of them knew about it: how to traverse, how to find.

He squeezed the back of her neck and she felt the strength of his hands, having always been gentle with her.

81

She thought of Terrell. They'd been the same hands he had used to murder their teacher.

To defend her.

"Jules, stop thinkin' about what Lily's gonna do. It'll be fine, you'll see." He looked at her quickly then parked the car above the slope that led to the beach.

The beach lay below, a steep ravine above it, lined with spruce trees which camouflaged the fire. They didn't need anything special to get down there but it would be a bad fall if they didn't watch it. Jason took her carefully by the elbow as they used the rigid and deeply grooved soles of their boots to assure their footing as they descended to the rocky beach.

* * *

Vampire

ANDREW AND ROBERT PAIRED, as did William and Pierce. Silently, having worked together as a quad before. They scented Julia easily. William never went anywhere without his quarry's scent. In this case he possessed a scrap of an original piece of clothing, never laundered. He allowed his runners a deep whiff before they picked up the faintest scent coming from their current position.

"I say one point two-four kilometers," William said, lowering his face from its position in the sky.

Pierce laughed. "So literal, William."

William gave him a look and Pierce's amusement faded.

He looked at the faces that studied him in turn. "Follow me."

They ran, staying to the border of the buildings' flanks. The shadows embracing them soundlessly, the peppering of blood splatter on their garments invisible in the dark.

* * *

before

THE DUSK LINGERED in Alaska forever it seemed like. Summer nights were one long siege of twilight. Julia didn't mind. The veil of false darkness provided the perfect backdrop for a sky the color of bruised violet, a sprinkling of the brightest stars flung about. Venus hanging like a shimmering anchor at the horizon.

She had planted her bony butt on a huge piece of driftwood Kev and Jason had hauled to a safe proximity next to the blazing inferno.

Cyn had been naughty and brought champagne. Julia would have loved to have argued but couldn't.

After all, they were celebrating her nuptials.

Hard as they tried it was inevitable that Lily would come up in conversation.

"I'm just sayin', you're not obligated to give a big defense, Jules," Cyn said, her legs crossed at the ankles, her chair rest was Kevin. The wash of the firelight warred with the sun burning low in the horizon, making a fiery halo around them.

Julia shrugged. Cyn wouldn't understand. She felt like she owed Lily. Moving in her eight-year old niece had never been her goal. Actually, Julia wasn't sure what *had* been her goal. She'd made it abundantly clear it wasn't having her brother's daughter to raise.

As a surprise family.

Jason kissed the top of her head and she buried her toes that were encased in woolly socks into the sand now warmed by the fire. Her XtraTufs were thrown to the side.

"She's got a point, Jules," Jason breathed against her temple.

"I know she does. But, she did take me in when my grandma couldn't. She's the only one that could. Beside a foster family."

Cyn shuddered. "That's like goddamned Russian Roulette."

Kev nodded, everyone knew you could get some shit family. "Yeah, Jules. I heard about some girl that was like Cinderella in her family. They made her label every scrap of food like she was gonna steal it or something. Big time lame. They just wanted the government money every month."

"See?" Julia said, looking at Cynthia. "It could've been worse."

Cyn shook her head, her huge hoops catching the light that swirled around them, a mix of burnt orange from the sky and fire, mingling together in an eerie wash. "If you say so. I still think she was a big time troll in her skirt to ya!"

She kinda was. But Julia still wanted to remember Lily in the best light she could and... "She's got all my stuff too."

Cyn's face broke into a grin. "Now that's worth some suck-up, Jules."

They laughed and then Cyn said, "I'm sorry your grandma isn't here anymore."

Julia was too. Summers at her place had been the only break from the grind of Living with Lily. Grandma had taught her things she'd never forget.

"Didn't she have your name?" Kev asked.

Julia smiled. "Yes, actually, I had *her* name."

Kev shrugged. "That's what I said." The little details of things like elders passing on namesakes sailing right over his head.

They smiled and made plans for tomorrow. Julia and Jason would go by her house and see if they could charm their way in after a hasty elopement and zero communication.

So not going to happen.

Cyn broke a mood that had slid far away from celebratory by jerking the champagne glasses out of her backpack. Kevin got the champagne out of his beat up cooler, the ice rattling and clinking.

Cyn put a cube in each plastic cylinder. The glasses had been made to looked like cut glass and winked like they were on fire from the light of the blaze. Julia smiled, Cyn had thought everything through to the last detail.

"Nice glasses," Julia said.

Cyn smirked. "I know, right? I couldn't let us be déclassé even at the beach!" Kevin filled hers to the brim and she plopped a full strawberry on the top, where it floated like a jewel inside the glass, the bubbles mesmerizing Julia as they floated in the golden liquid.

Everyone's glass fizzing with champagne, they lifted them as one, four glasses meeting in a clash of celebration. They took sips, eyeing each other above the rims.

Cyn did an obscene job of tonguing her strawberry in full view of Kevin, moving it back and forth in her mouth, twirling the stem like an provocative handle in her capable fingers.

"Come 'er," he said in a growl, grabbing her around her slender waist and pressing her against him. He put his lips to the half of the berry that lay between her teeth, jerking the stem with his teeth and spitting it on the pebbled beach. He met his lips with hers, eating the berry as he sucked the kiss right out of her.

Cyn groaned and flung her arms around Kev's neck, the two of them staggering over to their log of driftwood, oblivious to Jason and Julia as their audience. Kevin threw his arm behind him so they wouldn't topple, but as they sat down in a heap, he fell backward on the sand and we laughed at their lust ridden dance.

It would have been great if Kevin had not been on his back with his girlfriend when the werewolf appeared.

He was horribly vulnerable for what transpired next.

* * *

Vampire

STEALTH WAS the order of the night, as it were. He eyed the building carefully, taking in the ironic title of the structure itself: *Freedom Affirmed*.

William's lips curled. They wouldn't understand real freedom if it introduced itself with a handshake.

He spoke in a voice that could not be heard by humanity. The decibel level was too high for humans.

In the distance a stray dog lifted its ears and whined softly, taking off in the opposite direction of the disturbing tones of the Unnatural. Canines were instinctual. This one recognized the threat for what it was and ran in a direction of safety.

The other runners whipped their heads in the dog's direction, responding in like kind. They made their way to the structure, converging at roughly all four corners. Their progress was deliberate and insidious. They would not make a spectacle of their presence.

William had the barest sense of unease. He hoped that Julia's abilities continued to lay dormant. If they awoke during her acquisition, that would change things dramatically.

It would be very bad for all. Blood Singers were unpredictable at best. At worst, they were dangerous.

He hoped that Pierce and the others would heed his warning:

Be vigilant. Be aware. They may already be in the area, having scented her hours before themselves.

Werewolves.

* * *

JULIA'S EYES rolled wildly beneath lids that were clenched in horror.

Watching what had happened that fated evening as a movie before her.

Julia watched.

Her subconscious replay unrolling, unbidden and uninvited.

The werewolf came into full view, not in a crouch, but as a half-man, half-wolf creature, only partially changed. His advantage as a soldier of the Were was his form. He and the other soldiers of his race were aptly suited for the acquisition of Rare Ones. To do so, he would need to subdue the others. His keen sight, albeit in shades of gray to the deepest ebony, assisted him in his forward motion.

Immediately he allowed his senses to take in the threats. His night vision acclimated automatically, dismissing the glow of the fire, compensating in the orbital network that was unique to his kind. His nostrils flared, bringing the myriad of scents necessary for successful acquisition.

If he had been in human form he would have laughed. One of the males, who if he had been coupled with his comrade that stood beside the target, might have posed a problem. But he lay prone beneath a human female. A female clearly in heat, he scented.

He would dispatch him first, then move on to the primary target. The mate of the Rare One.

This assessment took mere seconds.

To Julia, from his appearance to his attack, it seemed to take hours.

As if in slow motion, the creature leaped forward in one long stride. The muscles underneath the dove gray fur were a ripple of sinew and tendon, perfectly synchronized.

Uniquely suited for harm and brutality.

Cynthia screamed when she saw the muzzle of a creature her mind could not name. Yellow eyes blazed out of its face as it flew through the air, body seemingly suspended. She tried to scramble off of Kevin but he was already reacting, pushing her away. It was his movement that kept the head she possessed on her shoulders.

Kevin was buried underneath a monster. A thing of legend come to life, the heat of the fire at his back. He tried to roll the creature off of him, using the thing's momentum against it but it was steel and fur, Kevin pinned underneath it.

In a moment of sickening clarity, Kevin realized that Cyn could be killed.

It was the last thought he ever had as his head was severed from the column of his neck, blood spouting out in a spray that splattered Cynthia, who lay on the sand behind him. She closed her eyes as the warm droplets of copper struck her in a wet splash. When she opened her eyes, her lashes felt gummy from the blood and she knew she would be sick even as she heard Jules screaming for her in the background.

Then Jason was there. He rammed the twisted metal rod they used for marshmallow roasting into the creature's side and it reared back from Kevin's body with a howl, backhanding Jason like he was as substantial as a feather.

Jason grunted as he landed on the sand six feet or so behind the creature. Then the werewolf was on him and he had just enough time to shout, "Julia, run!" before he felt talons like razor blades encircle his neck, squeezing.

Julia felt her bladder clench even as she ran to Jason's side, ignoring his directive.

Her husband.

The thing with fur, standing over seven feet tall on its hind legs, had a hand that was half paw, and all talons, surrounding the delicate flesh of Jason's neck. His other hand raised in a high arc, readying to deliver the killing blow, claws like spears poised.

"No!" Julia screamed.

Its eyes shifted to hers as she ran to Jason. It seemed to pause.

Then the hand swept down, the nails like knives glinting in the dying light of the fire.

In a blur of light gray, something barreled into the werewolf.

But not before a second mouth of gore opened in Jason's throat. Blood welling and falling as his neck was opened in a deep slash of crimson.

The main artery compromised, Julia ran, sliding in the sand on her knees as she crumpled beside him. Tearing off her jacket she ignored the rawness and finality the wound represented, crushing the soft material against it in a desperate attempt to stop the bleeding.

She could hear the creature fighting something she dared not look at directly behind her. The sounds of meaty flesh being battered was all around her. The lapping of the waves did nothing to silence the music of their violence.

Her eyes met Jason's. She saw his death laying in them.

"Run," he said out of his ruined esophagus.

Tears ran down her face in a stream, never stopping. "Shh... don't... talk, Jason," she said in a voice that trembled so badly she could hardly speak.

His eyes urged her to escape even as she stayed. Cyn wailed something in the background. But Julia didn't make out the words. She realized belatedly that shock was settling in like an old friend and she recognized it. Oh yes, she did.

It was hauntingly familiar.

The crash that had stolen her family.

Julia heard a sound and looked up.

A man met her gaze, his hands buried wrist deep in the bowels of the creature that had attacked Jason. The gore splatter reached his shoulders, his hands were entwined in the thing's entrails like bloody worms that pulsated and glowed pearlescent in the firelight. Julia swallowed, his deep cranberry gaze the last thing she saw as she turned her face away, heaving the contents of the airplane food as far away as she could from Jason's body. Her quaking hands pressed the cloth against his wounded throat.

Pressing.

Julia felt heat coalesce, rising from her feet and eclipsing at the roots of her hair as she collapsed in a dead faint next to her fallen husband.

Her hands fell away from the wound and the blood came alive again, soaking the cloth of her hoodie, turning it from gray to black.

The full moon rode the sky over them, a cruel governess.

The vampire runners closed in and scooped up the limp body of the Rare One.

The acquisition was a success.

They left in stealth, as they had arrived.

* * *

JULIA'S EYES SNAPPED OPEN, her mouth clamped to stifle the scream that had almost erupted. Tears that had dried in sticky lines on her cheeks were the evidence of a dream she had hoped to never face.

A nightmare.

She was so tired she ached. Looking at the glowing red numbers of the clock she saw that she'd only been asleep for a few hours. It read 2:16 a.m. Early.

She held her body still and listened. The sense of unease she had felt earlier, deepened. Julia knew that something was wrong even as she heard the barest noise in the hall. But it was the primal alert sounding off inside her breastbone that told her what had found her.

Vampire.

They had come. She had to get out of the building.

Now.

She rose, shoving her feet into her shoes. She didn't even put on pants. Running to the window she lifted it silently, the breeze ruffled the hem of her nightshirt, raising goose flesh on her skin in a rush. Looking down at the ground she was at least fifteen feet from the lawn below. She didn't think it was jumpable.

But as her skin began to itch in warning, she knew that it was a matter of time before they had her. She looked around her room quickly. If she survived tonight, she could return in the daylight when the vamps would have to rest and retrieve her things.

She fingered the ring on her neck like a talisman.

Julia looked down again and closing her eyes, crouching on the windowsill, she shoved off. She sailed through the air, preparing herself for the landing, her hair unraveling behind her.

As the ground rushed toward her Julia tried to brace her fall but landed hard, rolling her ankle as she fell. She screamed deep in her throat as ribs were bruised and her ankle sprained. Her head had landed on the soft ground, with an impact that would have crushed it had it been a hard surface.

Driven by fear, Julia leaped to her feet, swaying while her vision remained in triplicate. Her ankle shrieked in protest as she began a hobbling run. Her goal: the woods that bordered the back of the property. She made the treeline, shivering without clothes just shy of making her teeth chatter. She didn't want that.

They would hear.

Julia entered the forest, dragging her leg behind her, clutching her ribcage as she jogged in an ungainly lurch.

William palmed the lock on the door, thankful that it was of vintage origin. Those almost always yielded to his influence. The tumblers shifted against one another smoothly and unlocked at his behest. He opened the door and was greeted by the sight of gauzy curtains, like taunting fingers, waving their mocking salute to he and the other runners.

"She is gone," Pierce said.

"She could not have gone far," Andrews said for only the vampires to hear.

Robert said, shrugging, "We track her, it is not difficult, she is but a girl."

William turned glittering eyes to Robert, a newer runner. "I am sure that is what the Were are considering, even as we speak it." He made his way to the window that Julia had escaped from. As he gazed down, he estimated the distance as perhaps five meters. Too great a fall for one of her stature and disposition.

Blood Singer or no, she was but an evolved human. Swathed in fragility.

He turned in profile, the moonlight chiseling his features like marble. "She will be injured. Slow. Let us make haste, moonlight is wasting."

The runners converged at the window. William leaped

from inside the small room, exiting the portal with lithe grace, crouched in mid-air, he landed with the barest hop, his nose skyward.

His head snapped down, his face turned in the direction behind the building.

The woods stood in unrelieved black, jagged points meeting the skyscape. He felt the vampires land at his back, fully fed, energized to pursue. He thought of Julia.

Precious and vulnerable. Alone. He hovered over the possibility of the Werewolves presence. Without turning, he took the lead, running headlong, following the Rare One's scent like a moth to flame. Her fragrance a bell ringing like a clear chime for him to hear.

Only him.

CHAPTER 12

WERE

*J*oseph used his eyesight in the gloom as the tool it was. Piercing the darkness as a laser, he searched for their salvation. Lost over a year ago to a number of blunders, she would not be unrecovered again. Five Were strong, they had the upper hand, as the vamps generally traveled by quad.

And they were closing in fast.

The girl was crashing through the brush. They but waited for her to stumble into the meadow where they stood.

She would fall into their arms like a ripe plum. Joseph restrained a howl, turning his luminescent gaze to his first, Anthony, who nodded back, his muzzle lifting slightly, revealing teeth honed for killing.

By tearing and biting.

The other three Were flanked them, partially obscured by trees. They blended so well that it would take one of the supernaturals to see them without night vision or some such.

Joseph growled softly, "The blood drinkers draw close as well."

Tony snorted out his response, "Let them come." His paws

tightening into cruel fists, his talons still short, the battle's lust imminent.

Joseph's primary enforcer was fearless and not nearly as controlled as himself. He'd need to dig deep within himself for control once he was faced with a Rare One. They brought out the very basest primal urges within their kind. Tony had scoffed when told. But he had never been on the acquisition of a Rare One. Only Blood Singers. It was not the same. The comparison could be made that it was like an appetizer of Ritz crackers as opposed to caviar. Never the twain shall meet.

They waited.

As the breath stilled in their bodies, Julia burst out of the haven of the woods, the fingers of the branches reluctantly releasing her from their care.

Her injuries assaulted the acute olfactory senses of the Were, alerting and arousing them simultaneously

The Were advanced toward her position.

* * *

Julia

JULIA RUSHED FORWARD, her foot tangling on a root as she ran and she fell, her palms biting into the dirt. The needles and branches scraped her palms without mercy. She threw herself into running again, the fir boughs whipping her as she tore through, the smell of cedar filling her nose.

Her lungs burning, Julia could see through the gaps in the trees, an open meadow was just ahead. She ran toward the clearing, feeling if she could just get out of these woods, she'd be free.

She threw herself out of the treeline, her breathing ragged, her ankle a throbbing stump she dragged along. Julia was greeted by five werewolves. She knew exactly what they were.

Now.

Their eyes bored into hers and she felt something integral shift inside her and open, a flicker of emotions assailing her.

It took Julia but one confused moment before she understood that it was one of the Were soldiers within the tight group whose emotions were leaking on her like a wayward radio signal.

She felt lust, power and greed. Not in that order. She turned to run back into the safety of the woods and was met by William and his team.

Trapped.

They walked out of the forest's border using a smooth and unhurried gait.

Julia felt her bowels hiccup, her palms instantly glazed with sweat, her throat threatening to close. A fear so profound she could not breathe.

They did not look at her, rather, they looked beyond her.

At the Were.

Julia began to shake, she had nowhere to go and could feel anger from the vamps and a primal surge of adrenaline from the Were. The emotions collided with her in the middle.

Their emotional sandwich.

Overwhelmed, she collapsed to her knees, a pain in her chest. She met William's eyes. They flicked to hers then locked back on the Were. She began to crawl away, tears dropping to the grass that was already drenched with dew. The wetness soaked her knees and the hem of the nightshirt she wore. Julia was suddenly struck that she was out in the middle of nowhere, in a strange place with nine creatures of legend.

Half-naked.

She flipped over and in one motion, pulled the shirt over her knees to the tops of her feet. Her teeth did chatter then. Her ankle throbbed with the beat of her heart.

Julia watched the obvious leader of the Were step forward and William circle him. Their talons, almost identical, slid out from the tips of their fingers. In the moonlight the vampire's looked black, the werewolf's a light sable.

"Save yourself, Blood Drinker. No one need know that you released the Rare One this night," the Were ground out, the timbre of his voice sounding full of gravel.

William smiled. "We would never let this one go. We but lost sight of her for one moment," he spread his hands, feigning reason and continued, "she is our salvation."

"Ours as well. We can breed her. What do you offer?" The Were asked as a statement, his teeth revealed in a snout that was almost human, until you saw the teeth like ivory razors held in an alligator's grasp. Ready to close at the least provocation.

"It is an impasse, then?" William asked, already crouching.

The Were backed away, swishing a tail as a command.

With a gnashing of teeth, the Were sprung on the vampire and a war of fang and claw began.

Julia watched in horror as the vampires began to fight for their lives, outnumbered five to four.

The prize they fought over lay to the west. An injured and sodden mess, huddled in a ball with fear riding her like a shroud of mist as an uncertain dawn approached.

* * *

William

WILLIAM SPRANG, fangs unsheathed, launching himself at the leader of the Were. Wrapping himself around the torso of the

Were like a steel vise, his fangs sunk deep, the foul taste of its flesh like acid in his mouth. He hung on tenaciously.

Even as Joseph sunk all ten talons along his vulnerable flank, William worried the Were's shoulder like a dog with a bone, grinding his teeth closer to the vulnerable bone that lay beneath.

Joseph felt the horrible, burning bite of the blood drinker pierce his upper shoulder and stifled a howl of rage. Instead, he launched his claws into the vampire's side, digging deep. Like a handle he lifted the drinker in the air, a piece of his shoulder coming with it and flung him away, releasing and retracting his claws as he did. The vamp landed with a practiced roll, springing upright, blood trails leaking everywhere Joseph looked. All ten.

Like mini geysers they flowed, the blood looking like black oil in the moonlight.

Joseph howled in triumph. The drinker was wounded, quite badly. But he was distracted as one of his soldiers head's flew by his peripheral vision like an errant bowling ball. His nostrils flared and he was stung by the awful smell of a drinker quite close. He gave an instinctual evasive lean as claws missed his exposed throat by millimeters. He reacted even as he leaned, bringing the claws of his right paw and swiping in an upward arc, releasing their full length as he did. The talons sprang from the stubs of his fingers and gutted the vamp as he leaped to finish the swipe that had not been true.

Andrew's face had a surprised look as Joseph held him suspended, mid-leap. He retracted his claws and the vamp fell at his feet on the long grass of the meadow. With his left hand, he made the final cut to sever the head.

That bastard drinker could have healed a disembowelment. He could heal nothing without a head, Joseph thought with brief satisfaction.

The head rolled to join his fallen Were and Joseph turned in the melee, blood spray and gore littering the pathway as he began to move toward the girl. Belatedly he realized that Tony already made his way to her.

Against express orders.

Joseph was the only Were allowed to touch the girl.

Already Joseph could smell the unshakable lust of his first, riding an unstoppable urge. He would crush the girl if he reached her first.

The sharp claws of Joseph's feet sprung from the pads of his feet, spearing the soft earth beneath him. He spun, using the finely honed balance they gave him. On the balls of his feet, he surged forward, each landing paw, gripping and shoveling a spray of dirt behind him.

Even with his incredible speed, he could see he would not reach the girl in time. For the first time as a Soldier of the Were, he experienced an emotion he had only heard about.

Fear.

And underneath that. Panic.

Julia

AND JULIA THOUGHT she'd known fear. Tasted it. She had not. Sheer terror took hold of her now. Something even scarier than William approached. Not at a dead run, no. He advanced with purpose, a light in eyes that were reflected in the pale moonlight like a cat's. Glowing.

They were fixed on her with a look she couldn't recognize. Finally, as he was almost upon her she thought she knew what it was. What he wanted.

He looked like he wanted to consume her.

Julia gave in to her intense fear, screaming so loudly her

voice left her and hoarse shouts were all she could give out. Her terror was not diminished from the lack of their volume.

She scooted backward on her haunches with an energy Julia didn't realize she possessed. Her modesty forgotten, she scuttled like a spider backward, using just her hands and feet.

Still he came.

CHAPTER 13

WILLIAM

illiam's sides burned as if on fire, the wounds inflicted by the Were deep, the poison released from his talons delivered and flowing through his system, weakening him.

He needed blood.

And his group was outnumbered. Andrew gone.

He heard a hoarse voice, hysteria riding it like fine wine. Normally, a scream like the one he heard would incite a tornado of blood lust.

Not tonight.

The source of the screaming was his to protect with his life. By any means necessary.

William shifted into the form that would allow him to travel faster, his only gift. The singular thing that separated him, identified him as having the blood of a Singer running through his veins.

His already injured body fought the change. William forced it upon himself, his body losing shape and molding into the raven. It was twice the size of the majestic Bald Eagle.

The eyes remained a deep cranberry, a color not found in nature. His ebony wings unfolded to a span of nearly ten feet. He rose, partially healing as he lifted from the ground, his clothes in a shredded pile at his feet. Lack of blood, coupled with injury made William sway in the air. He sharpened when he was greeted with the image of Julia struggling in the brutal embrace of the Were.

Clearly in the grips of lust.

Breeding lust.

William pointed his sharp beak at the pair, folding his huge wings against his body, he sailed down as an onyx torpedo.

* * *

Julia

JULIA SPRUNG to her feet just as Tony grabbed at her. She used her elbow in an insightful move that surprised both of them, using the hardest part of her body as a weapon she threw it up into the half-human face that was so close to her. Tony helped her by leaning into her just as she jabbed it forward.

Her elbow connected with his jaw and it stunned him for a moment.

Julia spun and began to run, her ankle screamed and she ignored it. Something grabbed her hair from behind and lifted her off the ground by it, her scalp shrieking and burning. Torquing her neck, the Were wrapped hands that could have crushed the windpipe they held around her neck and drew her against his body, almost tenderly.

His other hand tore the nightshirt she was wearing collar to hem, using only the tip of one claw.

It fell at their feet in a pile and he moved his hold from her neck to wrap her upper arms.

"I will breed you... Blood Singer," it growled out between impossibly long teeth.

Julia was fully panicked now. Looking down she saw what made him male in full view and used her hand like a weapon, clawing at his face and kicking out. He shook her so hard her teeth rattled and she saw stars, her head lolling about on the stem of her neck like a fragile flower.

Out of her trembling side vision Julia felt air rush past her and another of his kind bore down on him, his hold releasing, the claws sliding away without purchase. She fell to the grass beneath, her knees folding under her like a chair put away.

As she gazed up at the night sky, the sounds of flesh being torn and ripped, growling and yipping reverberating in her ears, a great black shape descended above her.

Julia lay there, the wetness of the grass soaking through her panties and cami.

She saw that it was a great bird, the eyes piercing her as it hovered above her in ebony glory, revealed only in outline by the full moon.

She didn't even scream when the talons from its feet pierced her shoulders, lifting her body in the air. The pain was a numbing horror but her mind protected her as unconsciousness washed over her body.

The last thing Julia remembered was an unearthly howl of anguish reaching her ears.

Then there was only blackness, the pain a spiral that trailed after her.

* * *

Joseph

JOSEPH CLOSED his muzzle with a snap, the howl echoing in the openness of the clearing. The small body of the Rare One was clutched to the drinker like a dark token in the sky.

One Were and one vampire lay in bloody heaps, his first on the ground, heaving from exertion and in the throes of shaking off the breeding lust with effort.

The fool.

He watched as the remaining vampires bled back into the forest seamlessly, their bodies melding so closely with the shadows their forms were indecipherable.

Another failed mission.

He looked at Tony with unveiled disgust. Maybe it would have gone similarly without this transgression, he did not know. What he did know is that the drinker had shifted. His intel had not divulged that skill amongst the runners. He must have Singer's blood running in his veins.

The rat bastard.

They needed that Singer, badly. Before a fully blooded vampire could breed her. A thing the Were had heard as rumored legend only.

Joseph was beginning to wonder if there was some truth to it.

He jerked his head at the three Were who lived, indicating their dead comrade.

They hefted the body, the vampire's remains lifting in the light breeze as so much ash at the mercy of the wind.

Joseph and the others turned to go, Tony bringing up the rear, his hand buried in the hair of the head of the fallen Were, carrying it like a macabre purse.

Tony's unfriendly eyes latched onto the back of his leader, malice taking shape like slow-moving poison, insidious and progressive.

* * *

the kiss of Seattle

Burning.

On fire.

Julia was on fire.

Her eyes popped open and she wanted to scream. Instead, out of a mouth so parched her lips were cracked, she moaned. Her shoulders were one burning mass of flesh.

She cracked open an eyelid and saw fuzzy shapes moving silently around the room. Above her was filtered ambient light.

A presence came close to her and she flinched. "Shh, you're safe," a female voice said.

Right, Julia thought in exhaustion. She hadn't felt safe since the day Jason died.

Another blurry person, a male, came to stand next to the female, who made Julia feel a sense of comfort.

"We will have to put that shoulder back. Right it."

Julia watched as they looked at one another, her vision doubling.

She felt a gentle hand at her wrist and a bulging piece of cloth placed underneath her armpit, a fist wedged up underneath it and as her arm was pulled the fist punched upward and she shrieked. The pain at once piercing and awful.

Julia sunk back in to unconsciousness on a hitching sob.

William looked down at her, his hand sliding from its placement underneath her shoulder. The joint was back in its rightful place, that pinched look she had worn since her arrival was gone.

He breathed out and looked at Claire.

"She is so fragile..." she said. As she looked at Julia, she took in the bizarre hair color, the paleness of her skin, a touch of blue to her nostrils and lips. She had lost much blood. She looked at William.

"You will need to give her more blood," she said, her eyes searching his.

"Every drop I give her binds us tighter."

"Perhaps, but if you don't, she will heal humanly slow. In agony." She looked at him, knowing things that she should not and he scowled.

Claire knew what his life's goal had been, her eyes moving over the tell-tale mark on the girl's forehead.

What it had always been. It was in the Book of Blood. The vampire equivalent of the Bible. A Rare One would save the race from the brink of extinction. A union between a vampire of Singer descent and a Rare One brought the tenuous hope of offspring. One which William wanted.

Quite badly.

Children who were as strong as vampires. Possessing all the abilities but without the need to drink blood, living as the feral in the cover of darkness. Yes, who would not wish for that.

Long for it.

Julia bore the mark. A half-moon shaped scar like a small kiss of flesh hovered at her temple. It was the symbol of the Rare One. It looked very much like the moon, pure white.

William's hands balled into fists, guilt sweeping over him as he took in the gauze dressings, already discolored by Julia's blood.

He had almost torn her shoulders off in flight. When she fainted, well... it had been a near thing. The dead weight hanging her like meat off a hook. He clenched his eyes, willing the image of her broken body away as he had brought it into the bowels of the underground. The forgotten city that lay beneath Seattle.

The lair of his kiss.

He looked above him, watching the feet of the passing pedestrians as they walked over glass that was a foot thick.

Scuffed and cloudy, it had a vague purple hue, garnered by a century of sunlight he would never behold.

He sighed and looked at Claire, who had stubbornly folded her arms across her chest. The granddaughter of a Rare One, she should be renamed Stubborn One.

He came by his tenacious streak honestly. Claire was his cousin.

His fangs elongated, he placed the twin points against his wrist. Sweeping sideways, he made a clean cut like a razor thin line and blood welled, almost black.

Squeezing his wrist to prompt the flow, he used his other hand to massage Julia's throat. As the drops fell, her full lips parted and the first trembling drop held itself suspended for a moment like a glittering gem, then fell.

As the blood found its way inside her mouth, she stirred, her throat convulsing and swallowing. Without waking, her hands moved to the offered forearm, small and pale against even his flesh, like carved ivory, her grip weak as a kitten's. William leaned closer, the pull of her mouth against his flesh an erotic tether that bound him to her.

She drank.

William resisted his impulses.

They were many.

CHAPTER 14

*J*ulia awoke naturally, her body aching. As she became aware incrementally, her body didn't hum with fear, but with a subtle calmness.

She never felt calm.

Her eyes snapped open and were met by a stare that matched her own. She had never known anyone to have eyes the same shade as hers and was momentarily speechless.

Julia tried to sit up and the room spun. The woman's arm that was attached to that stare rose and pressed her back against the pillows that were stacked behind her.

She opened her mouth to speak and Claire stood, leaning forward she pressed a cup with a straw against Julia's chapped lips. "Drink. You're dehydrated."

Julia drank. It was the best water she'd ever had. It was refreshingly chilled and it coated her parched throat like the first spring rains in the desert.

She tried to gulp but the woman took the cup away when Julia would have had more.

"Small sips, we don't want that stomach of yours giving up the blood inside you."

Julia's expression changed and Claire saw it. "Don't even start, Julia."

Julia narrowed her eyes on the woman and she said, "The only reason you're not on that bed writhing around in pain is because of the blood William gave you." She cocked a brow.

"I'll bet," Julia croaked out, her voice raw from screaming.

"He didn't want to," Claire stood. "I forced him. It is bad enough for you to transition into our coven, we don't need an injury slowing that assimilation."

She looked at Julia. "I'm Claire."

Julia nodded in greeting. Claire obviously knew who she was.

Julia shrugged, she felt a comfort in her presence, true. But Julia had reason to distrust them. She could sense what was around her.

Vampires.

And not a few.

Legion.

* * *

Joseph

MAGGIE FUSSED over Tony when Joseph would have left the smallness of his injuries alone. Let him deal with it. He continued to seethe as she ministered to the long gashes that crisscrossed Tony's torso. She was disinfecting the open wounds.

Vampire venom was poisonous. Joseph smiled, thinking of the one he'd speared with his claws.

He'd have been feeling some serious pain. Delirium would be his friend as he flew with the Rare One. A troubling thought. What if he'd injured the Singer in his pain-induced stupor?

Maggie stood back, critically looking at the dressed wounds. "I think ya may live another day," she clucked like a mother hen.

Joseph looked at her, his expression softening. It was not her fault that he was pissed at his first. She was doing her job. Attending the Were soldiers. There was one less tonight. His headless body cooled in a shed on the Were compound. Lawrence would want a full report; then a ceremony would need to be arranged for his fallen comrade.

Now it was his horrible task to tell Colton's widow the news that her mate was gone. Joseph hung his head.

After a long moment of reflection, he planted massive hands on his jean-clad thighs. Standing, he stared at Tony, waiting until Maggie bustled out of the room. He watched the departure of her back and turned to Tony, stabbing a finger in his direction. "I have duties to attend to but you will answer to Lawrence. Your Packmaster will know what you elected to do, allowed yourself to do. It is *you* that jeopardized this mission."

"You can't blame me for everything," Tony said with derision, his upper lip curling back slightly.

Joseph came forward and Tony sprang to his feet, they crashed into each other, knocking a lamp off an end table. As it slammed to the floor, shards flying everywhere, Joseph took the six-foot three Tony down in an arm lock that drove his elbow into the other man's sternum, the windpipe compromised. Joseph felt the change hovering in a dim corner of his brain and his vision changed, his facial bones rearranging in a disconcerting clay like movement that had the room filling with the sounds of their shifting, tendons popping into their new arrangement.

But it was just his face and hands that changed. The rest of Joseph remained as it was. He slowly removed his arm from the throat of the soldier who had acted on impulse.

Joseph replaced it with a claw nearly a foot long in variegated and mottled browns, creams and tans.

"Do not," Joseph said on a growl, his throat partially changed, his teeth gleaming with killing intent in a mouth that now had a muzzle covered in gray fur.

"I can and I will blame you." His gold eyes round and large in his wolf form, peered at Tony. "You were without control so near the Singer. You begged me for this assignment, refused to be desensitized."

"I would not harm her!" Tony growled back, mindful of his own change, which bore down on him enough to make sweat bead on his upper lip, the restraint he employed ugly.

"Rape is harm!" Joseph barked at Tony.

He understood anyway.

"We are meant to breed her!" Tony said, exasperated.

"Not without the ceremony, not without the proper testing. She cannot be with *any* wolf. She must be properly matched, properly mated. Do you not see?"

Tony did not, narrowing his eyes on his Alpha. He would give anything to be the Alpha. He could not think for the scent of the Singer. How had Joseph stood it?

One day the position would be his.

By whatever means necessary.

There was a noise by the door and Adriana rushed in, landing a solid kick to Joseph's side with her full werewolf strength and his rib bruised instantly, robbing some of his breath.

"Goddammit! Adriana! It's not what it looks like!" Joseph said, removing the threatening claw from Tony's throat and leaping to his feet, one hand on his rib.

"Oh! You aren't over-disciplining one of our wolves?" his sister yelled at him from a foot shorter. Her eyes flashed and her small hands were planted on her hips. "Get rid of that ridiculous half-wolf face you're sporting and get your ass to Lawrence's chamber this instant!"

Tony smirked and Joseph whipped his head in Tony's direction and gave a low growl. Tony's smile faded.

"Ugh... you dummy! Why don't you just pee on him and get it over with? That's not how you do it. Watch me. Ya know, your smarter sibling."

Adriana turned to Tony, who she was not nuts over, but fair was fair. "Tony, would you please go to Lawrence and give him a full report of what happened on the mission in the next half hour?"

Tony struggled to his feet, giving as neutral a look at his Alpha that he could manage. "Happy to," he said, giving a stare that spoke volumes to Joseph.

Joseph sighed, his ribs squawking with the movement. "Adriana, you weren't there, you didn't participate in the mission..."

Her ponytail bobbed as she nodded her head. "Right, because I am a lowly female!" Her face reddened.

There was no way that Joseph wished to engage in this tired argument again. If she had been male, she would be Packmaster. As it was, she practically ran the den. Their father had made him promise to watch over her.

It was essentially a full time job. And she was vaguely nose-blind. His nose was the keener of the two and he wished that she'd trust him. She let her emotions run her actions sometimes.

Like now.

"Adi..." he began.

"No," she stomped her foot. "Tony is injured," she swung her palm to Tony, all but healed. After she turned back to Joseph, Tony grinned.

Sometimes wolves needed to sort things out. Physically.

Too bad the females were not seeing that necessity. He was the Alpha, he saw it.

He regretted what he must do. He opened his jaws wide and latched them onto her vulnerable neck, growling low in his throat.

"Argh..." Adriana yelped. Joseph was careful not to break the skin, as she thrashed around he subtly followed her movements so her skin would not tear. She grew still.

He unclamped his muzzle, regarding her with eyes like spun gold, his gaze gentle but stern. "Let me be Alpha, sister."

She rubbed her throat, where many small red indents marred the creaminess of it.

Tony was silent, letting the two siblings hash it out. He silently thanked whatever was Holy that *he* didn't have a sister. He shuddered.

"This is how an Alpha operates. You are Alpha as well, it should not come as a surprise."

"Ugh! You're so unreasonable! Such a He-Man! Hate it!" She flung her arms up in the air and stomped off.

That went so well.

Joseph sighed, making his ribs twinge.

"Move, soldier," he pointed ahead of him and Tony walked toward it.

Joseph followed the blazoned path his sister had scorched on her way out, moving to the Packmaster's chamber for debriefing.

What a joyous occasion would be had by all, he thought, as his face and hands melded back into their human mask.

* * *

Homer, Alaska

DETECTIVE TRUMAN WAS CROUCHED DOWN on his haunches, letting pewter sand run through his fingers slowly. A year later and he still couldn't get the scene out of his mind. The blood, the body... the aftermath.

They were still no further to solving the crime than when they first began. Truman stood, looking out over the vast ocean, the snow capped mountains of the Kenai Fjords in ominous grace, a backdrop to a tousled sea that had white-caps everywhere he looked. He sighed, standing. He kicked a large pebble, it bounced off a large piece of driftwood, the stains of blood that covered it looking like so much spilled coffee with the passage of time.

He'd go by the girl's apartment. He liked to visit Cynthia Adams.

She never got angry at his questions.

Unlike the Caldwell family. He couldn't force their cooperation, but a person would think that they'd want to find out who took their daughter-in-law. They didn't want to know. They no longer had a son, they'd said. And they'd certainly never considered Julia Wade part of their family.

Technically she was, the marriage license validated and duly noted.

She was Julia Caldwell now, wherever she was.

If she lived.

Detective Karl Truman hiked up the small ravine, swiping branches aside. Some of the larger ones were broken off at the trunk, sap covering their amputated stumps. He didn't pause on his climb to wonder what might have snapped a branch the size of a man's wrist off at the base.

The police had looked for rational explanations to the murder and disappearance.

When what they should have been looking for was anything but rational.

CHAPTER 15

*J*ulia was working into a routine of sorts, steering clear of the vampire that had "saved" her. Her arms were working again and she had full rotation, the scars from the talons that had sunk deep, almost gone.

She looked in the mirror, running a finger over the shiny pink wounds. They faded each day. Julia would brush her teeth and her eyes would move back to the reflection of them in the glass like a magnet to steel.

She knew more than she had before and wished she didn't.

There was no escaping this place. She felt the inevitability of her circumstances closing in around her and it gave her an almost suffocating feeling of claustrophobia.

Julia tapped the toothbrush on the edge of an old-fashioned pedestal sink, shedding the remaining water from the bristles. She turned the spigot sharply to the left and the water dried up, a tremulous drop falling and hitting the basin with a dull plop. She skewered the base of the brush through one of the four holes in the holder that was attached to the wall and without looking at her reflection again, she walked away.

Julia knew the routine. Claire would knock as she entered. They'd have breakfast together. Julia would fight panic attacks and Claire would lend some of that calm she had in abundance and Julia would live another day.

But she was just existing. She was good at inhaling and exhaling. She'd become almost expert since Jason died.

They were biding their time. Grooming her. You see, Julia knew what she was now. She was some prophesied genetic key.

The key that would unlock the prison of their existence. She was the answer to them not being vampires anymore. Julia didn't really think it was that damn simple, but they fed her what they wanted her to know.

Their version.

To listen to Claire explain it, it was some kind of honor. But she'd heard one of the vampire guards discussing humans.

Humans were cattle to them.

Food load. Without humans, they would die. Starve.

The Blood Singers were an essential element to the genetic diversity of the humans' blood. Without this superior faction, intermixed with the regular population, the blood quantum, its quality would be compromised.

In essence, Blood Singers brought the quality of the blood to a level that made all human blood palatable to the vampires.

All.

Vampires were ruled by blood and darkness; the Were by the moon. She was a jealous mistress, governing their changes at her whim. And that whim was when she was full. No more, no less.

Julia's lessons had begun. Through Claire, Julia began to understand her role. Why she never would have been allowed to live with Jason as a spouse.

Blood Singers did not intermarry. The purity of their blood was needed to balance the precious blood quantum. Mating with each other would upset this balance.

Singers were so rare that it was typically not a problem. Claire had mentioned a figure that was one, one hundredth of the global population. That meant Blood Singers numbered around nearly seven hundred thousand souls. A lot, right? No. Spread over the seven continents, it was barely sustaining the vampires. They numbered more.

That is why the two factions had converged on their group at the beach. They would never have allowed the union. But she and Jason did it in secret, so they hadn't known. But they'd been watching, accelerating their plan because of Jason and Julia's elopement.

Julia guessed the plan hadn't included Jason's death.

Claire had explained her parents to Julia. In detail. Both Blood Singers, they had been taken before they could have more children.

It hadn't been an accident, but providential.

As it happens, the one thing they did produce through the coupling of their gene pool was a daughter.

The manifestation of their combined recessive genes was Julia.

She was the Rare One. The unique female, promised to change the face of the races. Able to produce Lightwalkers. If bred to the Were their offspring would be moonless changers. The moon's control would be gone after several generations. The compulsion to be her slave no longer there.

Bred out.

Julia felt like the prized mule.

Then there were the supposed abilities. Supernatural

117

abilities. She remembered the conversation she and Claire had just yesterday.

* * *

"How can you stand it? Living here... with them?" Julia asked. Her arms folded across her chest, rubbing her skin as if she were cold. She wasn't, she was creeped out and unhinged. Everything Claire had told her reverberated around in her skull like a pin ball.

Rare One? Blood Singers? One of hundreds of thousands of people?

"I have little choice. This is the place that I have come to belong. I've been here many years."

"What about my parents? Were *they* expendable? Jason?" Julia asked in a low voice, her arms by her sides, trembling slightly in her anger.

Claire lifted a shoulder. "It is not typical. One in ten thousand is a Singer. That your parents found one another... that you found and married a Singer..." she looked at Julia. "It's unprecedented."

Wonderful. Julia's parents, dead. Jason, dead. All because vampires wanted their food all pretty and tasty.

Seemed legit to her.

Fancy cattle. That's all the Singers were to all of them, vampires and Were alike. Julia told Claire that.

She shook her head. "We are more. The quality of our blood and the fabric of our genetics are not the only things we have to offer, Julia." Her eyes searched Julia meaningfully. "Have you ever had flashes of intuition? Feelings of a precognitive nature?"

Julia sucked in her breath. She'd always known who was phoning as soon as her hand touched the receiver. What the next song would be on the radio. When there'd be a pop quiz in school. Now that everyone sent texts, she'd get a vibration before it rang.

Not from the cell, from within her body. She'd always just chalked it up to one of those things.

It sure the hell was one of those things. It just wasn't the thing she'd been thinking.

Can you hear me? Claire asked. Her lips weren't moving. Icy fingers brushed inside her head and Julia shivered. The feeling of an itch not quite being scratched hovered in her brain.

"What did you say?" Julia asked out loud. Sure as she was standing there that she was imagining things. People didn't have telepathy.

Can you do this? Claire asked, her voice breathing through Julia's mind.

I don't know, Julia replied, aiming her thoughts at Claire like a well trained archer.

She must have hit the bull's-eye because Claire smiled and responded, *I thought it might be possible. It is spoken that the Rare One will come to possess all the talents for our people.*

Julia backed away, stunned. It was too much to take in. A wave of calmness stole over her, making her feel slightly numb, drugged.

"Stop doing that!" Julia yelled.

"I only wish to help. I am part of you, we all are," Claire said, moving forward, her rich chestnut hair falling around her shoulders as she came at Julia.

Julia stumbled, falling backward. She felt something well inside of her, rushing to the surface like an errant bubble of oxygen sliding to the surface of a pool of water. She allowed it to leave her, bursting on Claire.

Julia hadn't meant to hurt her.

Claire looked like she'd had an invisible ripple plow into

her and she slammed into the wall. Just inches from the hearth that boasted an old fireplace.

Full of jagged rock.

Claire slid down the wall, stunned. Julia got up off the floor, rubbing her arms again, her body flushed, her head light. She began to move toward Claire when the door slammed open and William was there, glancing at his relative leaning against the wall where she'd been thrown. Julia hopped over the back of the couch where she'd been sitting and he was flying over it and underneath her before she could jump to the ground.

She screamed and he crushed her to him.

Her chest tightened painfully, the proximity to him unbearable.

She could feel it like silken tentacles pulling taut.

The call of her blood to his.

The consumption of his blood a pulsating thread that bound them.

Like a song.

A blood song.

The guard at the door took in the vampire Julia hated holding her against himself like she was the most precious treasure in the world.

To him, she was.

* * *

Julia

JULIA WAS GODDAMNED DONE with the coven. She was considered a flight risk.

Gee, ya think?

So, they had her guarded all the time. There were humans called "intimates," who were the day slaves of the vampire underworld. They guarded her when the vampire slept. While awake, they had the vampire guard. Day in and day out.

Julia was frustrated. She wanted to leave her room. It didn't matter that it was beautiful and all her needs were met. So what? She was little more than a bird in a gilded cage.

She and Claire had come to an uneasy truce. She would teach Julia to harness her abilities, Julia would not use them against Claire. Simple, right? Not really. Julia was already planning on honing said skills and getting the hell out of the coven. She wasn't stupid though. Julia knew that learning what these abilities were, practicing them with someone that also had them... well, it made sense. She decided to bide her time. *Not that there was a plethora of options*, she thought dejectedly.

Claire came to her the next day with the news that she had been there a month and it was time to meet the leader of the Seattle Coven, Gabriel.

He was Claire's brother, a Rare One.

If Julia had thought the odds of running into one of her kind slim, a Rare One was even slimmer. Claire had explained, out of the almost seven hundred thousand people who were potential Singers, only one percent of those were the coveted Rare Ones.

Wonderful. Julia didn't think that it had helped her in the slightest. It had just gotten the people she cared about dead. A tightening of her chest came on the heels of that marvelous revelation.

The vampires were old school. Claire told her there would be a ball of sorts. Like an old-fashioned "coming out." Julia would be the guest of honor. Their stolen prize.

The blue ribbon winner.

The prize Heifer.

They didn't need to milk her, just breed her. But to whom?

She'd never let one of the blood suckers touch her. It was only afterward that Claire told her William had "blood shared." Saving her indescribable agony from the wounds he inflicted on her, allowing her to heal quickly.

Not her problem. If they'd not chased her, he wouldn't have had to use everything he had to get her here. Julia thought of the feeling of the talons piercing her flesh, her bone the next layer beneath the biting claws and shuddered at the memory.

It was his fault she was here.

His.

* * *

debutant

WILLIAM STUDIED HIS REFLECTION, securing the matching cufflinks at the cuffs of his custom made button-down. It was burgundy silk, woven against the grain to produce a slight sheen with movement. Claire said it brought out his eyes. The eyes that met his reflection were the deepest shade of red, just shy of black, his pupils inky dots in their center. But they were not always so, depending on circumstance they could appear reflective, silver. He lowered his sleeves after adjusting the links just right. Sterling squares with a beveled and scalloped edge were pierced with a star burst that held a brilliant blue sapphire chip in its core. An heirloom from his father before him.

He sighed. Sometimes the pomp and circumstance of these ceremonies weighed heavily on him.

William thought of what Claire had told him. Julia was

resistant, distrustful. In her youth she thought that she could fool Claire into thinking she was compliant.

William had warned her this was not so. Julia had a steely resolve, never forgetting a wrong vested upon her.

That is why those whiskey-colored eyes followed him with indifference and sufferance.

Julia was not immune to the fire that burned in their veins from the blood share. Her blood called to him. She had tasted of his, so now she had a fraction of the feeling of the song that he held within himself for her.

She listened to his blood as a melody.

Her blood to him was a symphony.

There really was no comparison.

William turned from his reflection, forbidding his despair to take over. This was the Greeting Ceremony. Aside from Gabriel there had not been one in his kiss for three centuries.

Rare indeed.

He slipped quietly out of his chamber, hesitating slightly outside her door, apprehension at her proximity making his step falter. He drew himself together. He could not abide a slip of a girl commanding a warrior of the vampire.

William strode off, never glancing back.

His desire behind him, his plan ahead.

Julia

JULIA TURNED her head in mid-stroke of the hairbrush when she felt the familiar tightening inside her breastbone.

"What is it?" Claire asked, locking her gaze with Julia's in the mirror's reflection. Julia unconsciously rubbed her chest as she stared at the door, her breath held in her throat.

"I don't know," she whispered.

But she did. William stood outside the door. She was deathly afraid he'd come in.

She was even more afraid because she wanted him to.

Her body crawled with the need to be near him, the chemical aspects of the blood in her body more than they had been. Twice now he'd given her his blood. Each time, life saving. It was the quantity that mattered. When it reached critical mass, she would be left choiceless.

Claire had explained it was part of the mating process. That he had given her blood twice drove them closer to being mated. Whether he was right for her or not.d

Whether she wanted it or not.

"After the greeting ceremony is over then there will be a courtship within the circle of eligible vampires."

Julia couldn't believe how ridiculous it all sounded. A little more than a year ago she'd been a high school senior, secretly engaged.

Then married. Pretty unforgettable.

She'd been on a path of life so divergent from this one she could never reconcile the two, however much she thought about it.

Now, she would be handed over to the best mate of the vampire contingent. The one with whom she could produce the most likely offspring.

"The sooner you accept your placement here, the better off you'll be," Claire said, admiring Julia's gown. Trying to hide her scowl at Claire's words, even Julia had to admit it was the most beautiful thing she'd ever worn.

It was the palest champagne, almost a soft tangerine. Her ginger colored hair shone above it. Claire had seen to it that her hair had been expertly cut around her shoulders, where it curled softly.

"We keep your hair down for the greeting. No need to be

provocative this first time. It will be hard enough for them as it is."

Right, Julia thought, *the blood lust.*

Murmured voices reached Julia's ears as she swept in with Claire, the vampire guard and Clarence, trailing behind them soundlessly.

The voices stopped instantaneously, an ominous silence filling the cavernous space. Julia looked up, not being able to help noticing a central strip of ambient light that was perfectly spaced. Large grid-like skylights lined the ceiling of where she stood. Rectangular in size, they housed many thick glass circles. Dark spots would appear above them with regularity. It was mesmerizing.

The vampires stared at her as she brought her gaze down from the ceiling peppered by glass.

A man came forward and instantly Julia felt her body respond. It was not sexual. It was synchronicity. This man was kindred to her. She felt more related to him than she'd ever felt to her flesh and blood aunt.

He smiled and it was sun breaking through clouds. For the first time since her arrival she felt something slide into place.

Something that felt like home.

He was tall and she had plenty of time to assess him as he came toward her, his copper hair slicked back and tied in a navy silk band at the nape of his neck. He had a slight accent when he said, "You are Julia." He formed it as a statement when it was truly a question.

She nodded, the hair sliding around her bare shoulders. Her nervousness felt like a caged animal yearning for release.

"Welcome!" he said in a booming voice that echoed against the stone walls. Julia fought not to jump as he looked around and faced the crowd of vampires.

There were so many they lined the walls, some lingering

in the tall, bricked archways, two feet thick at the threshold. Julia's eyes searched the crowd, many faces expressionless, a few held contempt. Julia swallowed.

The faces lost their neutral expression as they tracked the small movement of her throat like vultures circling a dying meal.

In this case, it was she that they watched.

Gabriel continued, "Here is the one our warriors have brought to us. The first Rare One in three centuries. Here now. For the prophesied continuation of our race. It will be she that allows daywalking. And so much more."

He turned those golden eyes to hers, so much like Claire's, so much like Julia's.

"Please welcome Julia Wade into our kiss," he stepped back with a flourish and Julia sat there pegged, a butterfly's wings pinned to a board. Examined. Scrutinized. It was beyond awkward.

She wasn't anyone's savior. Julia was herself. That's all she was.

She stepped forward. And, brave beyond measure, or foolish, She didn't know which, Julia said, "It's Caldwell. Julia Caldwell."

At that moment, she met William's eyes and there was anger in his. Julia was sure that he wanted her to move on with her life. The husband she loved had been dead for over a year. The relationship never consummated. *Well... there was more to love than having sex*, Julia thought. If that was all there were then there'd be a ton of people married to more than one person.

In her heart, she was still married to Jason. Dead or alive, he still held it in his hands.

Warm and beating.

Her guts clenched thinking about being here. She swung her head to the leader, Gabriel.

He seemed to intuit where her emotional barometer was at that moment and said, "Caldwell then. Please," he looked over the crowd, who had begun to whisper amongst themselves at her correction, "make Julia feel welcome amongst us."

She sighed, giving one more glance to William and moved to Gabriel's side.

Resigned but not beaten.

Never that.

CHAPTER 16

*E*verywhere Julia looked she saw blood. It filled the elaborately cut crystal punchbowl in the center of a table easily twenty feet long. Stemmed glasses of every configuration stood around it like sentinels. The color wash cleverly hid what the glasses would contain once filled.

Blood.

Human blood.

The goblets looked like they were on fire, backlit from the sconces which lined the stone walls at a man's head height. In this case vampires.

But there were not just male vampires, but female as well. Not many, but they were there.

They were not happy with Julia's presence. She could feel their discontent like a weight on the nape of her neck, her skin crawling with it.

Well, neither was she. They could rein in their attitude, 'cause she didn't want to be here any more than they wanted her to be.

William came to Julia, taking her elbow and it felt like a match had been touched to flame, the heat of his contact with her bare arm igniting it neatly. It drove up her arm in a fine line of warmth, reaching the middle of her chest where it burst like a bubble. She gasped, catching her breath and watched William's jaw flutter as he clamped down on his reaction.

"Let go of me," Julia hissed quietly, her eyes flashing.

William turned to her, hissing back, "I will not coddle you." Her eyes narrowed on him and he continued, "I did what I must, to protect you. I am *so* sorry you do not see what is beneath your nose." His crimson eyes searched hers with anger, he wanted her to at least accept that he was doing his duty. The acquisition of her was something he had been tasked to accomplish. It was not personal.

Yet, on some level it was.

William did not kill her husband. That was the Were's interference, as was typical of their kind. No planning, just reactive brutality and passion. They could not have gotten a job done with finesse if a gun barrel had been pressed to their collective heads.

Julia ripped her elbow out of his grasp. It made her madder when she realized he could have kept her wherever he wanted. She thought of what happened with Claire. She immediately wanted to do the same with William. To him. But through the stone wall.

She smiled at her thoughts.

William looked at her and smiled back grimly. He could almost feel her intent, the blood union singing between them. Her thoughts were not known to him, but her emotional signature was loud and clear.

He removed his hand as if scorched. "Fine," William said. He leaned into her face from inches away. "Know this, Blood Singer, everything I do, I do for you. Not I. If it were for me, it would be so different." He ran a finger down her jawline and Julia shivered involuntarily.

William turned on his heel and stalked off. He left Julia just inside the threshold of one of the archways with vampires everywhere. She did not know any of them and suddenly felt like she'd been a little too dismissive of him. She glanced around uneasily, noticing Clarence of the guard was within ten feet.

He was ghosting her movements. He'd follow her into the bathroom if she'd let him. Maybe there was no letting him after all.

Julia wanted to tear her hair out. No privacy, nothing but living in a fishbowl.

Gabriel approached. He gazed at her intently for a moment, looking almost dashing in his navy suit. A crisp shirt in warm white was accented with a soft tangerine tie. Julia recognized the color immediately. It was the same as her dress. They matched.

Great.

Gabriel watched her with such tenderness Julia dropped her eyes. She was determined to not make friends here. She wanted to belong to herself.

Julia felt his finger before it touched the underside of her chin, lifting it to his gaze. "I know how you feel. I understand."

She moved her face away as his hand fell to his side. "You don't know how I feel. Claire told me that my parents and Jason were taken because Blood Singers can't intermarry. It was only a matter of time before they would've broken Jason and I up!" she whispered to him in a rush. Julia tried to be quiet but many of the vampires turned their faces to she and Gabriel, the conversation ringing in their ears.

"I do not wish for this to be the place for this conversation," he said, deftly swinging the conversation away from the heat of her anger.

Fine. So convenient for him.

Gabriel took Julia out of the archway of the pass through. She looked behind her at a long corridor filled with many wooden doors like the one that that kept her prisoner in her chamber. Thick, impenetrable.

Julia would leave this place. She straightened her spine and walked away with Gabriel. He took that as acquiescence and looped her arm through his.

Julia schemed as they approached a circular group of vampires.

She plastered a phony smile on her face, hoping William would not be amongst them. Hopefully, he was off sulking somewhere, licking the wounds she'd inflicted on him.

Julia's smile turned genuine.

William studied Julia covertly from the shadows. Seeing her expression change he wondered what she had been musing about.

* * *

Were

LAWRENCE WAS BEYOND DISPLEASED. The vampires would be extra vigilant now. Two failed missions. The reacquisition of the Rare One would need to be executed with the utmost stealth.

"It matters not that Tony behaved rashly. Ultimately, it was your responsibility as acting Alpha, Joseph."

Joseph knew that. Maybe he had not been clear enough.

"I don't want to see Tony receive discipline, Packmaster." Joseph watched Lawrence's nostrils flare and his eyes change from their standard brown to a liquid gold. The eyes they all held when the heart of the wolf beat inside their body.

"You speak true," the Packmaster intoned, his eyes becoming the flat human brown they usually were. "But he must be desensitized before the next mission." He looked at the two of them. "Which will be soon."

He stood, his lean body tall and graceful. Lawrence ran a hand through his unruly hair, wavy and untamed, he made it worse by combing it with his fingers. He pulled a map of sorts from his desk drawer and used his tapered fingers to smooth it out.

"Come," he told them.

They did, bending over to see what lay before them.

Joseph's face whipped up in shock. "This is where the coven is located? In the middle of downtown?" he scoffed.

Lawrence slowly nodded, tapping his nose. "As it has been since the great fire of 1898."

When he and Tony waited he sighed. "My grandsire trained me when I was but a wee wolf," Lawrence indicated a height of a human toddler. "He told me, 'Lawrence, you must know where your enemies hide'." He looked as serious as Joseph had ever seen him.

"But we don't fight them, Packmaster," Joseph stated the obvious, frustrated with the history lesson. He wanted the Packmaster to just elaborate on the plan of action. The rest was extraneous.

Tony laughed at Joseph's statement.

Joseph growled softly in his throat, heat infusing his esophagus. The change hovered, as it always did at the moon's zenith.

"We do not *challenge*, Alpha," he corrected, giving a growl that echoed Joseph's in Tony's direction and his eyes slid away from the both of them in a submissive response.

Satisfied, Joseph turned his attention back to Lawrence.

"There is a difference. You ken to what it is, eh?"

Joseph nodded. "I do, but I think we'll have to beat them at their own game." He looked at his Packmaster's face for a lingering moment then continued, "I have wolves that can gather intel, return to us with a method of acquisition for Julia Caldwell before they know what hit them," Joseph said as he punched a balled fist into his open palm, the sound of it filling the small space.

"Excellent. But first, you may be cognizant of the numbers."

"We need at least fifteen strong. We outnumbered them by one and still they escaped," Tony elaborated, speaking out of turn.

But he was right, Joseph thought and added, "It matters nothing. The one vampire had Singer blood. He shifted as an evasive tactic!"

Lawrence's brows shot to his hairline. "You would have captured her without this unexpected... event?"

"Abso-fucking-lute-ly," Tony said and Joseph frowned.

Lawrence chuckled, looking Tony square in the eyes. "We cannot afford to lose even one soldier." He turned his attention to his Alpha. "You are in charge of desensitizing your wolves. Do it. And do it quickly. We need to be ready for the soonest opportunity. Reconnaissance at the lair of the blood drinkers is essential. Establish time lines for their habits, follow their intimates."

"Yes, Packmaster," Joseph said. But he didn't like it. He had reservations about Tony. The image of Julia Caldwell struggling in his embrace was something that didn't leave him easily. Tony was a volatile wolf. Rash. He'd been that way since whelphood.

He bore watching.

The two werewolves strode out side by side. The Packmaster watched the pair, sensing the rancor between the two. He knew he had struck a match to their tempers.

That was the way of it. If Tony felt he was wolf enough to take Joseph in a fair challenge, let it happen. He would not cripple his unit of soldiers because the Alpha used caution as a shield. He would force their innate aggressiveness to the forefront.

Beside... Tony was obviously wanting a higher position in the pack.

Lawrence could smell it.

His nose never lied.

* * *

vampire

JULIA ALLOWED herself to be led by Gabriel's arm to the small group of vampires, their dark eyes tracking her like falcons. She could feel the material of her long gown swirl around her legs as she moved toward them, light and shadows lending their expressions a unity to one another.

"These are your potential suitors, Julia," Gabriel said, not even bothering to offer the introduction in a softer light.

He may as well have said, "Take your pick of breeding stock."

Julia crossed her arms underneath her breasts. She did not realize the posture moved her hair away from her bosom, offering the expansive creaminess of her skin as a delicacy before the vampires who were already looking at her like she was their favorite meal. One gasped in response to her subtle movement.

Gabriel chuckled, waggling his finger at the group. "I have said that when a female came amongst you, that you would have to sit on your fangs." He chuckled at his own joke.

Julia didn't, scowling at his words.

Not funny.

"Now, now, Julia... don't look like that, I was simply light-ening the mood."

Julia's attention returned to the loose circle. There were five of them. All dressed similarly. She studied the group... there was one that remained in the shadows. He came forward and the ambient light from the strange glass windows of the ceiling cast light like the moon on his face and she saw who it was, taking a step backward.

William.

William saw her sharp inhale and how she retreated a step. Was he so abhorrent? Wasn't their blood share supposed to feel good to a Singer? He fought not to clench his fists and appear relaxed. Even as his warrior brethren sniffed at her like the dogs of the Were. He swallowed the anger that threatened to engulf him.

Julia turned to Gabriel. "I will never consent to anyone here." She whipped her hand around at the vampires. "I don't want to be *bred*. I don't care if you boys never walk in the light. Maybe there's a good reason you don't?" She looked at each face, perfectly chiseled features, made out of the same mold, only William looked different... more human. She shoved that thought aside.

Gabriel's patience was thinning. "These are the vampire who possess the blood of a Singer in their lineage. Although, you may breed with *any* vampire, be mated with any. A Rare One may beget a child with any vampire. But it is the blood of a Singer that will allow the recessive genes to intermingle and produce the life blood of our coven."

"What?" Julia nearly yelled.

"Light Bringers," Gabriel said.

Tears threatening, Julia said, "You can't force me to do this! Why would you want to? You're a Rare One too!"

"I am not female," he said with a logic that made her want to slap his face.

She looked around for a face that understood, finally

landing on William's. His held compassion, but she didn't want that. Not from him.

She whirled away from the group, hiking the skirt up, the material a silken bunch in her fist and ran for the archway. She slapped the first door she saw and entered.

A bathroom. Small and private with a love seat just inside the door, she sank down on it. She cried into her hands and abandoned all hope.

Julia didn't know what to do. How she'd escape.

She made her sobs quiet. She wouldn't give the vampires in the hall the satisfaction of hearing her sadness.

They were the cause of it.

CHAPTER 17

*J*ulia dried her cheeks with a vicious swipe. Disgusted with herself and her feelings of hopelessness, she stood. Walking over to the mirror she looked at her red and swollen eyes, the tracks from her tears making streaks where makeup had been. Claire had insisted.

Her hands gripped the rolled porcelain edge of the sink basin, the coolness a contrast to her body's heat.

Her head hung almost to her breastbone. How many times had Jason held her up when she felt like she couldn't live another moment with Aunt Lily? When her constant nagging and distrust were more than Julia could bear?

Resolve took hold within Julia. She needed to get through each day here, formulate a plan. One day at a time. If she could gain their trust, even with some small measure, maybe she could find a way to escape. Especially as her powers grew. Without actually causing her harm, how would they stop the advancement of her abilities? Claire was the one that had told her she was entering her adolescence as a Blood

Singer. Almost twenty seemed too old for that but Singers lived longer.

They were immortal in some cases. Julia had not asked the burning question. The one that had trembled on her lips.

Was she?

Would she live forever?

It still seemed surreal to Julia. She kept going back in a mental circle to her last point of reference of a year ago. When the biggest plan was getting married to her high school sweetheart. Now paranormal powers? Vampires... werewolves. The enormity of it all was overwhelming. If the reality wasn't staring her in the face, she'd believe she was crazy.

Her skin began to crawl, prickling.

Julia jerked her head up and met the stare of a female vampire in the reflection a heartbeat before she struck, her fangs sinking into Julia's shoulder, the tips meeting her collarbone. She cried out, the pain more than even the claws had been.

"Hold her, Edna," a male voice said casually.

It burned like liquid fire. Acid in her flesh.

Julia was trying to scream around the fangs but with bulging eyes she saw the male that walked toward her, the scream dying in a mouth that had become dry with fear.

He had been one of the males in the group of "choices."

Julia crossed him off the list, she decided wildly, on the verge of hysteria.

"The female doesn't want you, fragile human. She hates you," he said, his eyes liquid pools of silver, reflecting like dull nickels. Those eyes tried to suck her under but Julia felt the pull slide off harmlessly.

"Thrall will not work, dolt," another male said, meeting her eyes in the mirror. Julia saw that the bloodied wound was leaking into the bodice of her tangerine dress, turning it red. An evil sunset bloomed on the gauzy fabric.

The other male's eyes widened and he bent over her shoulder, lapping at the blood like a cat with cream. "Ahh," he crooned. Lap, suck, gulp. Julia watched as the male's throat convulsed, licking at her skin while the other one watched. "Her blood is exquisite. I have never tasted the likes of it," his eyes rolled to meet hers in the reflection, a silver so light they looked glacial.

They were going to take Julia's blood where she stood. Edna the vampire anchoring her throbbing shoulder to force her placement.

They would feed.

The other male moved in, eyeing her throat as if mesmerized, his body one tight line of tension.

Julia became desperate. She had next to no training, having about bashed Claire's brains in the other day in a reaction so pure, so unexpected they'd been pacing themselves since. Panicked, Julia tried to remember what it felt like to engage that telekinetic ability. It was so new to her she didn't even know where to begin. Especially with her heart in her throat from sheer terror. Julia felt disjointed and lacking the cognitive reasoning for finesse.

When the vampire that licked at her met her eyes Julia let all her bottled up rage and emotions, out. Focusing them like a spear. The hell with finesse.

Choke, she thought with a mental shove.

She launched a counter strike at vamp number one. When he staggered back, blood spewing out of his mouth, she turned her attention to number two. Feeling an elemental push which echoed the other, Julia used that seething momentum and blasted the neck-biter when he would have sunk fangs into her erratically beating pulse.

She saved herself by seconds, his head having reared

back, twin spiked fangs that shone like creamy pearls, prepared for the strike.

The female latched onto her shoulder harder. Julia's arm went numb to the wrist and she couldn't suppress a whimper as the female gave Julia a smile around the fangs that were buried in the flesh of her shoulder.

There was a commotion outside and the door slammed open.

William's frantic eyes met hers and in a moment of profound weakness, blood covering her upper body, the loss of it more than she could adequately fight, Julia whispered, "Help me."

* * *

William

WILLIAM LOOKED AROUND FOR JULIA. Ah... there she went, stalking off to mope in the restroom. He sighed. He told himself for the hundredth time that she was but an infant. Still, her behavior took some getting used to. She did not see William as the protector he was. *If she would but allow it*, he thought, clenching his jaw.

He looked a moment longer to make sure that Clarence was a discreet distance from the restroom and went back to his conversation with Gabriel.

"Give her time, William," the coven leader said.

"I have watched her this past year. I fear she cares not for her own life. She still mourns the husband who is no longer." Just saying those words made William angry. He determined to speak his mind to Gabriel, "I think she uses his death as a crutch. He has been gone for one year past. She has been told the facts of his death. The Were delivered the death blow. Not vampire. She would not have been allowed the union in any event. Two Blood Singers together!" His expression mirrored Gabriel's.

Ridiculous.

Gabriel nodded in agreement. There could not be inbreeding amongst Singers, because of the negative impact on the blood quantum. And more importantly, to waste a Rare One in that way? Squander. Not during his reign.

He clapped William on the back. "She will understand more as time goes on. Julia will come to understand that she is too rare a jewel to wander about, taking her chances in the outside world. It is here that is her destiny. Here is her safety. Also," he looked into William's eyes, "now that her adolescence is upon her, every Were and vampire from here to the ends of the earth would smell it on her. Her childhood afforded her some protection. No longer." Gabriel made a severe cutting gesture with his hand at the exact moment that William felt pain pierce the highest area of his shoulder.

He stood so quickly the chair that he had sat upon turned over and fell, the wood hitting the cobblestone floor with a resounding crack, echoing in the space.

William met the eyes of his fellow vampire, their faces without expression. He whipped his head in the direction of the restroom.

A lone foot could be seen sticking out of the dark corridor.

Clarence's.

Julia was no longer under guard.

William sprinted in a burst of speed that made its own breeze, lifting the tablecloth that held the crystal and blood.

HE BURST THROUGH THE DOOR, the wooden frame bending under the force of the swing.

He was greeted by Julia's whiskey-colored eyes, strained

and wide in her paling face. William was struck by the tears that streamed down her cheeks.

Julia was unaware she was crying, her fear outweighing enlightenment.

William's eyes fell first on Edna, a viperous female. Then found the two that would have vied for the position of mate to Julia.

Two less contenders, William thought, before he picked the head off the interloper who had his fangs bared before Julia's exposed throat, venom for the change dripping from them as he prepared to strike.

The moment seemed to pause, Julia looking into his eyes with what he had longed for, had been beyond hoping for.

Fear filled their depth... and longing. She wanted him. In that moment, she gave in to the blood bond between them and her terror made her raw to it.

He answered with a look that took mere seconds to convey.

It was her voice though, her voice that struck his soul like a bell which chimed.

"Help me," she gasped out, her eyes deep pools of drowning amber.

He did not hesitate.

William punched his right hand into the back of Edna, talons extended. In gasping from the entry wounds, she inadvertently released her fangs from Julia's shoulder. Julia slid to the floor, using the pathway of the female vampire like a helpmate, her hands grasping along the female's gown.

Julia rolled over on her back, the blood from the wound running backward, pooling in the hollow of her collarbone and dripping to the floor where her burnished red hair lay like a fan atop the stone.

William hesitated, hating to kill a female of the vampire, but she had proved to be without scruples. He tore his talons from her back and she fell to his feet, gasping, all five having punctured her lungs in a most grievous manner.

William let Edna lay on the stone floor like a gasping fish. Turning his attention to the vampire that had hands around his throat in the universal choking gesture.

What was this?

He was choking on the blood he had consumed.

He swung his gaze to Julia, the fragrant smell of her blood filling the space, making William almost light-headed with blood lust, his throat tightening painfully.

And *he* was a quarter Singer.

The others would never be able to abstain from her as she lay vulnerable and bleeding.

There would be a blood riot.

The evidence of such lay at his feet. The vampire he had beheaded, laying as a pile of ash and blood was the eighth slayed.

Never having been exposed to a Rare One they were virtually helpless before the song for her blood.

William turned at the noise at the door, simultaneously moving toward where Julia lay.

The vampire moved as a unit, talons extended, fangs sprung free of their houses of flesh.

They came to where the delectable smell of fresh blood was released. A quality without compare. It was as if a thousand year old bottle of wine lay breathing.

On a cold stone floor mere paces away from consumption.

William leaped in front of the Julia just as the first vampire would have been upon her.

Julia

143

TAMARA ROSE BLODGETT

JULIA LOOKED up and saw a monster, fangs the size of her pinky fingers, dripping a clear fluid tinged with red, talons as long as her forearms standing at deadly attention.

And then like small swords they began to slice whoever drew near.

Their motion in a blur of darkness, too fast for her to follow, Julia became aware of moisture falling on her bare skin like rain.

She opened her eyes and a head fell beside her shoulder with a meaty thump. The dead eyes, once gray, turned into a collapsing wall of flesh and bone. As she looked on in horror, it began to disintegrate into a mass of ash.

It was the eyes she'd never forget.

Or the creature William had become, fighting the vampires that would have killed her.

They came, one after another, as blood drenched her gown and she lay helplessly at his feet.

William slashed and stabbed as injuries were rained down on him and then five overcame him. Julia whimpered, having never envisioned herself dying this way.

At that moment, Julia realized she wanted to live.

Had always wanted to live.

Her eyes met Williams, pleading.

She knew she didn't deserve his help.

But she was sorry. In that moment she didn't want this life, this existence.

Nevertheless, he was dying to defend her.

William was overcome. He had dispatched fifteen, losing all hope of the guards helping him through the crowd of rabid vampire overrun with blood lust.

The higher functioning of their cerebral cortex was gone.

When the five overcame him, he saw Julia torn from beneath his feet by two fanged brethren, one held her as the

144

other prepared to strike, losing his grip twice, her body slick with the blood of the massacred.

She was weak as a kitten, any fool could see, her wound not closing up. The blood clotting properties of the vampire saliva was not working.

Of course, Edna would have not used hers willingly. Julia was bleeding out.

William struggled against the vampire, beyond reason and rationale when he heard her soft whimper like a plea.

Bereft.

Hopeless.

Her eyes met his again, the blood bond reverberating in his body, pressing him to take action beyond his capabilities.

William did, smashing two of the vampires' heads together hard enough for their brains to splatter against the inside of their skulls and leak out their ears. He threw himself on his feet and launched to Julia's side in a fluid gymnastic movement, his fist punching out as he did.

The vampire who had fangs a millimeter away from her throat, lost them from the impact of William's fist even as his talons swung to take the head of the one that restrained her.

* * *

Julia

JULIA SAW WILLIAM COME. A shaky exhale escaped as she lay in the arms of one vampire while the other prepared to chew her throat out.

The one that held her dumped her head on the floor so hard she saw lights twinkle above her.

And then William was there.

Their heads fell on either side of her body and heat

145

suffused her. Julia knew she would pass out and had but moments to express herself.

William crouched above her protectively and she raised her arm, weakly. She clutched onto his clothing.

He glanced at her then away, prepared for the next onslaught.

She tugged again.

"Julia, lay still. You have lost much blood."

"Thank you," she whispered on her final breath. Her vision dimmed to a pinpoint.

The last coherent image was William.

A face she didn't hate anymore.

His mouth moved but she couldn't hear him, an enveloping softness encased her as she floated away.

Like dandelion seed on the wind.

Julia slept in a pool of her own blood.

And that of others.

Many others.

CHAPTER 18

THE DEN OF THE WERE - ONE MONTH LATER

"*D*o you see her?" Joseph asked impatiently. "Yes," Tony responded, dropping the night vision binoculars.

"It is easy to make her out, Joseph. She is so much smaller than the blood drinkers."

Right. Joseph knew that. But his anxiety was full-tilt. It had been a month since their orders from Lawrence to execute reconnaissance on the vampire kiss. They had.

It had been troubling to smell injuries on the Rare One.

When they had first begun their covert stake out, they could smell fresh wounds. They were concentrated on the female, but also one other.

The vampire that could turn into a raven. He had been injured as well.

It was only speculation but Joseph felt something terrible had happened within the coven. Something which allowed a freedom that was almost brazen in its regard to her safety.

Although, they flanked her five deep on either side.

Joseph was still sticking with the number fifteen.

Fifteen of his entire soldier contingent should be enough to bring her home.

The Rare One would assimilate into his den. She would not automatically be his. But he would butcher any Alpha who took challenge.

Joseph would be victor.

He must.

The whelp of the Were must evolve or the race would be lost.

He squeezed his hands into fists, mourning the moon's shape.

It was waxing. Two weeks yet until they could bring the change.

Joseph and Tony watched the small female figure bounce as she ran, the huge blood drinkers watching to the four corners of the earth.

Joseph growled low in his throat, the vampires unaware. Tony heard and answered.

It would have been a howl had the moon been full.

* * *

Julia

JULIA'S LUNGS BURNED. But in a good way. What had started out as nightly walks when the city slept had turned into jogging.

Now she ran. Her vitality returned incrementally night by night.

She shuddered, thinking about how her life had almost ended that fateful night on a floor of ancient cobblestone. Built for humans, infiltrated by vampires.

Claire had to provide blood to save her life. William could not give it.

The third blood share would have mated her to William. Whether she wanted it or not.

Forever was a long time to hold a grudge, Julia thought.

Because that's what it was. She was immortal only if she had blood quantum. Too much blood loss and her life would be gone.

Julia wasn't sure she believed them. There was no such thing as immortality? Right?

Then her mind burdened her with the facts of the past year.

Like the existence of werewolves and vampire. Check. Like that wasn't crazy-as-hell?

Julia wiped sweat from her brow and glanced at William, who didn't sweat, of course. He never broke stride.

Neither did the other nine which ran with her.

Excuse me, jogged. They could run, she could only do what she was doing now. It was hopelessly slow. She was a foot shorter than them.

"Are you well?" William asked.

She smiled shyly. He was beyond solicitous. Julia had allowed herself the barest crack in her plan. As she had begun to figure it, with all that time recuperating to help with her decisions, she had two evils. The one she knew and the one she did not. The vampires had come clean (or as clean as they ever would) explaining to her what her options were. Her alternative of escape seemed so remote. So unsuccessful. Julia couldn't help but feel defeated, beaten down. Her chances of survival if she were to get away would be slim.

For starters, there was no camouflaging the scent of what she was. That was by far the largest obstacle standing in the way of her freedom. True freedom.

Secondly, and this was a terrifying prospect, the Were searched for her just as hard as the vampires would. If she *did* escape, the likelihood of her being reacquired by another coven or den of the Were was high. She literally could not find sanctuary.

Her heart grieved for Jason. Her pragmatic nature instructed her thought processes. Survival. And it seemed she had many years to survive.

She'd been off a million miles away and finally answered William, "Yes, I"m fine."

He looked at the others and gave a command outside the decibel range of human hearing.

He took her by the elbow and they slowed.

She still felt slightly weak, but nothing like when they had taken the first, shuffling steps into the outside air. The smell of it had been cloying, foul.

And rich and wonderful.

Freedom had a smell and Julia breathed deeply of it.

So long she'd been underground, held captive in the original thirty-one blocks of Seattle's great city. While the cattle walked overhead, predators lived underneath their feet.

Julia remembered what Claire had told her over a month ago.

Julia came awake and met Claire's stare, her eyes steady on Julia's face.

She had never felt as weak as she did now. Not when she had refused to eat for months, when she had to be bathed like a baby by Susan.

She felt cold to her marrow.

"You've lost a tremendous amount of blood from the attack," Claire said in her calm way.

Julia looked at her, willing her lips to move, but they didn't cooperate.

Claire smiled and stood. She brought a cup with a bendy straw in it.

As Julia sucked on the plastic tube, cool, clean water saturated her mouth and tongue, swollen from lack of use and circulation anomalies.

Finally, when she'd had her fill she asked Claire, "What happened?"

Claire looked away for a moment, a blush of pink lighting on her cheekbones, her skin as fair as Julia's. Julia realized she was embarrassed.

"Things got out of hand. A few of the contenders... could not control their blood lust." She looked at Julia, who returned the stare without expression, willing her silently to go on. After a pause, she did. "We did not foresee it. But, they were quite premeditated. Gabriel and I," Julia huffed at the leader's name, immediately begrudging his authority. As Julia saw it, he had no authority over her. After all, he was nothing more than a glorified kidnapper, using the weapons at his disposal to manipulate the vampire outcome.

For their benefit, she thought sourly, not hers. His weapons of choice... the vampire of course.

Claire continued through Julia's insolence as if it didn't exist, "... thought there'd be sufficient protection because of their Singer lineage but it wasn't enough." Claire looked at the hands that were wringing themselves in her lap. When her eyes met Julia's she saw they were glistening, the tears held, unshed. "There are so few vampire that are capable of breeding with a Rare One." She gulped and struggled forward, "Now there are fewer."

So what? Julia thought. It's not like those were such great guys that had assaulted her? Whatever. She said as much to Claire and she nodded reluctantly.

"We know this now. It had been centuries since a female Rare One had entered the coven for this purpose. We didn't anticipate the pull..."

Julia crossed her arms again as she looked up at the shadows that passed across the glass skylight of her room. Why was sunlight allowed to penetrate their lair if it were such a problem?

Claire followed her gaze, smiling. "We have our technologies."

Julia's brow cocked in question.

Claire gave a little shrug. "They cannot live outside the confines of this space during the day. But, we have one that formulated a chemical wash for the glass..." she threw a palm in the direction of the only window that Julia had.

"So..." Julia's sudden realization of what the shadows were struck her almost dumb.

Almost.

"Those are people? They are walking over our heads?" she asked incredulously.

Claire nodded. "They do not know of our existence. It is like being hidden in plain sight. You understand this concept, no?"

Julia did. She had a babysitter before her parents were killed that would hide everyday objects in plain sight. Julia remembered at one point she'd hidden a sewing thimble on the top of an old TV antenna and it'd been an hour before she'd spied it. Metal on metal, almost invisible.

She couldn't suppress a small smile at the memory, nodding at Claire.

Claire returned the smile, not knowing its origin but happy for its appearance.

"It affords the kiss the greatest protection."

Julia looked at the shadowed feet, crossing the glass, a foot's separation between their life and death. They never knew.

Julia shivered.

"The solution blocks the UV rays."

"Couldn't that clever guy make a sunblock or something?" Julia asked, a little bit of snark creeping into her tone.

Claire's smile faded. "That was unsuccessful."

Julia didn't press but judging by the expression on her face, there'd been a few vampire-torches.

Julia withheld her smile. An image of William on fire came to her mind. Just a few days ago, that visual might have given her a lot of satisfaction. Now... her heart had shifted. And while she did not hate him any more, she wasn't sure what she felt. She thought of flying over the meadow, leaving the Were that had attacked her behind, the claws bound to her shoulders like excruciating hooks. His fierce expression as he fought the vampires that would have bled her dry.

Julia was ashamed. He was what he was, a freak of biology. As she was. Jason was gone.

Forever.

It was in that moment that Julia decided for neutrality with William. He had not shown her harm. On the contrary, he had shown much more.

What it was made her uncomfortable. That couldn't be held against him.

Her discomfort.

In the end, William had been right. Jason had been killed by the Were. Not vampire.

Julia sighed, looking once more above her head.

The cattle moved across their concrete pasture.

Unaware of the vampires below.

* * *

the present

WILLIAM SMILED DOWN AT JULIA. Cautious hope took hold of his soul. If a vampire had such.

She looked infinitely better than after the attack. He was right as rain in less than a fore-night. But Julia's tenuous situation was held in the fragile balance of the twilight of death. It took much to kill a Rare One. But the two that may have been in the race for betrothal ruined it by hurting her.

Forget that notion, William thought. Killing her. They almost killed her. He could hardly bear to think upon it. He had already claimed Julia in his heart. He had not the right. But love chose its own pathway, mindless of the change.

Love hath no master.

He took in her lush mouth, the pulse that beat at the hollow of her throat more attractive than any show of flesh could ever have been. He swallowed, reining in his emotions. He'd had two centuries to perfect his lack of expression.

William found that a year and some days with Julia had undone it all. The careful procedure of schooling one's expression in the way of the vampire, lost. He thought it might never be regained.

His heart seized with instant panic as a scent wafted through the night air.

In an instant, he pulled Julia against him, scenting their surroundings, her water bottle hitting the ground with a false thud, the water leaking out over the black pavement like a crystal well.

Broken.

* * *

Julia

JULIA'S HEART slammed into her ribcage, William's hands wrapped around her arms like steel bands, cool against her fevered skin, still warm from the run.

"What is it?" Julia asked.

Pierce lifted his nose to the air. "Wolves, William?"

"I do not know. But," he looked at the nine that were gathered together, his eyes glittering in the weakness of the lights that illuminated the street where they stood, "it is the only moment of my existence wherein I wish for their sense of smell."

There was uneasy laughter even as the vampires looked around them for the perceived danger. A few tense moments passed and William's shoulders finally dropped into a more relaxed posture.

"Well?" another vampire asked, Robert, Julia remembered.

William shrugged, his eyes tight. "I do not know what it was, but I very much wish to head back."

They agreed but Julia protested, "They would never think to find me here."

William looked down at her, his face cut marble in the whitish blue light of the streetlamp. "It is that mentality that will hasten your taking from our kiss. We do not underestimate the dogs. Their passion makes them dangerous." He looked into her eyes then elaborated, "Sometimes I will have a moment of..." William deliberated on his wording. Finally settling on, "intuition."

Julia looked at him. "Is that because of the Singer blood?"

He nodded. "The shifting to raven is the single most powerful element I gained from my genetics. Sometimes, although it is not always trustworthy, the moments of intuition have made me a better fighter."

"How?" Julia asked, allowing herself to be tugged along as they made their way back to the underground city.

"Instinctive."

"You fight with... training or...?"

He glanced her way then looked around again, still slightly tense. "I use what has been given to me. I know because of my Singer heritage that I can shift to raven form and sometimes I anticipate."

Julia had to ask, with nine other sets of vampire ears to the ground, honing in on her words she forged ahead, "Anticipate what?"

He stopped, looking down at her for a moment. His gaze uncomfortably intense, he answered, "Danger."

Oh, she looked around as well, sensing nothing.

"Let us be gone from this place."

And they left.

None of them saw the Were who tailed them discreetly.

The Were's sense of smell allowing a great distance to be maintained while still triangulating the vampire position.

The Were came upon the plastic bottle that had been dumped.

It was too perfect to believe. The vampires had been sloppy by allowing anything she touched to be discarded by any means other than fire.

Of course, vampires did not like fire. A grim smile overcame his face.

He reached to pick up the discarded bottle, scenting it for the Rare One.

Julia Caldwell's scent floated around the mouth of the bottle like the most exquisite fragrance imaginable. He held the bottle triumphantly while motioning with his hand for the four other Were to gather round him.

They did, each scenting the bottle. Familiarizing themselves with her smell.

The scent of the Rare One. The Mistress even over the moon.

As her unique signature filled their flared nostrils, five pairs of eyes spun to gold in faces that were no longer quite human.

Joseph brought his face up to gaze at the moon. Its mocking form half gone to full.

As small yips of excitement broke out in the circle of men, the tone changed to a quality that caused the pigeons to flee their roosts.

The noise caused the fear and flight reaction as surely as a primal alarm going off.

The Were returned to their den.

An empty bottle as so much trash, carried in the fist of the Alpha.

Joseph clutched it tighter as he ran.

CHAPTER 19

TWO WEEKS LATER

*J*ulia stretched until every vertebrae cooperated by popping. Ah... so much better. She wasn't happy, yet. But for the first time since Jason's death she felt a form of contentment. She was sure it had a lot to do with the daily runs. Her body was knitting itself stronger each day and she was thankful.

William had not pressed his advantage when it would have been easy to and Julia had noticed.

William and she had lunch together each day now. Actually, she ate lunch and he drank blood. It was an uneasy alliance but he had to receive nourishment too. And she couldn't negate what he had done for her.

With his blood.

It was yesterday's lunch that rolled around in her mind. She couldn't believe what he'd told her. The revelation.

That Claire was his cousin. William was one quarter Blood Singer. His ancestry lent him the paranormal stripe that allowed him to shapeshift, to have those little moments of awareness that were *other*.

Julia had been curious, picking at the meal before her,

salad and salmon. The coven provided only the finest meal for their trophy. Julia squelched the thought even as it formed. She knew that she needed to think of the coven as her benefactors. Or she'd never achieve any happiness, joy.

She had sighed and Williams's brows had rose in question.

"It's about Claire..." she looked at him.

Stared actually, trying not to notice how handsome he was, how well-built, how... everything. Heat rose to her face and she knew without a mirror she was blushing.

"Well... she is my cousin." He dropped the bomb like it was of the least consequence.

"Are you kidding?" Julia nearly shouted.

He shook his head, the corners of his mouth already turning up.

"You are!" she huffed, folding her arms across her body.

"I promise, I'm not having you on. It is true."

Julia searched his eyes for the joke, and finding none, went on, "How is that? She looks like she's ten years older than me?"

William paused, then said, "Once a Singer mates a vampire, if there is enough blood quantum, they take on some of the properties of their mate. In this case," his eyes met hers, "immortality."

Julia thought about it, almost stunned into speechlessness. "So Claire's like... hundreds of years old?"

"Technically that is accurate." William said, thinking he was enjoying having her pull information from him like hen's teeth.

The tables turned for once.

Julia huffed. "Just tell me William."

"She is three hundred six."

Julia gasped. That made William...

"I am only two hundred twenty."

So young, Julia thought, rolling her eyes.

William laughed from his gut. Usually serious, he found Julia lightened him considerably. She added a buoyancy to his life where none had been before.

"Yes, she is quite wise."

Julia turned her fork over and under, over and under until William put his finger on the tines. He met her gaze. "What are you thinking?"

"I wonder why we look a little alike, Claire and I?"

William leaned back in the chair he sat on, drumming his tapered fingers on the bare wood of the table, thinking.

Unaware that he smoldered at her, in her. The blood share's tenacious grasp still clung like reluctant glue.

"Gabriel has said there is a common region that the Singers hail from antiquity."

Julia waited.

William shrugged. "It is just a hypothesis. But it may explain the similarities in their looks." He looked at her briefly, then glancing at her half-eaten plate finished his thought, "Blood Singers are generally fair-complexioned, with some degree of red hair. But not all. Some can be quite dark."

"How do you know this?" Julia was thinking that Jason hadn't had that coloring.

"It was a cross-checking method we employed as runners. If the scent did not convince us, the coloring being as it were... well, it was almost fool proof."

Julia was fascinated, remembering her mother's hair ablaze with copper fire. She remembered perfectly. Memories of the accident crowded the inside of her skull in a dull press but she shoved them away forcefully.

"Gabriel is originally from Scotland."

Ah... Julia remembered wondering about that brogue he had.

"Have you heard of Stonehenge? Located in England?"

She nodded, it was pretty famous. In high school they'd studied it briefly in World History.

"That is where the biggest concentration of Singers reside. They fan out in many directions, but it is there that they proliferate."

Julia smiled, not really successful in reining in her sarcasm. "Then why don't you guys do a road trip and net 'em all?"

Williams's smile faded, shaking his head. "They become powerful in concentrations as big as that one." His eyes were serious again.

"So, they can bring a can of whoop-ass?"

William smiled at her vernacular. "Yes, they can bring whatever they please. That is why we concentrate on mostly immigrants, diluted by centuries of out breeding. Sometimes, as in your case, we strike a pureblood. Any Singer over half pure is worth acquisition."

Julia thought about all that he'd said. "So, why am I not... psychic or some other cool thing like that?"

William chuckled, crossing his legs at the ankle. "You will be many things." He shrugged, "It is different with each Singer. A Rare One is an anomaly. Hard to find, more diffi-cult to speculate about."

"What can Gabriel do? He's the coven leader... he's a Rare One," Julia said, thinking he may have mojo. A buttload.

Julia watched William think about his words and was struck anew by how very deliberate he was with his thoughts. He never just blurted stuff out.

Like her.

She smiled unconsciously and he returned her grin, his fangs hidden.

"He is male." William looked down to his long-stemmed glass, the bagged blood distributed inside the glass as an affectation. Like a beer out of a frosted mug as opposed to straight out of the bottle.

She waited and he continued. "He has some paranormal talents," he paused, looking at her then continued, "but it is the females that possess all of what a Rare One could offer. Eventually, you will be many things. Manifest many things."

Julia looked at him. "Besides being able to make vampires choke on my blood and heave helpful people against walls, what else is there?"

She was only half-joking. Julia wanted to know what to expect.

William shrugged a muscular shoulder, the button-down shirt hiding nothing. She'd give vampires this, they were all pretty spiffy to eyeball.

"It has been some time since a Rare One has been... in residence. It will be all conjecture at this point. But," he paused, "there have been things in legend. Those are: tele-kinetic ability, telepathy, super-human strength..." He finished, ticking off each ability on his fingers then resting his hands on his thighs.

Julia liked the last one and smiled.

He chuckled, "That's usually reserved for males."

Oh.

"Limited healing. And of course, there are the genetic properties of the Rare Ones. They will allow the supernatu-rals to become more, better." William leaned forward, all intensity. "Just think of the ramifications of being vampire, but not ruled by bloodlust, by the night." He swung his palm to encompass their immediate area.

Julia watched an internal fire ignite in his eyes and real-ized the vampires felt trapped by their existence. That what made them *other*, also stifled them in isolation.

It made Julia profoundly uncomfortable to realize two factions thought of her as a savior. But she hadn't asked to be a Rare One. Instead, she had just wanted a normal life. She looked in William's earnest eyes and sighed. At least she hadn't been taken by the Were. From what William told her, they cared very little for the Rare One's comfort. She remembered what he had told her on one of their many runs before she'd been able to do much but shuffle along.

* * *

William

WILLIAM LOOKED DOWN with tenderness at the top of Julia's head. He allowed himself that luxury when she was not aware of his regard. She looked up and he instantly schooled his expression into one of neutrality.

"You ask of the Were. They also find the Blood Singers critical. Even a Singer who has as little as one quarter blood quantum can give them additional days to make the change. They cannot aspire to be moonless changers. But, they can have more days to use her call." He kicked a random pebble and Julia stopped, turning to look at him. The streetlamp reflected off the damp patches of asphalt, the city still humming all around them. The deadest hour of the night had the least people but still cars were rushing past, dim noise and the smells of a city that never quite rested a backdrop to their hushed conversation.

She crossed her arms and huffed out a breath while the other vampires formed a loose circle around them, maintaining an ever-vigilant protective perimeter. "So what you're saying is, that both vampire and Were compete? They run around, gathering up the purest of the Singers to what? Make sure they have more power?"

William thought it sounded dire when she put it like that. "It is for the betterment of both. We think their methods are heathen. But the consequence is identical. What they gain, what we gain..." he let his sentence trail off.

TAMARA ROSE BLODGETT

"What do we gain, William?" Julia asked, her eyes searching his, her palm on the center of her chest.

He did not drop his gaze but not without effort. There was little that the Singer gained. Except, their mate would be devoted. There was additional protection. He sighed, raking a distracted hand through his hair, frustrated.

"You have the security and protection of the coven," he finally answered.

Julia snorted, "Oh yeah! That's worked so well," she said significantly. She thought of the fangs that had been sunk into her collarbone, adding to the healing scars of William's claws from when he was in raven form. Unreal. She felt so protected.

Julia told him so, with sarcasm.

William gripped her shoulders, cupping them firmly in hands that wrapped them front to back. "There will always be rogue vampire. There will always be vampire amongst our kind that take, that do not follow rules, hierarchy. You do ken to that? Is it not the same in the human population?" he asked, unblinking. His eyes, so blood red in certain lighting, were silvered and reflective in the dark.

"It's true," Julia responded, trying to not squirm in his grasp. "But if I'm so special, why did they try to hurt me? Believe me, it hurt."

William knew. He had been barred from giving blood a third time. As her kind said, the third time would have been the charm. It would bind her to him without choice, without consent. A union filled with resentful compliance was not acceptable.

Not to him.

In the end, she had been given a transfusion. She smelled off for two weeks afterward. He had mentioned she had smelled like someone else until her body's natural cycles and rhythms had righted themselves.

"I'm so sorry that I didn't smell tasty for a week or two," she'd said, rolling her beautiful eyes at him. William had smiled.

"It is better for me. Not your pain, your suffering at their transgression," he mentioned quickly to avoid confusion as her brows came together in a frown. "But because their attack on you proved my mettle. You know the man I am."

Julia shook her head in correction. "You are not a man. You're something else."

William's face took on a sad countenance. "I am more man than you could ever know."

Julia looked into a face filled with sincerity and an expression she'd seen on Jason's face before.

Desire.

She shifted her gaze from his as they walked away together, the vampire guard swarming around them.

TAKING

JOSEPH GAVE Tony a subtle flick of his tail, but it was scent, not motion that let Tony know to flank the group of vampires. One amongst the Were remained unchanged.

A new threat faced them. They had smelled what threatened during their last reconnaissance.

The Rare One was entering her awakening. She would be dangerous. One of his wolves would nail her with the gun. A gun that had a dart filled with a sedative. It could stop an ox. In this case, it would stop the Singer. Stop her from using what made her unique against them. That she stayed willingly with the kiss of drinkers was worrisome. Very.

She was unmated. Joseph knew. Her smell told him.

They moved toward the group, stealthily. Sure and confident.

Ready for combat.

* * *

Julia

JULIA WAS NERVOUS. She was usually anxious now. Gone was the easygoing nonchalance of her former life. Knowing what she was had stripped her of that. Not knowing what her future held, or knowing the expectation others had for her future had cloaked her as surely as the warm puffy coats of her Alaskan existence before.

William watched her pace, her unease a contagious thing. Finally, he could bear it no more. "What is it? What is troubling you?" His arms were crossed, his face in shadows as he leaned against the wall in her chamber. She took in his form, his athletic build accentuated by the casual attire. His tight black T-shirt stretched across a broadly muscled chest, black sweatpants hugged hips and legs finely honed by exercise and the perfection of what he was.

Julia stopped. Looking at him she felt the pull there between them, like a rope of warm taffy, always taut, never breaking. She felt dumb explaining it. "I know that the exercise is good." His expression encouraged her and she realized she was starting to care a little for William. She didn't know how she felt about it. But after almost eighteen months, he and Claire were really all the contact she had.

She went on, stumbling over the next part, "Before the thing... happened." Julia flicked her eyes to his.

William knew she meant Jason's death.

She swallowed and he waited in pregnant silence. "I felt a sense of..."

He arched his eyebrows. "Foreboding?" he intuited.

She nodded, relieved he understood. "Yes."

He straightened. "You sense that now?"

She nodded again, it was a vibration in her body,

humming in an ominous way she hated. And the headaches were back.

Turning, she walked toward him voluntarily for the first time.

William watched her come, a graceful slow-burning flame, eyes and hair a liquid gold that ignited a torch within his soul. He stuffed his emotions deep inside, giving her his pleasantly neutral face. It was something that was now a daily challenge. Before, it had been made easier by her indifference. He did not feel that from her right now, in this moment.

Julia came very close to him. Reaching out she placed a small hand on his arm and he stifled the gasp that tore from inside him as their flesh connected. Her eyes moved to his. "I'm not afraid of you anymore. I don't know how I feel, but I know you'd protect me."

It took every ounce of willpower not to touch her back, caress that face he had caressed mentally a thousand times before with his eyes. How badly he wished to do it with his hands. Instead, he forced them against his side, remaining unmoved.

"Today, I'm afraid. Even this near, this protected. I don't want to be with the Were." Julia knew however bad this new life was, that the alternative with them would be worse.

William stiffened. "We would never allow that. They have tried for you twice, and failed. They would never succeed."

She shook her head, the ginger of her hair sliding over shoulders encased in the smooth nylon material of her exercise gear. He watched the silken strands and wanted to run his fingers through it. The low light of the skylight caused it to glow a soft red. William suddenly wished he could see it in the sun. He imagined it would be quite red.

"They may succeed," she said.

He looked down at her as she looked up at him. "No," he

said fiercely, his emotion overwhelming his sense. Wrapping both his hands around her forearms. "It cannot be precognitive. If that were so, they would have tried for you months ago, when you were more vulnerable."

Julia stared at him. He wasn't believing her. She'd be given her nightly exercise, regardless. Maybe she had a case of nerves.

Maybe her unbearable loneliness was in the way. She felt the heat from her body warming his. Still, that small space separated them. She noticed his hands encasing her arms and suddenly her eyes were on his lips.

Julia's mind trembled at the possibility. Her emotions and intellect warred in a heated battle.

William felt her gaze shift from his eyes to his mouth.

He waited. She must decide.

He had never had a greater challenge, his nerve endings on fire.

Julia felt her emotions unraveling, guilt over Jason, his death, their unconsummated marriage. Missing him like a pit of misery in her stomach. She knew what she was beginning to feel for William was wrong. But she could only go on so long with the constant loneliness. William was right, he had proven himself. She was the one that needed to move on.

Her decision made, Julia stood on tiptoe, using lips that hadn't kissed in almost two years, she brushed a featherweight's press over the softness of his mouth.

Julia's eyes were closed, one hand on his chest for balance. She didn't feel his response and her skin flushed with embarrassment. She began to draw away.

Until she felt his hands move off of her arms and snap around her body, jerking her against him. His mouth moved over hers with a barely contained hunger, eating at it until she opened it for him.

He lifted his mouth just long enough to say, "I will always protect you, Julia."

"I know…" she began but his mouth came down on hers again and she twined her arms around his neck. The heat that moved between their embrace felt overwhelmingly natural.

Too natural.

Julia pulled away just as there was a knock on the door and she felt his arms release her reluctantly. She watched William's face as he followed the progress of her hand as it touched her mouth, swollen from his kiss. Bruised from his affection.

Guilt assailed her. "Come in," she said, relieved for the interruption.

"It's time," Pierce said, looking from one to the other, sensing the broken tension like shards of glass laying dangerously all around them.

* * *

William

WILLIAM WAS angry at the knocking, the sweet scent of Julia filling his nose, his senses wailing to take her, to make her his. Their first contact was more overwhelming than even he could have imagined. That she initiated it, that their blood share was all but washed away, made it all the sweeter.

He looked upon her as she pulled away, guilt and desire mixed up in her features. He had a pang of regret, then shoved it away. He had not taken what she'd loved away from her. It was the Were that had stolen her husband's life. In their haste to acquire her, they'd killed a Singer unnecessarily. It had been long, almost two years of patience and frustration. If he could finally be joined with her. If she would possibly be open to a courtship, he would not dissuade her. And his competitors were less.

Actually, the horrible attack of Julia had tightened things up considerably in the coven.

He glanced at Pierce, coming to his senses as if in a fog. He shook off the lethargy of his desire with difficulty. Gabriel wished for Julia to exercise, to be away from the coven. He did not think she was coping well. Even William had to admit that she was progressing better with the exercise.

Her words of disquiet were troubling. William did not assume everything. He wished to be as confident as possible but to discount a Rare One was not prudent.

William considered himself pragmatic. And ruthless.

Always that.

He turned to Pierce, "Let us take an additional five runners."

Pierce's brows came together.

William answered his unspoken question, "It will ease Julia."

He turned and smiled at her. She gave him one of her rare genuine smiles. He loved seeing it on her face and smiled back.

William wished he had put more weight in her comment. It would haunt him in the months to come.

Julia looked at William and was instantly relieved. He had not discounted her warning. He was more than a protector now. She wasn't sure what he was becoming, but in that moment a small space in her heart softened, a fissure formed, allowing William in.

CHAPTER 20

RUN

*J*ulia wiped sweat of her brow, running with a thousand vampires at her side.

Not really. That's just what it felt like.

She'd told William that the Were were sniffing around and so far, nothing.

Julia was feeling foolish. She decided to tell him so.

She knew that they didn't need fifteen anymore. Five was probably enough. He'd smiled and kissed her forehead casually, calling off the vampires for the following evening's run. Her sense of impending doom had lessened.

It had been a full week since she'd mentioned her uneasy feelings to William. It was so similar to what she'd felt before Terrell went madder than a March hare, as Aunt Lily would have said, that she'd felt compelled to speak. Now, she just felt like a dumbass. Getting the vampires wound up because she had an emotional hiccup. Julia needed to be stronger.

She smiled at William. Julia thought there would be a ton of awkwardness between them but he'd been solicitous, touching her subtly day by day. A slow bridge of small intimacies were building one on top of the other.

She came to find herself looking forward to the subtle touches and glances, anticipating them. If anyone had told her that she was going to be crushing on a vampire two years ago, she would have written the letter to have them committed herself.

Yet, here she was. She hadn't forgotten Jason, but the pain was less acute.

Julia was also not certain of her path. She knew in her mind that Jason was gone. That this weird new life, however much she hadn't wanted, it was what she had now. Julia realized she needed to move on. A vision of Jason's face, once so clear, had turned fuzzy at the edges. She felt herself all at once profoundly sad again. It was not just losing him in reality. It was the memory of him slipping away day by day that tore at her heart.

William stood watching the myriad of emotions play over her face and having made a study of humanity in the past two hundred years he knew some of what she reconciled.

Damn the Were, William thought for the hundredth time. She would have been separated from her husband regardless. However, his death had marked her. Even now she struggled.

"Julia," William said. He looked at her, the sadness clinging to her like greedy fingers and thought that she looked so fragile and small standing there. The hopes of his race depended on a young woman barely more than a girl.

Julia looked at William and the blanket of memories slid away for the moment. She swung her face to Pierce and the other three. Julia nodded. She was ready. She focused her considerable will on the moment, not on the past.

They were deep into the run, her body singing in muscular tension and heat. The vamps were barely on a jog. Julia felt like she was practically sprinting. They used the steep hills of the city and climbed them like the Swiss Alps. An occasional car sputtered by, the gears grinding together in the ascent. When they reached the area the famous Nordstrom's occupied they stopped. The loneliest part of the night embracing them as they stood in a loose group. William grabbed the water bottle from a small backpack that lay between his shoulder blades. Handing it to her she gulped a few swigs, admiring the building. Cyn would have died ten deaths to go shopping there, Julia's melancholy stealing its way inside her again. Her face tilted to take in the vertical sign. It was completely black, save for the letters in ivory. She noticed it was lit from the sides, the characters softly illuminated.

William watched Julia grapple for a life that was no more and broke into her thoughts, "Let us go back."

She nodded and was struck dumb with a pain so acute, so widespread she gasped and fell to her knees.

The five vampire took their eyes from their posts to assist her.

As Julia lay sideways on the concrete sidewalk, the sign poised above her head like a guillotine, she saw the Were slide out from the dark corners the city provided.

There were many.

Julia whispered through her pain, which she now recognized as an alarm come too late, "Werewolves..."

Joseph and Tony watched, alongside the remaining nine Were, as the small group of vampires allowed Julia Caldwell to rest.

Six long days they had waited for the vampires' complacency to reestablish itself. For their perfect moment of opportunity.

Finally, it had come.

Joseph took in the sight of her. The golden hair swept back in a ponytail, the navy athletic gear looking black to his wolf vision, so soft a color in the darkness he knew it was blue. He felt her awareness before she did, watching her drink water.

"She will know we are here soon. Be ready," he gave Tony a significant glance and he raised the dart gun in acknowledgment.

"I'm not gonna fuck this up, I told ya," he said in a growl.

Joseph turned his snout to Tony, their golden eyes locked on each other. "See that you don't. We won't get another opportunity like this one." Their eyes held for two heartbeats more and Tony broke the stare, his status in the group firmly set at first. Not Alpha.

Not yet.

Joseph swept his eyes amongst the other Were soldiers and they gave him the subtle eye contact he required. The affirmation that let him know they were ready to battle the vampires.

On his scent command, they released their bodies from the shadows and stepped out into the open.

William knelt beside Julia, stifling his rising panic. The first thing that flooded his mind was her warning, nary a week old in which she had told him of her unease. He had listened, acted. But now he saw the alarm on her face and realized that the Were had chosen their time.

And it was now.

William brushed the hair that had come undone away from Julia's temple.

Tenderly.

He stood and readied himself for what the Were would bring.

The four that were with him spread and flanked his position. With a last look at Julia, he stepped in front of her. The look blazing in her eyes scorched a path in his mental imagery. What he had seen in them clenched his insides.

Trust.

Julia trusted him.

As he looked out and counted eleven of the enemy, he hoped that the sentiment was not misplaced.

Julia reclaimed tenuous control of her body and stood on shaky legs. She was fatigued by the run but was numb with fear. She backed away from the vampire that stood in front of her and her eyes met the Were that stood in front of them.

One in particular captured her attention.

The rapist.

Julia backed away until her butt collided with the Travertine façade of the building.

It was dark as they came, the streetlights illuminating the Were in patches of streetlight then disappearing as the dark embraced them again. Julia didn't take her eyes off the one.

He was the biggest. The most intense. She immediately understood that he wasn't the leader. Then she saw it. In his hand he held something.

A gun.

What? They were here to kill her? Julia was utterly confused. The two groups were not, however. As she held herself up against the wall they wordlessly charged each other, the Were making excited yips as their supple muscles clenched and bunched, readying to spring against the vampire.

Julia thought she'd just slip away while they fought. She couldn't be taken by the Were, her mind shuddered at the possibility. She began to feel her way along the building's façade, until her hand curved around the corner. She turned her face into an alley so dark she couldn't see where it ended, how high the sides were.

She stepped into the darkness, the war behind her raging in a clash of supernatural strength and will.

William advanced on the leader, swiping with talons that sprung from his fingertips in a blur of motion faster than anything he had mastered before. The pulse of his protection for Julia a thing that beat in his brain independently of his heart. The need to protect her was instinctive.

He saw in his periphery one of the runners fall, his gaping wound a hole in his body. *Still he would heal,* William thought as he leaned away from a strike and simultaneously punched a hole of his own in the chest of the nearest Were.

Fear gripped him. Julia was no longer a warm presence at his back. At the same time he saw one of the largest of the dogs break from the group and lope off to the side, a spider gait with fur, he pursued something else.

Someone else.

William turned in the direction of the lone Were just as Joseph used his half-wolf paws in a swinging arc, bringing them down across William's back, knocking him forward into a rough patch of cobblestone, revealed by newer asphalt. William's hands bit into the unforgiving street as two more of the Were assailed him. They pummeled him into submission.

Before he lost consciousness, he tore the head from the neck of one and warm blood sprayed his face. He gulped without thinking, the grievous wounds inflicted by the Were repairing as he drank the arterial spray of the enemy. His death repairing the worst of William's injuries as they occurred. A cycle of rejuvenation that was as old as time.

Joseph saw the vampire leader take the head from his third and howled. Before he could kill the vampire covered in blood at his feet Joseph's second growled, "Tony."

It was enough. Joseph shot away from the vampire, his soldiers tearing the other vampire limb from limb in an hour when humanity slumbered.

While humans slept peacefully, proof of the battle ran in the city street, painting it with inky blood.

. . .

JULIA RAN ALONGSIDE THE WALL, more tired than when she'd been running for exercise. The terror at being taken pouring an adrenaline nightmare in her body, her extremities numb with it.

She clipped her ankle on a pallet that was standing upright before she could see it and yelped softly.

She heard a noise behind her, the softest scrape and put on a burst of speed, her hand leaving the wall behind her.

Julia sprinted, the heat and lack of air in her lungs whistling a tune as she tore forward Up ahead she could see a tall fence. Without a backward glance or thought she grabbed on to the smooth, circular metal fencing and jumped the first row, digging her shoe into the hole and climbing.

Julia didn't hesitate when the first piercing sting of something in her shoulder twanged and bounced.

When the second bit her in her upper thigh as she climbed, tears began to run down her face, the fence design in sharp contrast to the streetlamps that were beyond. The holes from the fence made shapes on her face, circles of light spearing her as she climbed.

She climbed slower now, she realized with soft horror.

Julia told her hands to grip the cold metal. Her foot missed the next hole and slipped.

The tears came harder now, dripping off her jaw and falling to the ground before her.

She stopped, seven feet above the ground, three more yet to finish. The razor wire at the top formed a spiral of hopelessness she couldn't overcome.

Julia's vision began to dim, the grayness of the night encroaching on her. She clung to the fence, her body no longer climbing, pressing herself against it, she clung.

As her legs folded beneath her and her fingertips slipped

away she fell in a graceful arc to the concrete below.

To her death.

Julia didn't react when she heard the excited yelps and yips of the Were beneath her.

Jason dead.

William gone.

She was in the same position she had been when she started.

Sole protector.

Of herself.

Julia didn't land on the unforgiving concrete below, but in a steel cocoon, lined with fur and muscle. She looked up into eyes that shone like liquid gold. Her vision dimmed as she threw up her arm to defend herself in the last way she could before she faded into drug-induced oblivion.

Joseph stared at Julia for the moment of wakefulness she had before she sunk into the sleep of the drugged. His stony heart had squeezed at her weak attempt to defend herself against him. Did she not know that she could not? That there was no need? Joseph gave the signal to move out of the area even as he tightened his hold on the Rare One. They must exit. The blood drinkers would come en masse when the others didn't return with the Singer. Their margin for error this night was slim to none.

He ran, the light burden of the girl negligible.

Tony ran beside him, managing to carry out the task without a hitch.

Perhaps a first.

As he passed where they'd warred he saw the ash and blood lifting in the wind as a light rain began to fall. Cleansing the proof of their battle. One troubling thing remained.

A single vampire lay undisturbed, covered in his were-brother's blood.

Joseph faltered, debating on whether or not to return and finish him. His experience whispered at the possibility that this one would be a problem in the future. Then he looked down at the sleeping girl in his arms. He clutched her tighter. Better to fight the devil that you know rather than the one you do not.

He re-hastened his gait, smoothly leaving the city behind for the mountains beyond. They would address that worry if it came.

For now, the Rare One would become part of the pack.

The den would be balanced once again.

Joseph would have smiled as a human.

As it were, he was not.

He lifted his snout to the sky and howled a baleful note.

It resonated in the city as they left the buildings of concrete behind, the others, a symphony in chorus with him.

They ran to the den.

To freedom from their warden.

The moon.

CHAPTER 21

UNDERGROUND SEATTLE

*W*illiam's abused body struggled to heal even as he debriefed Gabriel and Claire. Their eyes and bodies were dread-filled.

But not as much as he.

William was so full of self-recrimination he could hardly breathe. A thousand what if's swirled in his mind. Not the least of which was the elaborate plan the Were had executed. The instant he had stood down, allowed less runners for the daily exercise, the Were had pounced.

As it was, when the runners had been sent after they did not return, it had been only William they had found. Four runners, dead. Only two of the Were killed.

They had woefully underestimated the cunning of the Were. They thought them without the intelligence for strategy.

They had been quite wrong. And now, because of assumptions, the Were had Julia.

It had taken the blood of three humans to allow William's recuperation. Even with that much, a gorge-worthy amount, William was still not at his peak.

Gabriel paced in front of him. "It does no good at this point to place blame. It is I that wished for Julia's exercise, for some semblance of normalcy."

Claire placed a hand on his shoulder and he stopped the frenetic path he'd worn in the floor of William's chamber. "None of us could have known this would occur," she pleaded with him to see reason, to not blame himself. Easier said than done.

"Julia knew," William said quietly. "She knew what was about. But she was so young in her ability, so new to trust..." he let that last trail off.

It was her newfound trust that cut deepest for William. What had it been? A mere week of them moving toward the end that he had envisioned for them all along. Now... she faced a situation that was not ordered but unprotected and unfit. A Rare One who would be treated without regard. Her abilities and genetic makeup used as a tool to further the dogs.

Of course, she had seen the vampires in a similar light. Not that William blamed her, yet... he had never been forthright enough about his feelings for her. He had thought it too soon to regale her with his regard. He'd only hinted at it. Now he wished he had been more bold. He startled Gabriel and Claire as he punched one fist into his open palm in anger, sitting up from his hunched position in the seat of his room.

Nausea and dizziness swirled around him but he hung on, he would not succumb. He would keep his focus on the rescue of the Singer.

Julia.

His future bride.

* * *

Julia

JULIA WOKE UP SLOWLY, feeling like she'd been run in the washing machine on the spin cycle.

Like a hundred times.

She sat up and her head spun and throbbing pain latched into her temples immediately.

Julia felt like hell, her mouth a sandpaper legacy with a chaser of dragon breath. God, yuk. Julia slowly opened her eyes, taking in her surroundings. She was so disoriented she forgot where she was for those few seconds, the pain of her head and acute thirst the distractions that called her attention.

Not anymore.

The thing that greeted her as the memories of yesterday crashed into her consciousness like a train without a brake was a huge pane of glass. A forest beyond stretched without end. Huge Western Red Cedars stretched as far as the eye could see, filling her vision. The sweep of their emerald green branches caressing the ground with an unseen wind that lifted and moved them in a soundless dance.

Julia looked down at her body, the tracksuit was gone. Instead she wore a cami and pajama bottoms. In one of the most surreal moments of her life she saw there were sparkly unicorns covering the material in the palest blue and silver.

Huh. She was being held by werewolves that had dressed her in unicorn pajamas.

Irony-much.

A single tear escaped her eye and made a pathway down her face. The weirdness of her life was making her so claustrophobic she wanted to go back to sleep and never wake up.

A knock came at the door and Julia ripped the sheet from the bed up to her chin, turning to face the door at the same time.

A girl came through the entrance, maybe about her age but oh, so different.

She wasn't human.

How did Julia know? It was those spinning golden eyes, their slow rotations screaming *other*... other worldly.

Julia just stared. Rude, but at this point it didn't matter. She was tired, she felt like she'd been beaten she ached so bad. Instead, she waited quietly.

"Hey," the girl said.

Julia sat there, saying nothing.

The girl fumed, finally sighing in a huff. "Listen, I know my brother put the he-man moves on ya. I tried to tell them it was the wrong way to do it." She flung up her hands and started pacing the room. "He's such a pain in the ass! Alpha this, Alpha that. Well eff that," she spun on her heel and faced Julia.

Julia leaned away.

She waffled her hand in front of Julia. "You don't need to worry about me," she plunged her hand against her chest earnestly.

Right, Julia thought, doing an internal eye roll, *that's what all the supernaturals said.* Clearly, that'd worked out so well in the past.

She shoved her hand out for Julia to shake. "My name's Adriana. I already know who you are, of course," she said rolling her eyes. Julia put a tentative hand out to shake and Adriana pumped it vigorously.

"This is awesome, finally they will quit talking about battles, acquisitions and all that happy horse shit. I'm so completely sick of all their chest beating bullshit I could puke."

Julia did a slow blink, gradually taking back her hand.

She thought Cyn might have been reincarnated in Adriana. Or they were secret cousins or something. However, there was the matter of a small difference.

She didn't think Adriana had a filter. Ya know, that thing that pings when you've said too much or you're going to? No, she didn't have one of those. And... Julia was certain that Cyn hadn't been a werewolf.

Julia ignored all the really important questions and gulping she asked, "Are these..." she picked up some of the loose pajama material in her hand and met Adriana's now-brown eyes (that was a relief that the wolf inside her wasn't threatening to spring out any moment), "yours?"

Adriana nodded enthusiastically. "Yeah. You were in some hot-ass jogging get-up so I thought you should be in some-thing more comfortable after being nailed with the juice."

"The juice?"

"Yeah, that crap they stuck ya with that makes you conk out." She looked at Julia for dawning comprehension. Seeing none she frowned, going on.

"Here's the deal. They pegged ya with the mega-tranquil-izers to getcha from the vamps, right?"

Julia nodded, slightly dazed at the Force that was Adriana.

"So now you've got a colossal headache and you're so thirsty you could die, right?"

"Yes," Julia nodded, her thirst roaring back to life at the mention of it.

"You can borrow those as long as ya want and I've got water." From behind her back she brought a water bottle. She gave it to Julia who uncapped it and started to chug it down.

"Whoa, pony. No gulping. My brother'll have my ass if you start doing the psychedelic yawn all over the place."

Julia gave her wide eyes. Brother, personality squared on this girl.

Adriana chuckled, mimicking what must be her brother, "I need you to be as disarming as possible, Adriana. Do not do your normal..." she mimed choking herself and went on in his presumed voice, "energetic behavior. The Rare One needs time to transition..."

"Blah, effing blah." She whipped her palm around dismissively. "You'll be fine, right?"

Was there another option?

Adriana stared at Julia, taking in her attire, the wild hair, God knows what else.

"Huh. Well... let's get you cleaned up, ya look like ass."

Definitely like Cyn.

Tell me how you really feel, Julia thought, following Adriana as she pushed open the adjacent bathroom door.

* * *

Were

LAWRENCE, Tony and Joseph were in a heated debate. As usual, Tony was the one questioning each decision.

"I took the Rare One down, she was escaping!" Tony said, his teeth barred in his human form, the wolf peeking out around the edges.

Well goddamn... *bring it*, Joseph thought as the muscles of his neck and shoulders corded and bunched in response to the subtle posturing.

"Enough!" Lawrence roared. The Packmaster's face was etched with grim lines of fury.

He took in the Alpha and his first, seconds passing. The moment swelled awkwardly, a palpable pressure building, on the verge of bursting. He broke it, "Save it for the ritual. That is the time to fight for the Rare One. Right now," he swung his direct look to Joseph, tense with the fighting instinct, "your sister is with Julia Caldwell?"

Joseph gave a terse nod, thinking of all that could mean. His sister was... willful.

Tony grunted.

They looked at him and he threw his muscular arms up in the air. "She is not the best at being *welcoming*. She is the most Alpha of all the females." He had a look on his face like, *clearly she is the least mild choice*.

"But, she is female. That is what the Singer needs, reassurances. Another female will bring her a measure of comfort," Lawrence said.

Joseph winced. He wasn't sure if Maggie wouldn't have been a better choice. Too late now. Adriana had roared in there like a flaming inferno, singeing everything in her path. He shook his head.

Lawrence shrugged, looking at the two men. "She will not intimidate. That is what the goal is here."

"She will still hold us responsible because of the dead Singer," Tony clarified.

Lawrence palmed his chin, thinking. "She may hold us to blame, if our soldier had not attacked her mate." He nodded, continuing. "But much time has passed. Perhaps her love for him fades." He shrugged. "It does not matter. She is here now, she has not been claimed by the vampire."

Tony and Joseph exhaled sighs of relief. That would have been an unbreakable bond, her relationship with a vampire, negating her abilities to assist them. It had been a near thing. The entire pack knew it.

Lawrence looked from one to the other of them. "She has one month. Even now I smell her readiness. Her becoming..."

They nodded. Her presence was at once exciting and unbearable. He didn't know what it had been like for the blood drinkers but she was a heady thing amongst the pack.

"Yes, Packmaster," Joseph said and Tony chorused the goodbye simultaneously.

They walked away together, their shoulders touching. Soon, it would be fists in the ring. A fight between them and others bringing the den closer to the reality of a moonless tide.

A lone howl broke the stillness of the woods where the den thrived. Joseph and Tony gave a wary look at each other, looking in the direction of the call. They looked away, neither commenting on the sound.

Its origin.

The call of the feral.

* * *

William

A HANDFUL of days gone and William felt himself again, sparring with some of the other runners. The ones lost in the battle with the Were a void in the ranks that would not be easily replaced. Especially Pierce. He had been a true warrior, responsible for the deaths of two during the siege that ripped Julia from their hands.

He lunged forward, with both hands meeting in a destructive vee toward the vampire runner who grappled with him. He was met with impervious resistance as their arms collided like flesh-encased steel, the smack of the hit resounding in the acoustics of the underground. The brick and mortar of the cavernous accommodations echoed hollowly in the space.

Vampires did not breathe but one breath to a human's four. That was not the case when fighting. Both runner's actions and speed a blur of muted color as they swung at each other underneath the ambient glow of the skylights that acted as a fractured ceiling of light. The humans that walked the surface lived unaware of the predators that fought below.

"Again!" William shouted as the runner tried to beg off another round. William lost his temper, grabbing his comrade around the throat and jerking him against him, his fists like clamps of unbreakable titanium, buried in the folds of the shirt he wore, tearing it as he pulled.

Suddenly, Gabriel was there and William straightened. He turned to the runner, "Go."

He went.

Gabriel looked at William, chest heaving, his fist clenched like battle ready hammers. "Enough, beating your fellow runners into the ground will not return her to you." His eyes searched William's and he began pacing, the shadowed feet of the humans walking above them throwing speckles of darkness over his face as he moved.

Gabriel stared at William, his expression half in shadow. He glanced upward at the skylight where the humans walked all day and sighed. He knew what the loss of Julia meant to the kiss. He could not imagine what the loss meant when love was twisted inside it.

"I understand the loss of Julia... may be more..."

"You do not," William said on a hiss, his hand planted on his hips, his breathing finally settling into the normal rhythms of his kind. "You cannot. I waited for her. I was patient," he seethed. "And now this!" William threw up his hand. "She is with the dogs now. Being subjected to..." William's expression was thunder contained.

Gabriel strode to William until their chests almost touched. "We *will* reclaim her."

"When?" William asked, his brows falling like a brick over his eyes.

"Before the moon comes full again."

They both understood the significance of the moon's cycle. The dogs would try for her. The ritual coming full circle.

There would be no choice for Julia in their world. It was the Alpha that would be her mate. Whatever one killed the other. It was their way.

Uncivilized mongrels.

* * *

the Feral

THE MEAT APPEARED AGAIN *like clockwork, his tortured mind dismissing its grief for the greater need of sustenance. He leaped forward just as the arm retracted through the hole. The only light and air in the place where they kept him.*

He growled low in his throat. Talons leapt free of his fingertips and he plunged them into the prey that squirmed on the end of his talons, sharp as finely-honed razors. He cut its throat with his dominant left hand and caught the lifeblood as it sprayed from the death slice. When its life hung from a string, he sliced the body open, neck to crotch, the steaming entrails his next feast.

He fed.

Satisfied, he flung the corpse in the pile in the corner of the metal room he was kept in.

The food settled and began to work its magic on his body, his senses springing to life, his sense of smell the most keen of all.

A dim memory was upon him and he felt compelled to move. He did, dropping to the ground he reversed his wolf into his human form again. His hands bit the ground and he allowed his body to assume a plank-like position. He raised and lowered himself until he lost count and the rivulets of sweat ran off his face and pooled beneath him.

When the female returned to collect his dead meals, their eyes met and she looked away. He was above her. Even he understood that. She was behind a partition that was clear.

His mind knew somewhere from Before that it was called acrylic. At two feet thick, even he could not overcome its strength.

He was very strong now. He smelled the fear on the female through the holes that were drilled like Swiss cheese in the clear wall.

When he lifted his nose to scent her, he smelled another scent, very faint.

It caused the wolf that rippled underneath his human flesh to roar to the surface in a grinding purge that blew his body apart, skin and tendons tearing in a sickeningly painful mesh of wolf and human flesh.

His half form emerged, seven feet tall and covered with a deep wine-colored coat of fur. In the light of day it would have looked like the sun set on his back.

He howled, the scent of the female was one he knew.

He despaired.

He rushed the partition, his talons scraping the acrylic where deep grooves appeared like quartz scars on its surface.

The female backed away, running outside the door and closing the bolt that barred entry.

And escape.

The werewolf howled and bayed until his voice box no longer cooperated.

The female covered her ears and ran away, hot tears beating a burning trail down a face that held but one expression.

Shame.

CHAPTER 22

*J*ulia undressed and stepped into the shower, the hot spray hitting her body, the aches lessened but the headache remained.

There was absolutely no peace as Adriana kept talking while she bathed. Thank God for opaque glass.

"You're probably wonderin' why I can't be somewhere else while you're de-scuzzing."

Actually, Julia totally was.

"Gotta keep an eye on ya. The boys are all frothing at the mouth about you escaping. Like that's even remotely possible. Duh." Julia could feel Adriana rolling her eyes.

Julia rinsed her hair and body off, eyeing the razor. She'd love to do a full groom. Now wasn't the time though. How could she even give a crap about shaving when a pack of werewolves were sniffing around? Julia guessed that she was getting used to her strange life as normal.

It made her want to cry again.

Just as she thought she might lose it, a skinny arm stuck a towel through the shower curtain.

"For your hair," Adriana said.

Huh.

Julia wrapped her head in the towel and stepped out.

Naked.

Adriana tossed a second towel in her hand and walked to the vanity, busying herself with getting the necessities out: toothbrush, paste, floss, comb...

Julia patted dry and wrapped herself in a towel that had been washed with the same detergent Aunt Lily used and Julia bit the inside of her lip to keep from crying again, the taste of copper filling her mouth.

She widened her eyes to keep the tears from falling.

Adriana turned with a grin. It dropped like a sack of stones when she saw Julia's expression. "You're not gonna start bawling or something? Like, right now? 'Cuz, I'm not equipped for female sniveling."

That stopped Julia's tears and made a grin appear despite herself.

"Good, you had me worried."

Julia said, "You don't seem very..."

"Were-wolfy?" Adriana asked with a sarcastic lilt to her voice.

Julia nodded. "Yeah, that."

"Well, what didya expect anyway? All shaggy mutts howling at the moon or some shit like that?" Her hand pegged her hip, eyebrows to her hairline, ready to fight.

She was hell on wheels Julia thought helplessly. "I didn't know... I just woke up," she shrugged. It was impossible to explain.

Adriana smiled. "It's okay, you'll get used to me. It's the boys you'll have to keep an eye on. You're like their bitch in heat."

So subtle too, Julia thought. Hell.

Adriana saw her expression. "Nah, it's not that bad. Can't you feel her?"

192

"Feel who?"

"The moon, silly. She's not full. You're safe till then." Her eyes became warm, the brown fading to a molten chocolate and Julia saw the wolf she was underneath her human flesh.

It was disconcerting as hell.

She knew she shouldn't ask.

Julia did anyway. "Ah... what happens then?"

"Nothing special. My brother and a bunch of other wolves will fight to the death to mate with you."

Julia's hand flung out and grabbed the vanity to steady her sudden vertigo, the other hand clamped onto the knotted towel at her breast.

"Are ya okay?"

No. She was definitely not okay, she thought, starting a slow stagger that led to her falling.

The wisp of a werewolf caught her and looked down on her with a flicker of compassion. Just as Julia was sucked under into unconsciousness she said, "We're gonna have to toughen you up."

Julia's eyes fluttered closed and she slept.

Dreamlessly and deep.

* * *

Were

THEY LOOKED DOWN at Julia as she slept. New jammie bottoms replaced the others, now dirty.

"How'd she do?" Joseph asked his sister, resisting the urge to tuck her dark blond hair behind her ear like he'd done when she was a whelpling.

She wouldn't appreciate it now. He smiled at his reflection.

Adriana looked up at him and scowled. "Obviously, so great! She fainted when I glossed over the mating ritual."

"Glossed over?" Tony asked.

She waved her hand around. "I just mentioned, ya know, you guys were gonna fight to the death over her and she'd be with one of ya. No. Big. Deal." Adriana put her hands on her hips, daring them to contradict her logic.

Tony's mouth opened and closed and Joseph put his a palm on his forehead and scrubbed his face.

"What?" she all-but-shrieked and Julia turned, moaning in her sleep.

"See! She's gonna be fine. Better to have radical honesty, guys. You should try it sometime, works like a charm on the chicks."

"Yeah, I see that!" Tony said, pissed at Adriana.

Joseph knew it had been a mistake to have his sister be the first one that greeted the Rare One.

Julia opened her eyes and saw two men standing over her bed and scuttled into the corner where the wall met one side of the headboard. She clutched the sheet and hoped for some handy telekinesis. And why the hell hadn't that come when she needed it last night as the tranquilizer darts flew? She winced where she'd bitten the inside of her cheek to keep from crying.

No worry over tears right now. She was pissed instead.

"Who are you?" Julia ground out, her voice hoarse, her body tensed.

Adriana grinned. "See, she's just fine. You jackasses got her off on the wrong foot and now you're gonna have to romance her," Adriana finished, supremely satisfied with herself.

Julia, Tony and Joseph glared at her from separate corners.

"Fine!" She fumed. "You guys can figure it out on your

own. Good luck with that!" Adriana took a look at Julia, shook her head and marched out the door, slamming it off its hinges on the way out.

Joseph cringed when the wood slapped together with a resounding thwack.

"That ah..." he began.

"Nice family," Julia said.

Tony laughed and Julia looked at him and his smile faded.

She was acutely aware of being in a bedroom with two men she knew to be werewolves in nothing but a cami and jammie bottoms. She pulled the sheet up higher, clutching it underneath her chin.

Joseph watched how she moved into the corner defensively and was distressed about it. There was nothing he could do but explain their position.

"Julia..." he started, then abruptly changed his mind, "let's get some food."

"Yeah, okay. Just as soon as you gents get out of this room and let me get dressed." Her eyes searched theirs, the one that hadn't said much giving her pause. He was a big guy even without being a werewolf. Julia was guessing he had a foot and over a hundred pounds on her. There was something in his eyes, the predator never really left them, she decided. She was going to keep him in her sights for sure.

All of them.

They left the room and Julia ran over to the door and slid the bolt to lock it. Like that was going to be any help. She took her hand away, a slight tremor making it quake.

Julia spied some clothes on a lone chair in the corner and pulled the drape as she passed in front of the window, shutting out the forest from sight.

Her head snapped up a few seconds later when a plaintive howl sounded.

It pierced her gut, there was something so sad about it, tears actually flooded her eyes at the mournful call.

What was wrong with her? She shook it off with difficulty.

Julia dressed. Moving toward the door she put the flat of her palm against the wood, calming her wildly beating heart. She pressed her forehead to the wood for a moment, clenching her eyes, her mind touching on William and just as quickly shoving the thought away.

He couldn't help her now.

She slid the bolt back and opened it, walking out of the only sanctuary she knew, into the unknown.

He knew the routine and would bide his time. They assumed that he was crazy. They were right. But he was also determined. He had something worth escaping for. He now knew so much more than he had, the memories of others a part of the fabric of who he was now, centuries of genetic thought processes and experiences crowding his skull.

They kept him here in this holding cell to study him. They fed him, allowed him to kill, forced him to exercise and maintain a standard of hygiene.

Not that he cared.

He had died that night.

Now he waited to be reborn.

The feral watched the lock turn and three of his kind came inside. They used more now. After he had taken the head of one, they now used three.

"Time for your bath, feral," Tony said without compassion.

That would be the first of them he would kill, he thought with satisfaction. His patience had become its own force to be reckoned with. Soon, they would taste it. He repressed a low growl, some of it escaping like a breeze in the quiet room.

Joseph looked at the feral warily, his eyes flicking to Tony's. "That's not helpful and you know it. He can't help what he is any more than you can. Now let's herd him in there and get it over with. And be careful." Joseph said, eyeing the wolf in front of them. Big in human form, he was huge as a wolf, and one of the rare reds. It was a shame that he couldn't be part of the pack. But he'd been turned, not born. That branded him *other* in the pack's eyes. All the benefits of the Were but without the protection of the den at his back. An anomaly.

And feral, his mind nearly gone.

Who could blame him?

Tony snorted a laugh. "He is not Alpha to me!" He rolled his big shoulders into a muscular shrug of irritation that would have been impressive, but next to the huge red wolf, it just wasn't.

"Are you sure?"

Tony looked at the rare red Were that stood in front of him, spinning emerald eyes laying an unspoken challenge at his feet. *He* thought he was Alpha enough, those eyes said. He flicked a glance at his Alpha. He wasn't sure but he'd sure like to test the theory.

Sooner rather than later.

Instead, Tony threw a palm out at the large, walk in shower meant to accommodate all things not human.

The feral allowed his shape to melt into human form again, so seamless a transition Joseph sighed.

Joseph and Tony looked at him with envy.

The moon did not rule his Change.

Only theirs.

* * *

Julia

JULIA LET her legs swing back and forth as she pushed scrambled eggs around on a plate with big blue flowers on it. The cook, or mom-of-everyone, started to chatter again but Julia was only half-listening.

"Eat up now, hun. Keep your strength up!" she busied herself, wiping her practical hands, toughened by a thousand meals, ten thousand dishes cleaned, off on her apron. She plopped her elbows on the breakfast bar opposite Julia and said, "Dontcha like what I made ya?"

Julia did, but the appetite wasn't top notch. Not by a long shot. *Let's recap*, Julia thought. Husband killed almost two years ago... best friend, gone. Taken by crazy vampires because she was some kind of genetic prodigy. Check. Then kidnapped by crazier werewolves.

Please eat and exchange pleasantries.

Riggghhht.

She was so into that.

Not.

She did anyway. "I do... like it. I'm just a little tired after the whole getting kidnapped thing. That'll make hunger..." she trailed off and Maggie picked up the thread of her thoughts easily. "Unimportant?"

Julia's eyebrows quirked.

Maggie smiled.

"Oh right. Yeah, I guess." Julia forced another bite in her mouth, everything tasting the same when Adriana stalked in, grabbing a couple of grapes from a fruit bowl and popping them inside her mouth. Chewing vigorously she said, "Hey Maggie, what's for breakfast?"

Maggie slapped her hand as she went for more fruit. "Good for ya but you need some protein in your craw. You know the routine."

Adriana glared at Maggie and she glared right back.

Interesting dynamics with the werewolves, Julia thought,

remembering how civilized everything was with the vampire. With the Were everyone was passionate, yelling and boisterous, hitting each other... different.

Julia thought about it more. She had almost forgotten the blood letting episode with the vampires.

That hadn't been civilized. She repressed a shudder.

She watched the girl and the older woman circle each other warily and Julia resisted the urge to push away from the bar and get out of the way.

"Sit your rear end down and stuff some breakfast down your pipe before the men come. They'll clean everything out, ya know."

Adriana parked her butt next to Julia's, sullen. "K."

"Humph!" Maggie said, ladling a plate with twice as much as she'd given Julia and slid it across to Adriana.

She dug in with gusto. When half the plate was put away she caught Julia staring.

"What?" she asked, shoveling in more food.

"It's just... so much food..." Julia began, looking at her own barely eaten food.

She shrugged a slender shoulder. "Gotta fuel up. Eat more as the moon waxes."

Julia cocked a brow.

"Ya know," slurp-gulp, "gettin' bigger?" She looked at Julia like she was mildly retarded.

"I understand what a waxing moon means," Julia said, insulted despite herself.

"Well thank God, I was startin' to really worry about ya!" she said, giving Maggie a significant look and she nodded back.

What? They thought she was dumb or something? Julia frowned as the two werewolves from before came into the kitchen.

Julia did get up then. Backing up against the wall closest

to the door she had used to enter the kitchen.

Their eyes flicked to hers and she did not miss the subtle flare of their nostrils.

That was a creeper factor of about one thousand.

They were scenting her.

Her eyes met Adriana's and she smirked then added, like Julia needed clarity, "Bitch in heat, baby, bitch in heat."

Nice. Julia flattened herself even harder against the wall.

Joseph glared at his sister and she blithely ignored him, gulping some more orange juice and stabbing a sausage, now impaled on the tines of her fork.

While he smoldered at his sister, Tony's eyes bored into Julia's.

She shifted uncomfortably underneath that gaze.

His eyes weren't right.

Tony watched the Rare One with barely contained ownership. She'd have to bow to him. He would be Alpha to her. He didn't care what Lawrence said. Maybe he was Alpha enough to take him but because of him being the Packmaster, he didn't get to play in the sandbox. Tony's lips curled in a predatory smile. The bitch Rare One would free him of his status in the pack. He would be able to Change at Will, the moon nothing to him. No pull, no more domination. He could taste the freedom that she'd provide. And all that bullshit about honoring Singers. That was for the old ways.

It was gonna be his way.

Tony looked at her again and saw that she interpreted some of what he thought from the expression in his eyes. He hooded his gaze and looked away, better not to let her in on his plan. As it was, Joseph was Alpha enough to understand what he wanted. He hated looking away from her first. He didn't want to give her the impression that her gaze was dominant to his.

After all, she was a weak female. She was of rare blood, but female nonetheless.

Julia backed further against the wall. The look the big Were gave her scared her. She saw Adriana catch the glance between the two and shoot her arm out in a sucker punch that landed expertly in Tony's solar plexus.

He issued a satisfying grunt that caused his gaze to swing away in anger toward Adriana.

Tony felt the swing a moment too late, his gut unprepared. That bitch Adriana swung at him and landed a nice one in his bread basket, stealing most of his breath.

Embarrassment washed over him instantly and before he knew what he was doing he was after her.

With his Alpha who was also her brother in the room.

He saw red, a lesser wolf and female having humiliated him in front of a potential mate of the most important order.

Tony would crush her.

Julia responded without thinking, watching a huge hand ball into a fist as it raised above the mouthy Adriana while her brother was across the room.

The power that was not harnessed correctly, without finesse, without will came to the surface in a surge of brilliance, bursting inside her in a flash of interior light. Without thinking, Julia directed it at Tony and he spun where he stood, like an invisible wood plank had been leveled at his raised fist and swung hard, making brutal contact.

He staggered against the breakfast bar and away from Adriana, his back slamming into the fridge, a storm of magnets clattering to the floor like hail.

His eyes snapped up and met Julia's. She knew the remnants of what she'd done stood in the room between them. Hell, even she could feel an almost static energy zooming and ricocheting around them, pinging off the walls.

"Holy shit! That rocked! You clocked his ass!" Adriana said, jumping up and raising her fist into the air.

Joseph was on Julia before she could move, sweeping her behind him as Tony fell on the spot where she'd been standing.

Julia screamed in response, held against one Were while the other's jaws snapped around him to get at her.

She saw his face between the sliver of the one's arm and the wall that he stood against.

Tony had changed, the eyes luminescent and golden in a face that had elongated into a snout with silver fur and many teeth.

Like a crocodile. Except this one didn't crawl on the ground, but was nearing seven feet tall.

"She's shown defiance!" Tony roared, drool and spittle flying out of a mouth filled with teeth the size of her pinky finger.

Adriana yipped behind him and he whirled on her, pathetically small compared to him, all white with silver-tipped fur, her eyes were an unnerving glacial color, gold blazing through them like lightning.

"Adriana, no!" Joseph said, going for his sister in protection even as he left Julia there in the doorway threshold.

Vulnerable and unprotected with a half-Were in anger.

Directed at her.

Tony turned and saw his opportunity to subdue this female. Now, before she embraced ideas of superiority. Her fragility was attractive. He would not crush her but she would feel the sting of his superiority.

Oh yes.

He sprung from clawed feet that missed purchase on the tile floor of the kitchen and as he slipped, he regained his balance at the last moment and leaped for her.

Julia saw that muzzle coming for her and couldn't get

whatever telekinetic power she possessed to work. It was like she was out of gas. She turned and ran.

The wolf's hot breath on her neck, her fear tightened her bladder and made the food she'd just eaten rise in a tide of gorge.

He paced the cage they kept him in and when his acute hearing heard raised shouts he allowed his nose and facial alignments to shift to wolf. Only those. That was all he needed to gain an answer for what was happening outside the confines of this place.

His nose became a snout and many layers of scent came to him instantly. He pressed his new wolf snout against one of the many holes in the wall and fear touched him.

Female fear.

He knew the flavor of it.

He knew who was frightened.

The wolf burst out of his human form, the force of his change spraying what he had been moments before around the room in a splattering gunk of flesh and bone. The blood mixed with the liquid that facilitated the change landing against the clear wall and slipping down to pool at the ground.

He howled a warning of such contained rage and power that the birds roosted in the trees in midday, avoiding whatever had made that sound by seeking refuge at the highest point of the forest.

Julia heard a howl of rage that made her steps falter just as clawed hands that were now half-paws as big as her head wrapped her upper arms and jerked Julia back against a body that emanated an impossible heat. It blazed against her back as she struggled to get away.

Then the other Were stood in front of her.

Joseph, the brother of Adriana she thought with random wildness.

"Let her go!" Joseph growled out.

The need to mark the Rare One pounded a steady beat in Tony's head, he could hear nothing else. He knew the Alpha had spoken but the fragrance of the Singer had sunk its talons into his soul and the call of the wolf was on him. He couldn't shake it and began to tremble with his needs.

They were many.

He opened his jaws wide to take her throat into his mouth. She must submit.

The pain was immediate. He felt something strike him in the back of his head and his hands loosened on the Singer, trying to take her to the ground with him. But as he fell sideways in slow motion, he saw the Alpha grab her to him and press her against himself.

Adriana held the cast iron skillet in delicate hands that were half-wolf. With grace, Adriana had skipped up behind the werewolf, twice her size and arced the pan above his head even as she jumped vertically, landing it soundly on the crown of his head.

He began to slip, his hold coming away from her arms and Joseph grabbed her when she would have fallen with Tony to the floor.

He pressed her to his chest and murmured the things people say to soothe when there isn't a hope of it.

She met Adriana's wide eyes and thought maybe she'd bitten off more than she could chew.

Hardy-har-har.

Julia pressed her eyes shut, smelling the male aroma of the wolf; pine, earth and the faint smell of cinnamon.

But it was the haunting shout of another wolf that echoed in her mind, the sound of it still following her thoughts. Somehow he had interfered with Tony hurting her.

It had sounded so sure.

Like a warning.

CHAPTER 23

*A*driana looked down at a semi-conscious Tony and said, "Bull's-eye!"

Julia looked at her with big eyes and Adriana laughed. "He gets kinda enthusiastic and needed a slow-down."

Yeah, Julia thought, *a cast iron skillet would do it.*

Joseph slowly released Julia and turned her to face him. She was immediately struck by his eyes, an impossible hazel, at once gold, green and a rich, root beer brown. Rainbow eyes.

She realized she'd been staring and cast her eyes down. He chuckled. "You're not afraid of me?" Joseph asked.

Julia shook her head, but oh yeah, she was. But given that he'd just rescued her from Enthusiastic Tony... she guessed he was okay.

He looked at his sister, his hands leaving Julia's arms with a caress and she shivered, like a goose just walked over her grave. It was a creepy sensation but also like a itch on your back had just been scratched. Totally weird.

"That'll be a helluva thing to smooth over, Adi," he said to her, exasperated. Joseph looked at Tony on the floor, writhing around and scrubbed his face again.

Julia had an idea he did a lot of that when it came to his sister.

She smiled at him. "He was outta control and your ass was too slow so... Adriana to the rescue!" she shouted to the rooftops.

Julia stood awkwardly between them in the kitchen. A werewolf at her feet, one beside her and a possible female ally.

Funny how life works.

* * *

one week later

MOONLIGHT STREAMED THROUGH THE SKYLIGHTS, shattered pieces like shards of glass on the cobblestone floor of the underground of the Seattle kiss. William looked at the pass through which led into one of the long halls, the bricked archway perfectly framing Gabriel.

He had an abiding scowl planted on his face.

For good reason. William was busy packing in readiness to reacquire Julia. It was but one week from the full moon. They were not yet ready for acquisition but each moment they drew closer to the moon's zenith their enemy grew stronger.

And on their territory, no less. No, the time was now. He and Gabriel had argued. But, as the leading runner, he had pull, his thoughts held weight.

And, as her potential mate, even more so. Claire had sided with him.

Gabriel pushed away from the brick and walked over to where William stood, shouldering a small backpack. "You do this at your own peril. You realize how closely guarded she will be?"

William nodded. "I do. Even now, kept by the mongrels, day by day they grow closer to their heathen ceremony. No," he shook his head at the multiple visions that greeted him, "she will not have that end. Not Julia."

Not his Julia.

* * *

Julia

JULIA WAS in her room again at the Were compound. That is how she saw it. Her routine was the same and it reminded her eerily of the vampire. Except for William. She found she missed him. At first, he'd been nothing but a captor. But now... he was someone that she had grown to care about. To... have an easy friendship with. She was acutely aware that she'd grown to depend on his protection. She had not felt that sense of security since Jason.

Her chest got tight and Julia took deep breaths. Her capture and his death combined in a memory of unbearable agony.

One bright spot was Adriana. She liked Adi, so Julia called her that. Julia remembered the conversation exactly.

* * *

"YOU CAN CALL me Adi too, ya know," she'd said, putting some clothes away in the drawer, her eyes doing a peripheral check of Julia's reaction.

"Okay, thanks," Julia said.

"Do you... do you always go by Julia?" Adi had asked.

Julia looked down, feeling sad. Finally, she shook her

head. "No... I had a friend," Julia covered her mouth with her cupped hand for a moment and Adi broke the sadness with, "No waterworks, just tell me your nickname."

Her whiskey colored eyes met Adi's brown ones. "Jules. That's what my friends called me."

"Tell me about them."

It was the first time someone had actually given a crap about Jason, Cyn and Kev.

She told Adi all of it. How cool they'd been, how much she missed them, how she and Jason had gotten married in the Gnome Chapel. That brought an instant smile.

"Really? That's a no-shitter." Adi had thought for a moment, her chin planted in her palm. Then she brightened. "At least it wasn't in that creepy Elvis Chapel." She grimaced and Julia laughed.

She laughed until her sides hurt and tears were streaming down her face.

Adi looked at her with curiosity, "What the hell, Jules? Doesn't everyone think there's something alarming about a dude in white polyester and tassels?" Adi asked reasonably, her palms spread at her sides. "And the man tits? Ugh!" She hissed in emphasis.

That made Julia laugh harder. When she had some semblance of restraint, she held up a finger and replied, "That was my only requirement," she said, wiping the tears.

"What?" Adi asked, confused.

"I didn't want to get married at that damn chapel with The King in attendance."

"King my ass," Adi muttered.

"Cyn didn't like him either," Julia said, remembering.

"Was she pretty cool?"

Julia nodded, their gazes locking. "She was the best," she said wistfully.

* * *

Homer

TRUMAN SLAPPED the file against his thigh as an officer approached him, "Detective Truman!"

He shifted his weight in the large chair that swiveled behind his desk.

"Yeah?" Karl asked, looking at the disheveled beat cop. The name on his tag read, *Daugherty.* He'd sent him on a last-ditch wild goose chase. The seasons were changing and after almost two years, the weather was finally cooperating for his purposes. Truman had thought of something, something that had been missed when the Caldwell scene was canvassed two years ago. Well, almost two years.

Those trees.

The trees that stood on either side of the rugged path that led down to the beach. He'd seen them a thousand times but the dream he'd received last night had been a revelation, the break he hadn't been able to get from returning to the scene of the Caldwell murder a hundred times.

Daugherty jerked up the evidence bag like a prize won at the carnival. It was clear, inside it were three or four long hairs.

Truman didn't know it then but they weren't left by a bear.

They weren't human.

That dandy little footnote would be inscribed later.

The first real smile of the day broke over Truman's weathered face and the beat cop smiled in return, relieved beyond words that his boss wasn't gonna chew his ass.

Today.

They smiled at each other and Karl reached for the bag, its precious cargo so light but oh, *so* heavy.

* * *

3 months prior

THE TALONS STROKED Cynthia's throat and she shuddered. She'd been asleep in her bed, on the day that the cop... Turner, Tucker... whatever his name was, had come by to visit her and ask questions again, about Jason's murder.

Jules' disappearance.

Her answers were always the same. The visits from the creatures were always the same.

The day after Jules was taken they'd come inside her bedroom window and silenced her immediately.

They said things. Terrible things. But she believed them when they told her if she said anything about what *really* happened, she would get the same fate as her boyfriend.

Now this one came again.

Cynthia didn't care what it said. She thought it liked causing her pain and fear.

Her only consolation was that if they had Julia... really had her... they wouldn't be so worried about discovery.

Cynthia wasn't the same girl she'd been before. She didn't care about fashion or fun. She wanted to escape from Homer. Move somewhere new.

Somewhere *they* couldn't find her.

As she lay pinned on her bed by the creature that ground out its demands, its filthy half-paw wrapped around her throat, its fetid breath encasing her in rot, he instructed her on what to say.

"Keep to the story. Repeat what it is," it growled at her. At least it was only the one this time.

"I... it was a bear attack." Her eyes flicked to its, golden and spinning in an immense head with fur the color of the sea on an stormy day. "That's why there was so much... *blo*...

blood," Cynthia said, her voice trembling from the memory of the blood, the carnage, her boyfriend's decapitated body, paces from hers.

He squeezed her throat and the breath wheezed out of it. "And...," the werewolf that held her on the bed asked, giving her a teeth rattling shake.

He released the pressure so she could utter the final lie, "I passed out from the shock. I never saw what happened," Cynthia said mechanically.

It smiled a grin filled with teeth meant to maim, tear and kill. It suddenly released her throat and her hand went to it automatically. The tears fell in rivulets, dampening her pillow.

Cynthia had seen everything that happened. All of it.

She didn't like slasher flicks anymore.

She knew horror was real.

Cynthia watched the Were leave through the window like before.

She made a promise to herself in that moment. She'd move to where they couldn't find her. Somewhere different, anonymous... big.

Like Seattle.

Perfect.

She'd forget what had happened with a fresh environment, Cynthia told herself.

Her eyes fixed on her meager belongings in her studio apartment. She rose from her bed and began to pack at three o'clock in the morning.

Long past the witching hour.

* * *

Julia

ADI AND JULIA RAN.

No privacy of course, but they ran anyway. It felt so like the exercise she'd taken with William and the other runners. But the Were could keep up in their human form.

Julia hated Tony at her back. Because she knew, deep down, that he really didn't *have* her back. William had been open about his intentions, about the history. The vampire Book of Blood.

The Were had been covert, not that it helped. Adi told Julia everything she wanted to know and things she didn't. She was a treasure. If Julia had met her in other circumstances they could have been friends.

But even now, Julia planned her escape.

She ran on a dirt path, made wide by use, the dappled shade from the trees making the ground look like a puzzle of light. Julia felt the heat of the sun even through the trees and felt how different it was from Alaska. There was a distance in that part of the world. As if the sun held its rays back, stingy in its warmth. Here in Washington, the kiss of its heat was all around them and she reveled in it.

She'd miss it.

Julia didn't care if she was important. She wanted freedom, liberty. She had stayed awake these past few nights thinking about that one, one hundredth percent of Rare Ones that breathed the air on this earth. Why couldn't she belong to them?

Why couldn't she belong to herself?

Be free to choose her own path, her own destiny. There was no one to give her any council. They all wanted a piece of her.

Of her blood. A song that rivaled all others. A genetic match of perfection to balance their needs.

What about hers?

They drove up the last hill, their legs pumping furiously,

Adi barely breathing as she whispered to Julia, "Ya know that swine Tony?"

Julia huffed out, her legs grinding up the incline, "Yeah?"

"He put me in the dog house and now I'm off babysitting your precious ass," she said, sprinting ahead.

Oh shit.

Julia poured on the speed and caught up, running along-side her. "What do you mean? He scares me," Julia said quietly, mindful of the ears pricked behind them.

"He's made me give a squirt of pee on occasion," Adi said dryly. "But not without payback if you feel me." She gave a smug smile and Julia nodded. She felt her. It'd only been a couple of weeks here in the den but already she wondered why Adi wasn't in charge. She sure thought she was.

Adi hadn't gotten the memo.

But in reality Julia had grudging respect for Joseph. He was stern, gentle and supervised the pack with great fairness. The Packmaster... he was a different story. Julia hadn't liked him much better than Tony. Julia remembered their brief meeting.

* * *

LAWRENCE CIRCLED the Rare One and was surprised at her. Hardly more than a girl, she looked no different than any other female.

But for her smell she could have been any college-aged student, roaming around.

She certainly was not. Her smell was like the most rare perfume, small in quantity and potently lethal.

Agitating. Julia Caldwell drove under his skin and stayed there. The moon as his witness he would be most glad when the Ritual of Luna and the mating was finished. He would lose one of his wolves and gain a legend. Freedom was within their grasp. Having a Rare One would solidify their leadership in the Pacific Northwest Region.

Forever.

A self-satisfied smile curled his lips as he met Julia.

He saw that she regarded him with distrust. No matter, hers had been an easy life.

Julia watched him assume everything about her in a glance and knew that he may be Packmaster here, but to her, he was presumptuous. And just plain wrong. She had a trick or two up her sleeve. They thought her awakening powers were not fully formed. That when she'd heaved Tony against the fridge that she was too much of a novice to do anything to defend herself.

They were wrong. Julia was executing the equivalent of push-ups when she was alone in her room. Levitating herself and all that was in her space.

She'd become quite good at it, developing finesse, pushing herself for control in the short time she'd been there.

Claire would have been proud, gulping against the lump that formed in her throat.

Julia glanced at Adi and she nodded back. Time to turn back. They turned where a great log had fallen, its form caved in with a secondary seedling growing out of the decomposition. Julia looked beyond it, into the deeper woods.

It was there that her escape lay.

As they ran the werewolves fell in beside them and Julia could feel the emotions around her. There was no way to block it out. She could not gain one ability without others showing up. She had never wished for something more in her whole life. Another one like her.

A Blood Singer.

* * *

four days

HE HEARD *them as they came back from exercise and pressed his snout against the acrylic partition, a vile material that smelled like rotting plastic to his most sensitive organ. He smelled the female of his kind that fed him and the other.*

He would know her fragrance anywhere. But it had changed. Something about that familiar scent was altered.

It didn't matter. Soon enough, when the moon was ripe and full, he would escape this place. He mourned what would be done to see it through.

But in the end, it would be worth it.

one day

ADRIANA SLIPPED into the kennel where the feral was kept and instantly felt the guilt grip her.

She hated seeing him.

He was the most beautiful of the Were she'd ever seen. A coat so deep a red it was like wine, eyes so green they shimmered like emeralds. In fact, Adi didn't think there were jewels that looked as good as his eyes. But she'd been there the day he'd knocked off the head of her whelpmate.

He was dangerous.

And crazier than a June bug, as her grandpa would say.

She had extra feral duty. Because she'd walloped that shitwad Tony in the head with the pan. No thanks that she'd saved the precious Rare One from a mauling. Oh-no. It was, "Adriana, Tony is superior, you need to show deference..." Blah, effing blah. Deference her ass. Tony was a pain-in-all-their-butts. She figured she did everyone a favor. He had a very small brain and when she'd thwacked his head, maybe the swelling would enlarge it enough so he'd think.

Nah, that'd been a fat damn chance. He was back to asshat status as soon as he woke up.

The dick. Why he was even in line for the Ritual was beyond her. None of the men could see his cruelty? He wasn't good with the whelplings. He had to remind them constantly that he was dominant. Yeah? So what. They knew that. They didn't need their asses handed to them day in and day out to catch a clue.

Adi fumed inside the kennel, which was really a huge outbuilding. Her eyes went at once to the feral. He was in human form and she thought that unusual. He could partially change at will and didn't need the moon. However, he was invincible when it was full. Nobody entered then, unless there were three or more.

They'd learned that the hard way.

Adi felt guilty that he didn't get food or water one day a month. Actually, she didn't agree with keeping him like a zoo animal. Just because he was turned didn't mean that he was less than them.

Lesser.

He watched her approach him warily, very small for a female of his kind but wily, yes... very clever.

She looked at him in his human form, six foot two, athletic build, sandy blonde hair. But the eyes were not green. She didn't know why they were not gold during the Change like her pack. The Packmaster didn't know why he was a red. There were so few.

Adi had a speculation about it. The Alphas weren't keen on listening. Her brother would though. She would tell him tonight.

Adi looked behind her for a moment, thinking of Julia... what if? No, it was too weird for words. It was impossible.

Sacrilegious.

She went forward with the food, it squirmed and whimpered in her clasp, its fate etched in its eyes.

He began to salivate before she pushed it through the slot, her wrist and part of her forearm vulnerable to injury.

The man sprung forward, scooping the prey out of her grasp and lightly scratched her with his talon as she withdrew.

Their eyes met for a moment as she snatched her arm back through the narrow distribution slot. She cradled the arm against her chest, the blood from the scratch soaking her T-shirt beneath.

Adi had never been more glad for the two foot thick partition. She knew who would be the victor between the two of them if he escaped...

For the first time in her life, Adriana was scared. Scared of another wolf.

He was more Alpha than any she'd ever known.

And she didn't scare easy.

CHAPTER 24

William did not have the kiss at his back. Gabriel wanted Julia back, but not at any cost. It was a conditional desire.

William's was not. She would be his. Not the dogs', not some other hapless runner with Singer ancestry. His.

He waited in the woods, the night but a promise, his brazenness in the darkest part of of the forest a testimony to his desire to retrieve her from the clutches of the mongrels. For tonight was their ritual. When the moon wept her fullness on the Were, they would change. They would feed and they would consummate their hold on the Rare One.

For as long as William took breath, they would not.

* * *

Brendan

The Singer looked both directions and turned to his sister. "I smell a vamp in these here parts!"

Jen rolled her eyes, not everything was a joke! "Shut up,

218

they'll hear you..." she folded her arms across her chest and gave him a look like, *are you kidding me?*

Brendan chuckled, grabbing Jen in a bear hug that left her without enough oxygen. "Knock it off!" she hissed. "This is serious!"

Brendan nodded soberly, then went off in a hysterical fit of laughing.

Jen stalked off.

Brothers. She oughta know, she had three. All Singers, all with plenty of air between their ears. She was the only sane one in the family.

Brendan stood behind her. "Don't be mad... it's just," he shrugged then continued, "the intel says we've got a 'big deal' Singer wrapped up with the Were but they've been wrong before." Brendan made a bunch of noise kicking a stone that lay in a nest of leaves.

William turned his head, hearing a small sound not of nature, half a mile east from his position. He stood, trapped in the shadows, the sun a dangerous heat, high and bright above the safety of the forest's canopy.

Had it been night, he would have discovered who made the racket.

As it were, he must remain where he was, steeped in frustration and anxious for the next step. His nemesis, the sun, rode above him.

All thoughts lead to one:

Julia.

"Would you stop being so loud? If you know there's a vamp around why would you provoke him?"

Brendan grinned, she took all the fun out of his antagonizing. "He'll fry like a tiki torch, sis. I want a front seat for that performance." He smiled wistfully and Jen rolled her eyes again. Her brothers had a death wish!

He saw Jen's face and laughed. "Nah. He'll have to park

his ass in the woods or some skulk-position like that until twilight comes. There's no moving until then. I'm just yanking his undead chain." Brendan stretched his long body and tight muscles corded and flexed with the movement.

Jen wanted to punch him. It was a two-part reason. One, he was just *that* sure of himself. Two, he could eat enough food for five people and still look like a GQ model. She scowled at him and he grinned wider, his teeth flashing white in the semi-gloom of where they stood in the woods.

"You remember I've never been wrong before, right? Smart-ass!"

"Ooh... language!" Brendan warned, the smile still plastered on his arrogant mug.

Jen contained herself with effort. "Listen here, buster. I'm part of that 'intel' you blithely discounted. I'm precog..."

Brendan muttered under his breath... "A helluva a lot more than that..."

"Huh?" Jen said, narrowing her eyes on his.

Brendan threw his hand against his chest, fingers splayed. "What? I didn't say anything."

Right, Jen thought.

There was a noise down low from their position and Jen caught the flare of Brendan's nostrils just as he swung his head toward where the Were poured through a wide pathway, opposite their position with two females.

The siblings crouched down simultaneously. Peering through the thick foliage hugging the base of fir and cedar trees which grew like mighty companions, the fragrance thicker than the air around them, their eyes stayed trained on the enemy.

"What are they?" Jen asked in the softest voice, barely above a whisper.

"Were... and..." Brendan extended his neck, lifting his

chin, nose in the air. "All Were but one of the females. She's Singer..."

Jen huffed in triumph. No kidding? Singer, huh? *Like she'd said.*

Brendan caught her self-satisfied smirk and continued, stuffing his irritation at his know-it-all sibling, "... there's something more."

But when they looked again, the group had disappeared inside the compound.

"Damn!" Brendan said, pounding a fist on his jean-clad thigh. "Almost had it."

"Had what?"

"What flavor she was," he said, grinning again.

"Girls aren't ice cream!" Jen huffed.

Brendan's smile widened. "News to me."

Jen punched him a good one in the arm.

She used her knuckles like he'd taught her. He leaped back as she swung and it was a glancing blow but she'd made him flinch.

Felt good.

Brendan looked at his tiger of a sibling. On the prowl.

Girls, he thought, rubbing the red spot she'd made, his smile returning as he looked at her.

* * *

The Ritual of Luna

ADRIANA LOOKED at Julia and thought she cleaned up pretty good. She eyed her critically, taking in the all-white ensemble. She couldn't help but connect the dots of symbolism here. Virginal lamb led to slaughter. Actually, she didn't really know about Jules' background except she was still sorta hung up on her husband. The guy had been dead, what?

For-freakin'-ever. Like get over it yesterday. But, she'd hardly been able to get through talking about him to tell Adriana what her story was. Even she had to admit Julia hadn't had the greatest life. Parents dead at eight, lived with crappy and resentful relative. Soulmate husband bled out by rogue Were.

That was troubling to Adriana. Why had the Were taken out the Singer? It was an amateur's move. She couldn't understand why he'd been a target at all. Any idiot whelpling knew that a werewolf could subdue a human without killing them. Hell! One of the Were could subdue four humans. It puzzled her. Something smelled funky and she'd love to find out the cause of it. Of course, Adriana knew from experience that when she started sniffing around, her nose got slapped.

That pissed her right the hell off.

"Adi?" Julia asked, her champagne-colored hair finally free of the black hair dye and well past her shoulders again.

"Huh?" Adriana jerked her head up. She'd really been a million miles away.

"What were you thinking about?"

Lots of secret speculation. "Just distracting crap." Partial truth.

Julia had the distinct impression that Adi had been thinking about something interesting. She turned and looked at her reflection in the mirror and couldn't help but think of Cyn. She'd have died about Julia wearing white. It just wasn't her color.

She'd been told it was symbolic.

The dress had been made for her. Actually, it had been a standard size and altered to fit her. The bodice was simple and crossed underneath her breasts, leaving the tops exposed, narrowing to her waist, where the full skirt flared at the hip and came to what Aunt Lily had called "ballerina length." That was just above the ankle to the uninitiated. That had been her. Uh-huh. Not anymore. Cyn had seen to it. The material was some kind of chiffon, filmy and light, opaque and lovely.

Julia wasn't nervous about their ritual. Her plan had been the same all along. She had her telekinetic skills down. When the werewolves were distracted by their fighting, she'd split. The get-up was as retarded as they come for her badly hatched Escape Plan but she'd spied keys and she would use them. Couldn't she hop in a car and drive away in princess white?

Yeah, she could.

She'd miss Adi. It figured that she'd bond with a female werewolf in the Den of Iniquity. Geez.

She turned away from her reflection but couldn't help asking Adi, "You promise your brother will... beat Tony?"

Adi nodded her head enthusiastically. "He'll kick his ass."

Julia gulped. "What if he kills him?"

Adi shrugged. "No loss for me. Besides, if he thinks he's Alpha enough to fight the big dogs, he can get all froggy and jump on the lily pad."

Julia smiled. Adi was so like Cyn it made her heart ache. She turned away before Adi could see her expression.

But Adriana did see it.

She frowned as she followed Julia outside toward the pavilion. Unease was forming in her mind.

Something was wrong.

Adriana would be watchful. But first, she had one final chore to screw with after she settled Julia in her position within the ring of the pavilion.

* * *

William

WILLIAM STAYED UPWIND of the mongrels and prayed for the breeze to stay as it was. He watched the sun sink low in the sky, washing the branches a sunset color.

The trees looked like they were weeping.

Crying tears of blood.

A small smile formed on William's face at the visual analogy.

Time grew short.

He was ready.

Julia stood by herself as people began to fill a great open gazebo. It was actually ancient in its composition. Great pillars held the roof above it, a hammered copper, so green not an ounce of its original bronze color showed through. The pillars had been made of marble and the materials used were the most incongruous she'd ever seen. Here, in the middle of an old forest full of trees over one hundred years old, stood a structure that would have been more at home in Rome.

She looked at the scarred marble tiles at her feet, streaked with veins of grey and speckles of gold. The grout must have been some white color at one time, but now had a dove grey hue from age.

All eyes were upon her when Lawrence approached. Julia took a step backward, his physical presence was so overbearing, his personality the same. *Mega creeper*, Julia thought. And not for the first time. Goose flesh broke out on the skin of her arms, bare to the weather. It was warm enough for what she wore but in the presence of the Packmaster, it was cold.

The chill of death sunk its bite into her bones.

He ignored her unease and turned Julia in the direction of the crowd.

Like a prize. A prize breeding mule. How flattering for her.

Julia had an excellent view of the seating that was built-in all around her in a circular presentation. It rose out of the ground as an integral part of the pavilion, each seat a curved unit, higher than the last. None of the faces were friendly, all somber.

Julia guessed that some were not happy with the fighting and death.

Or... with her.

She'd never been popular.

Tony and Joseph watched the fragile beauty of the Rare One showcased in her rightful position in the pavilion, the Ritual of Luna nearly begun.

Their faces turned to the sun sinking behind the mountains, night and day balanced on the finest scale.

Finally it tipped to night and the moon winked into existence.

The glory of her fullness exerted an irresistible pull as the men changed into their otherness in unfurling brutality. Flesh and bone burst, shifted and sloughed onto the ground at their feet.

Their snouts came together, five in all. The challenge in their eyes unmet but for a few moments more.

They trod out to the pavilion, to their destiny.

Julia watched them come and her arms gripped the side rails of the great chair the Packmaster had forced her into.

Like she was royalty or something.

She guessed she was to them.

Soon, she thought.

Soon.

The feral heard the fight begin just as the female entered his prison. He swung his head in her direction as she looked around in confusion. Obviously distracted.

Normally, full moon duty on the feral would have gone to someone else... several someones for the danger factor, but she'd gotten nailed with it because of her stunt. It'd been worth it. Adriana entered through the heavy door, her eyes sweeping the cage.

Adriana panicked, where had the feral gone? Oh no! He'd escaped? Without thinking about anything... her safety, protocol, anything... Adi slapped the slot open and felt around for the alarm when a steel band of screaming pain latched on to her wrist.

Her arm was pulled through the slot with such vicious-ness that it dislocated her shoulder. Adi howled in warning and pain, her voice reverberating in the cloistered space.

No one came.

The wolves fought in the ritual. No werewolf was within range to assist her.

Adriana opened her eyes as tears ran down her face for the first time in her life.

She grimaced and stared into the green eyes of the red wolf.

"Sorry," he ground out, snagging the code card off her neck with a jerk. It snapped the tether and he stood, pressing the slick thinness of it into the locking mechanism.

The door slid away with a whisper and he stepped through.

He glanced down at the female Were and hesitated... he hated he'd hurt a female. It had been frighteningly easy. And very wrong.

But a female that he knew lay beyond this point.

He turned and followed the scent of fighting, the moon lending her energy to him.

All of it.

It thrummed through his body and made his muscles align for finer dexterity in motion.

Preparing him for fighting.

His form became all wolf seamlessly, a rare transition of speed and smoothness.

He growled low in his throat.

He was ready.

William stepped out of the tree line at the same time a great red werewolf, one that he had never seen in battle or otherwise, appeared at the same time.

They stood opposite each other and their gazes locked for a swollen moment of consideration.

William sprinted to the pavilion at the same time the feral rushed toward the exact point.

Neither noticed the pair of Singers that calmly walked toward the stage.

Where blood ran like a river, dripping down steps that had been white marble but moments before.

Veins that had run grey now ran red.

Crimson with blood.

CHAPTER 25

*T*wo of the werewolves lay dead in a pile of their own gore. Wounds so deep their bodies had been eviscerated while three others circled each other, swiping and surging froward in a dangerous game of avoidance that no one could win.

It wasn't a game, Julia wailed inside her head, feeling shock eat away at the edges of her mind.

Joseph was wounded, Tony more so. The third Were had rolled into a submissive posture when Tony went toward his throat, merciless and opportunistic. He stilled as if halted by an invisible hand and turned as Joseph did. Their noses alerted them to the new danger at hand.

Julia turned to look at what could distract them from the important task of killing each other when the biggest and scariest creature entered the stage, bigger than Tony.

Bigger than life.

Julia gasped and got up from the chair, unsteady from the trauma of the fight. Watching it play out in front of her like a surreal movie had been almost more than she could stand.

But Julia *had* stood it.

Joseph yelped a plaintive command, "Adi!" Even in his half wolf form, the worry for her was apparent.

Tony spared him a glance as knowledge filled eyes that were only half-wolf. Both Were stood on their hind legs, nearly seven feet. Mirroring the giant red Were that faced them.

Julia skittered behind the tall chair, her hands gripping the back until they turned white and grew numb.

The wolf looked at her and Julia felt something stir deep within her, the fear melting away as they continued to gaze at each other. She was on the edge of an epiphany when the Packmaster yelled, "The feral, I call total rights!"

What? Julia thought, her hands having fallen away from the chair.

She'd actually taken a step toward the great creature, the emerald eyes sucking her in when she heard a voice she knew so well.

"Julia!"

William. Relief poured through her, suffusing her body with renewed energy.

She snapped her head in the direction of that voice, seeking his eyes, reflective silver staring her down.

As she did pandemonium erupted all around her, the melee closing in with the sureness of the cycle of the moon.

* * *

Singers

BRENDAN SAW the wolves tearing into each other and thought that for all their fierce strength they weren't the brightest bulbs in the shop. He and Jen had waltzed into the pavilion hardly noticed.

Thanks to the rabid Were and the loner vamp.

Interesting combo, those two.

Brendan scented the area, counting what the odds were when he hit on a scent he could not identify. Puzzle pieces of scent recognition sifted through his massive storage banks of finer scents.

Then he knew.

His gaze fell on Julia. Brendan felt like he'd been hit between the eyes with a two by four. All thoughts ground to a screeching halt, sucker-punched.

But he hadn't.

His head swiveled to Jen's. She didn't know.

Brendan said the words, "She's the one." His hands trembled with the knowledge.

"What?" Jen shrieked over the noise. They didn't have time for his melodramatic crap right now. They needed to get the Singer and get out!

Jen looked into his eyes and grabbed his forearm. A pathway of emotion flowed between them and her eyes widened, her head snapping in the direction of the girl in white.

"No way," she breathed.

"Way," Brendan nodded.

"Shit, we needed more back up," Jen said.

"Yeah," Brendan agreed. He didn't correct her on her language.

They moved toward Julia, the rarest of them all. The one that was prophesied to lead their people to autonomy and freedom.

The visual of the small girl in white didn't match the version of fairy tales they'd been raised with.

A powerful Singer would be revealed. A woman. Their queen.

Brendan gulped, thinking about how many of the enemy were around them. He would have to bring out the big guns.

Julia took everything in and then her chest tightened and she searched the faces even as wolves circled the great red Were she had been mesmerized by. William came for her as wolves attempted to restrain him. It was impossible, with the distraction of the feral wolf, the vamp and then...

Julia saw the pair. A girl with strawberry blonde hair and freckles and a man with bronze hair and deep brown eyes, dusky skin that was so striking against the deep red of his hair. But it wasn't those things that caused her breath to hitch. She knew what they were instinctively.

Singers.

Like her.

Julia moved toward them. It felt like she was coming home.

William had a moment's regret that he would need to dispatch the pair of Singers, obvious relatives of each other. He stabbed a Were in the middle of its Change and the blood of the fallen made the marble slick at his feet.

He went for the Singers who had almost reached Julia. She moved to meet them.

That would be very unfortunate were they to touch one another.

Julia's eyes widened as she saw William sprint for the backs of the Singers who advanced in her direction, it would be seconds and they would meet her. She called out a warning, loyalties torn. She cared for William but these were her people, she couldn't let William hurt them.

Brendan scented the vamp and turning casually, almost too late, he flung his hand out at the soles of the vampire's feet as he sprinted for them.

His intent was clear. Killing intent.

Fire leaped and drove its heat up the legs of the vamp. That'd get his full attention. Brendan turned dismissively, his eyes already searching for the Singer.

Blood Singer royalty.

That's when the feral Were barreled into him, knocking him off his feet and crashing into one of the marble columns. There was no give to stone, Brendan realized, his bell soundly rung.

He lit this dude up too, with the last of his consciousness.

Nothing happened but he saw the Were fling away, but not before he scented him.

The recognition of what he was causing Brendan to halt in surprise, everything else falling away.

It couldn't be.

But it was.

Jen hollered, "Come on! That's the best I can do... I can't hold that sucker!" She had a hand wrapped on the Singer's wrist, huge amber-colored eyes in a small oval-shaped face stared up at him.

Holy hell, Brendan thought, *maybe it's love.*

He was drowning in a sea of gold.

"Snap out of it!" Jen shrieked.

Right.

Brendan saw the vamp on fire and the red Were struggling against ten of his own.

The two wolves who restrained him best were tracking Brendan with their eyes.

Time to shake and bake.

Joseph broke away from the feral and bounded after Julia and the two others of her kind. But he was in full wolf form, his paws slipping on the gore of the marbled surface of the pavilion. He fell twice, then finally gained purchase. He was almost upon them when the other Singer flicked her palm at him and he was thrown backward against one of the pillars of the pavilion. A fissure formed, running from the impact of Joseph's body and climbing to the roof.

Julia ran, the manacle of the girl's hand hurting her wrist. What hurt more was the lone howl from the pavilion.

It made Julia's heart ache. She clenched her eyes tight and felt strong arms come around her, picking her up even as they jogged, the girl's hand releasing her.

She didn't look back. Visions of William on fire and the red Were struggling to get to her kept swirling in her head.

Julia didn't know why it mattered. But it did.

She gazed up into the face of the person who held her, seeing only a strong jaw and eyes trained straight ahead. She felt the heat rise from her toes and let it overwhelm her, consciousness slipping away like a leaf on the wind.

Brendan felt the Singer's weight change as it went from live to dead weight and grunted with the stress as he jogged. He was profoundly strong, as all post-puberty Singers were. But an almost full run with dead weight? Challenging-much.

"Don't fuss, brother," Jen said, sprinting with him to keep up, a smile locked into place. "Besides, we've got company."

Jen said it like there were some flies that needed swatting instead of fifteen Were chasing after them.

And gaining.

Brendan redoubled his efforts, sprinting. His lungs were a burning inferno, begging him to stop. But this was where it counted. This is what he'd trained for, he wasn't going to give back this precious cargo. She was the final hope for his people.

The brush crashed behind them as they reached their transport. The night's coolness had moved in and he could scent the exhaust that plumed into the air like a spiral of smoke before he saw it. Brendan instantly identified it as theirs.

The door was already flung open, Michael screamed, "They're up your ass!"

Thanks for the clue, braniac! Brendan thought.

He reached the open door, slid open to accommodate the Singer, shoved her into waiting arms and turned, a downward arc of talons making a breeze next to his face.

Hell! That was close. There was no fighting at close range unless Brendan had the element of surprise.

He didn't. That was long-gone. A big monster was coming for him now, half-wolf form, all the dexterity of full human shape, but the strength and speed of pure wolf form.

He was up shit creek, then Jen was there. Her face was a sweaty mask as her palm was straight out in front of her body, her arm plank-stiff.

She held back the first siege of the Were by her will alone. Her body trembled with the effort, sweat gliding down her neck and soaking her shirt.

"How long?" Brendan shouted beside her, trying to light as many on fire as he could. They all got nailed at the feet. It was a temporary measure at best, he was a Tracker, not a Pyro. The secondary ability was awesome sometimes. For deflection.

Like now, when they needed a mondo distraction.

"Get in!" she hissed.

Okay, hell... so touchy.

He saw around ten more burst out of the woods. As he got in he grabbed Jen around the waist and hauled her against him, slamming the door closed. He banged on the drivers seat, "Go!"

Rafael floored it even as the van rocked with the first Were hitting the side with enough force to partially lift the wheels off the trail.

Shit! He looked down at Jen, swiping hair away from her temple. She was totally spent.

"Can she?" Michael asked, an unconscious Singer in his lap.

"Nah!" Brendan shouted over the gnashing of teeth and

talons on the exterior of the van, nails on a chalkboard of metal. "She's totally gassed!"

"Dammit!" Michael laid the Singer on the blanket at his feet and got busy. Throwing himself in the front seat his face mired in concentration... and ten vamps appeared in front of the van.

Rafael had laid on the gas but the wheels were spinning without purchase. The Were crawling over it like their own anthill. He hissed in a breath, "What the hell?"

"It's okay, it's me," Michael said. "Just drive!"

Rafael did, even as the Were slid off the van to deal with the perceived threat of their primary enemy.

The Were attacked the vamps even as the van slid through them like ghosts. Because that's what they were. Michael had executed his tactical advantage to perfection.

He was one of their best Illusionists.

The van screamed out of the Were stronghold, spinning up dirt as it roared off. The four Singers and their treasure, barely hanging on to tenuous liberty.

CHAPTER 26

SINGERS

*J*ulia felt like she'd been run over by a truck. A couple of times. She cracked open one eyelid, feeling the heat of the sunlight before it fell on where she lay. She looked around at yet another bedroom, her surroundings different than the vampire, than the Were.

She was in a funky-shaped room. The bed stood in a portion of room that jutted out, three windows facing the outside, her headboard against the central one. She rolled over, gazing outside. She moved a gauzy white curtain aside and sunlight struck her like a weapon. Julia squinted.

Rolling hills of green carpeted valleys that kissed a far away forest greeted her stare. It was beautiful. A small lake or pond shimmered in the distance, swans floating on the surface like feathered jewels.

Julia sat back on her haunches, her heels digging into her butt. She looked down at what she was wearing and was beyond thrilled to see that she was still wearing the white gown. So... they'd dumped her in a bed with the dress on and the whole deal.

Perfect.

She swung her feet over the bed and stood on a wood floor that had planks that were five inches wide and very red in color. Her gaze swept the room and she noticed two doors. Julia guessed one led to a bathroom. As she approached them she tried door number one and turned a crystal knob, faceted like a large diamond. It turned smoothly, slightly loose in its brass housing and swung it open.

A tall narrow window with jewel-toned stained glass let in sunlight broken by the colored patterns in the glass. The light cast on the floor looked like a shattered rainbow. Julia spied the commode, a pedestal sink and a sinfully large claw foot tub.

Awesome.

She used the facilities and caught a glimpse of herself in the mirror and grimaced. That's when she noticed an army of trolls had marched through her mouth and longed for a toothbrush. More than that though, she wanted to know where she was. For the first time, she was happy to be somewhere new.

These were her people.

Julia had finally come home.

Jen folded her arms across her chest. "You're not going up there," she said, hearing Julia walking around, using the bathroom. Exploring.

Brendan shrugged. "Why not? Don't want me to hog your find?"

They'd been arguing all morning. Which wasn't too atypical because she was so goddamned stubborn. Brendan was busy seething when Michael breezed in.

"Is hotness awake yet?" he asked, rooting around in the ancient fridge for something to snag. He was so hungry, Michael was pretty sure that he was digesting his own spine. His whole head was in the fridge when he heard Jen's reply,

"None of you doofuses need to go hassle her. She's new, we... heck, we kidnapped her! Maybe she needs time to... I don't know, acclimate or something?"

Michael jerked his head out of the fridge, banging it a good one on the top. He grimaced, looking at the dent there from the other one hundred and twelve times he'd done it. Huh.

"Listen," he held up a finger. "We saved her precious ass so she better be grateful. I say socialization is in order. And... who'd want to do the Were Bride routine?" Michael rolled his eyes, gulping juice out of the carton.

Brendan narrowed his eyes on his brother. "Listen, I got dibs. I did all the hard work. You just poofed some vamps to distract the Were. I ran with her!" he rolled his eyes at him.

Brendan's keen sense of smell alerted him too late.

Julia had appeared in the doorway, the most forlorn and sad expression he had ever seen covering her face.

Shit.

They all started to talk at once but she stopped all conversation with, "I'm sorry. I thought that you... that I was..." she burst into tears. Julia thought that they had wanted to rescue her from the Were but from the sounds of it they were pissed to have to deal with her. Someone they had to shuffle around.

Jen glowered at her brothers.

God! They were so inept! And Brendan! He was the big deal Tracker... he couldn't scent her fast enough to curb his words?

Idiots. Jen popped off the kitchen stool, punching Michael as she walked past.

"Hey!" he mock-yelled at her.

Julia looked up, tears shimmering in those eyes. They were like gold topaz Brendan noted, a little dreamily.

Jen grabbed the hands that Julia was trying to use to cover

her face. She was so embarrassed to be somewhere that she wasn't wanted, in the ridiculous white dress, her hair six ways to Sunday.

"No, no," Jen crooned, throwing a dirty glance at the two guys that stood behind her looking contrite. "Don't listen to my stupid brothers..." she looked up at Julia earnestly. "They always sound dumb."

"Yeah, that's us. Dumb," Brendan said dryly.

"Yeah, that," Michael agreed, swinging his longish dirty blond hair out of his eyes.

Julia gave a small smile. "So, you guys... do you want me to leave?" Her lip trembled again. "Because I can't go back there," Julia said in a low voice.

Brendan was alarmed and approached her too quickly. She backed up and he stopped. "No. You don't... we don't want you to go back to the Were... or the vampire. We're all about sucking you into our world. It's where ya belong."

Michael nodded. "Why would ya think that we wouldn't want you?"

Julia shrugged. "You sounded like... that you were kinda mad?"

Jen shook her head. "Nah! That's the way they always sound."

"Like smart ass meets anger management?" Julia asked. She was definitely okay now, Brendan noticed with relief, a smile breaking through her tears like they'd never been.

Jen smiled in return. "I'm Jen," she said, sticking her hand out and Julia shook it.

Brendan and Michael came forward. "And these are the dummy duo, who you've had the misfortune of meeting already," she said, but the humor in her voice took away the sting.

"We're not always dumb," Michael said, taking her hand and giving it a gentle squeeze, then dropping it.

"I wouldn't know how to be dumb," Brendan said and winked. But he didn't shake her hand, instead he drew her into a hug which pressed her against his body, melding her form to his. He said against her hair, "We've been looking for you for a long time." He drew away, the happiness radiating from every pore.

"Me?" Julia asked, putting her hand to her chest, trying to let the heat from his embrace fade like a still-hot brand.

They nodded.

"Why? I mean, I don't know you guys." She looked at them expectantly.

"It's not who you are it's what you are," Michael explained cryptically.

Julia folded her arms, impatience seeping in a little. "Okay, I give. What am I?"

They looked at each other uneasily and Julia asked again, "Come on, spill the secret! I know I'm a Singer..." she threw out her hands. She'd known that for awhile. "I know I'm the 'Rare One'," she said, her hands dropping against the fabric of the dress after the air quotes.

"Rare One?" Michael shook his head. "I don't know what that is but you're not that to us."

Jen said, "You're more than that."

Julia looked at them. She opened her mouth, impatience on her tongue when Brendan spoke, "You are Queen."

Julia staggered back a step. "What?" she asked dully, her voice coming from a distance. "Queen of whom?" Julia heard herself asking.

"The Singers. You are Queen of the Blood Singers."

The room began to tilt and she heard many voices at once. She fell into strong arms.

Fainting for the second time.

It was becoming a trend.

Brendan looked down at the girl in his arms and felt his heart clench. He hated feeling weak.

She already had a piece of it.

His heart. It beat slower for the loss of that chunk.

Brendan didn't even know her name.

Not that it mattered. Love was an errant master, choosing who it would without reason.

Without rationale.

* * *

pack

ADRIANA SCREAMED AT HER BROTHER. For him, at him.

"Hold still, Adi!" He jammed his leg into her armpit and wrenched the arm back in before she could stiffen up more than she already was.

Tears of pain rolled down her face and Joseph swiped them away with the pad of his thumb. "Shhh... it's okay," Joseph said, gathering her against his chest.

"It's not okay, Joseph and you fucking know it!" Tony paced and Joseph felt the small bones of his face shift. That was automatic when an Alpha felt challenged. The Change asserted itself subtly beneath his skin.

Adi felt it and looked up at her brother.

"It is at your feet where the fault lies. You insisted that Lawrence give her the worst punishment!" he responded, his anger roiling underneath his skin with weight, with purpose.

Tony turned to face him, his posture wary and tight.

Joseph carefully untangled himself from Adriana, shifting her weight against the acrylic wall that had held the feral.

But no longer.

He faced Tony, walking toward him on a slow prowl.

Adi watched as her brother's body shifted to bursting, the moon's power waning but not enough. Not nearly enough.

"Me? She is the one that pushed the boundaries! It's always her. And she is always coddled. Now the Rare One has escaped with the Singers, the feral has escaped and that vamp runner killed five of us! Five!"

Tony's scathing stare burned a pathway across Adriana and she growled low in her throat. She didn't care that he outmatched her by a hundred pounds and a foot of height. She hated Tony.

He smelled bad.

She smacked her palm of the uninjured side of her body against the clear wall and boosted herself to standing. "I will take responsibility for the feral, I panicked. I thought he'd already escaped. But," her stare gave dominant weight to her words and she watched Tony visibly bristle at its significance, "I will not accept the strange shit that went down while I was injured substituting for *you* so you could fight my brother and also stick me with that chore on the full moon!" Her eyes shifted from one to the other. "I am not a 'favorite'," Adi said, using air quotes. "I was pressed to do the worst chore at the worst time because I let my alligator mouth overload my canary ass."

Joseph barked out a laugh. "She's right."

The tension in the empty holding cell slipped down a notch.

"Like any one of us could have known a vamp was skulking around, all Lone Ranger and then the coincidence of the feral escaping? Oh!" she yelled into the strange acoustics of the room, "let's not forget the darling Singers that waltzed in, during the bloodiest and most distracting ritual ever conceived, and snatched Jules right from underneath our very noses," she seethed, the fingers of her index and thumb a hair's breadth apart.

They'd been that close to not losing Julia.

"And!" she continued to rant and Tony crossed his muscular arms, rolling his eyes, "Shut up and listen!" Tony growled, this female never knew when to shut up. Hell, if that brother of hers wasn't always around, he'd teach her a lesson that'd stay with her permanently.

Tony smiled at his thoughts and her lips pulled away from her teeth, another growl reverberating from between them.

"Enough!" Joseph roared, startling them both. His eyes landed on his sister. "Finish now, then we go to Lawrence. This whole incompetent mess will need to be explained."

"I was just going to say, that fifteen of our wolves trailed the Singers, and still... we didn't get her back."

"So?" Tony said with derision.

"So... I think they're more powerful than we've been trying to convince ourselves."

"Ha! Bullshit. They're human, they can do some parlor tricks. It's not real strength. Who do they call leader?" Tony asked, palms spread with his superior omniscience.

Adi rolled her eyes. He was such a goddamned know-it-all.

"What of the Book of Luna?" Joseph asked into the stillness, Tony's words echoing into silence.

Tony didn't bother with reading that old crap. It was the new order. The only thing he'd wanted was to become a moonless changer. That, he'd believed in plenty. And now that little Singer had slipped between his claws like water through a sieve.

She would be within his grasp again.

Adi nodded. "They are a force of their own. You know that! Look what happened a few hours ago? They fooled *you*, Tony!"

Tony glowered at her. He'd almost had that Singer but it's

as if the Singer had eyes in the back of of his head. Tony shook his head, thinking about it.

"Yeah," he ground out. "Don't know how, I almost had him." He smacked his fist into his opposite palm, his dark eyes flashing.

"Scent Tracker," Joseph said in a flat voice.

Tony whipped his head in Joseph's direction, his brows raised.

Joseph and Adriana nodded. They'd both been trained in the precepts held within the Book.

Tony threw his hands up. "I give. Drop this secretive shit. Just. Tell. Me." He pegged his hands on his powerful hips, frowning at them.

"A sense of smell a thousand times more powerful than ours," Joseph said.

"Impossible," Tony breathed out, thinking of his multi-layered scent awareness. It was so overwhelming he had trained himself to tune out most scents. It was too much. But one thousand times more sensitive? He couldn't wrap his mind around it. He scoffed at the possibility.

"I know, right? It's..." Adi began.

"Unbelievable!" Joseph agreed, nodding.

"Yeah... okay. Whatever. But what about the ten vampires that just flashed into existence and were ghosts when we attacked?" Tony said like, *explain that.*

Adriana laughed and the men turned to her. When she finally stopped she said, "Vampire mirage."

Joseph sighed. Not helpful.

"What was it?"

Joseph shook his head. They weren't sure. But it had been a superb deflection on their part. Too good.

"Don't know," he answered.

"Well, it was pretty fucking effective!" Tony said. "I could smell the vamps. *Smell them,*" he said through clenched teeth.

Joseph gave a sound low in his throat. "No, that was the Tracker, assisting... the other one."

"They can work in tandem?" Adi asked, stunned.

Joseph nodded. "Looks like." Then he paused. "But a more likely reason for the two is family."

"What?" Tony asked, his eyes narrowing.

"I speculate for that pair to work as seamlessly together as they did, they'd have to be family."

"What about the bitch with them?" Tony asked. He conjured up an image of her in his mind. Small, pixie-like features, hair blondish, he guessed. Hard to know with the moon, it silvered everything.

Except the Red Feral.

His fur had shone like blood spilled.

"Her too," Joseph said.

But Tony's nose was unaffected by his sight. He'd know her the next time he smelled her. Hell, he'd know them all. Tony's fists curled. "I'd love to have another chance at those three."

"Soon," Joseph promised.

"What about the female?" Adi asked suspiciously. She trusted Tony about as far as she could throw him.

"Especially her," he said with barely contained desire.

Joseph scowled at him just as another Were entered the holding pen.

They looked at him. "Lawrence is waiting," he said, shyly glancing at Adriana.

Brother! she thought... *men!*

Adi flounced out, pushing by the Were. His eyes followed her form as she disappeared.

Joseph followed behind and Tony came last.

As he passed the other Were, slightly younger than himself he whispered, "You don't want her."

He leaned back with a puzzled expression. There were

few Were females and she was a good looking one too. "Why?" he asked, genuinely puzzled.

"Untrainable," Tony said, stalking off behind the siblings.

* * *

the Feral

THE FERAL LIFTED *his head from the fragrant entrails of the deer, the meat a fresh and tasty smell that permeated his olfactory senses, stirring a deep and profound hunger.*

He howled.

Then fed.

The moon, on the wane but not headlong, hung above him in a blanket of velvet, the stars as diamonds. They glittered as she supervised her charge.

When at last he finished, his body demanded rest. He dug out a place of safety in the deepest part of the forest. The Feral burrowed underneath his self-made nest. Finally satisfied, he needed to ready himself for the next leg of his journey. Sleep came for him and just as he slid into the embrace of unconsciousness, he thought of her.

The female.

He must have her.

And she, him.

He was certain when they had connected under the roof of the great structure that she felt it too.

The pull of one to the other.

They were meant to be together.

Forever.

He slept, the moon keeping her own counsel.

* * *

the pavilion

WILLIAM SCREAMED inside his head as the Were held him, their talons biting into his dead flesh. He saw the Singers tear Julia out of his grasp and that of the Were.

Hope slid away like rain on a tin roof.

William Changed were he stood, his raven form protecting him, assuring his survival.

The Were let go in surprise, not ready for the smallness of his form. As they rushed to grab him at the same time he rose with a sharp caw, circling above their position. His eyesight, many times sharpened from his vampire form, tracked the Singers. And the pursuit of them by the Were.

He followed, his blackness the perfect camouflage against the night sky. He saw all:

When Julia fainted in the arms of the Singer as he ran.

When the fetid breath of the Were caressed the back of the one who held her.

When the ten of his kind suddenly appeared then vanished like they had never been.

Defeated, William flew to a safe distance, then Changed back into the form that would return him to the kiss with the least effort.

Even as he ran, his mind turned over his next move.

If he had been one to play chess, his sight would be set on one piece. And one alone.

The queen.

* * *

Julia

JULIA OPENED her eyes and was instantly met with melted chocolate.

His eyes, her thoughts still muddled and fuzzy.

Oh, wow. She'd fainted again. Could she like... find a rock and crawl underneath it?

"Hey you," Brendan said, pushing a stray hair away from her temple.

"I feel beyond stupid," Julia said.

"Well, we're even then," he said, his lips curling up at the corners.

She smiled at him and he grinned back.

Suddenly, Jen's face showed beside his. "You're okay. Big shock is all."

Yeah, that. Biiiigggg shock. Two hunky dudes, also Singers, kidnap her and squire her away to... where the hell was she anyway?

Michael said from the foot of her bed. "You're somewhere in the Olympic Peninsula."

Julia frowned. "Kinda cagey."

"Kinda cautious," Michael quipped.

Brendan patted her head like she was a small dog and stood. "Gotta keep things secure. Nobody knows anything. That's how we like it..."

"Uh-huh, uh-huh. That's the way we like it, uh-huh, uh-huh..." Michael said, swiveling his hips in a distracting way.

"God... ewww... I hope that's not actual singing you're attempting?" Jen asked, beyond embarrassed by her retarded brothers.

"Oh yeah, I can do Karaoke with the best of them," he said with a hip thrust and hop. Julia giggled and Brendan frowned. "Are ya okay? Ya asshat, 'cuz..."

Brendan looked expectantly at her.

"Julia," she supplied her name by way of introduction.

"Julia," he smiled and gave her a wink, "is not impressed by your..." he swung his palm around, "gyrations and attempts at singing."

"I don't know," Julia began in a drawl.

All eyes went to her.

"For pure entertainment value, it's about a seven."

"Out of what?" Michael asked hopefully.

"Fifty, retard!" Jen yelled, punching him in the arm again.

"Ow!" Michael raged, then turned to Julia. "Did ya see that abuse?"

Julia nodded cooperatively. She had. She grinned.

Jen grabbed the boys and dragged them out of the room. "Get ye out!" she yelled, shoving them outside and turning the lock.

"Sheesh!" Jen fumed. "They're so... so..."

"Funny?" Julia asked.

Jen sighed, then gave her a sidelong glance. "Maybe." Then looked at her. "But if you tell them I'll poke your eyes out. Their heads are so fat as it is they couldn't get through doorways if you stroked their egos even the tiniest bit." Jen looked at her.

Julia smiled. "I promise, no fat head air pumps allowed."

"Right!" Jen said, stabbing the air with a finger held high.

"Now," she looked at Julia critically. "Can we deposit the dress in file thirteen?"

"Huh?" Julia asked, bewildered.

Jen laughed, "Sorry, I have some strange expressions."

She sure did.

"Trash... let's throw it away." She looked at Julia. "Unless you want to keep it for some reason?"

Julia looked down at the soft folds of pure white. "No." No reason at all. But as she said it she was reminded of Adi and felt a stab of guilt and sadness. She sure would have liked to say goodbye to her.

She was relieved not to have to be in some whacked-out forced union with the Were but... she missed having Cyn. She missed Adi.

Shit, Julia realized she'd put out an engraved invitation for a pity party and she'd just RSVP'd for herself.

Dammit.

Jen seemed to pick up on her mood. "Hey!"

Julia turned to look at her, the melancholy riding her like an unwanted friend. "Get out of the get-up and get a shower. We'll suck up some grub and walk around the complex some. I betcha got a ton of questions." Jen looked at her expectantly.

Yeah, that sounded good. "Sure." Julia walked to the bathroom and Jen handed her some clothes. "You'll have to wear my stuff until we figure some clothes out for ya." She looked up at Julia. "I guess my pants will be Capris on you," she said, winking.

Then she was gone.

Julia stood under the spray, taking the longest shower of her life, the colors from the window casting puzzle pieces of color across her body as she washed.

Julia cried in the shower, the rain from the shower head washing away her tears. She cried for everything.

William.

Cyn.

Adi.

But the heaviest tears were for Jason.

Always him.

* * *

"Did ya get a good cry?" Jen asked Julia.

She thought about lying. For about three seconds. "Yeah."

"Good," Jen said, clapping her on the back. "Let's have a look-see, k?"

After a breakfast consisting of fruit and scrambled eggs they walked outside. There were so many places to look Julia didn't even know where to begin. The first thing that caught her eye was when they exited the house. Julia turned around and immediately located where her bedroom was.

The house was breathtaking.

It looked like a house of gingerbread but on a big scale. It was Victorian, maybe turn of the last century. Julia knew because she'd lived in an old house.

Before.

When her parents were alive. She waited a moment to let the grief dissipate, then returned to studying the structure.

It rose like a brightly colored wooden jewel, the forest an emerald backdrop behind it. On the extreme left was a turret that flowed from ground to roof. Three windows formed a "bay" of sorts that were eight foot tall, each one. It looked as if water coated the surface of the glass, wavy from age. At the turret's peak spun a weather vane, the arrow pointing in whatever direction the breeze blew.

"Wow," Julia breathed reverently.

"Ah! That old thing..." Jen said, unimpressed.

Julia swung her head in Jen's direction. "What!? That's like the most gorgeous house ever! And I have the best room in the house," Julia noted. She couldn't believe she was actually here. When just yesterday she'd been with the Were. Julia shook her head, freeing the remaining cobwebs of her memories, her life.

"Maybe that's true. But the house? Ugh! Nothing works, it moans, it moves, it creaks!" She threw up her hands. "I think it needs to be razed and we get something in here so when my brother flushes a commode my shower doesn't scorch my butt off!"

"Noooo! I love it!" Julia said as she felt Jen pull her arm, leading her away from the stately home. "Forget it. Look on your own time at the rust bucket. For now, let's go to the paranormal school."

Julia stopped, tugging her arm back. "What?"

Jen looked at her. "Ya know. It's where us Singers train. Learn... etc." She put her hands on her hips, staring at Julia, waiting for the light bulb to go on.

Wait a second, Julia thought. "Train, for what?"

"To nail the vamps and shifters. They can't tame our rears. We're independent."

Julia was getting that part.

"To 'nail the vamps and the shifters'...?"

Jen nodded like Julia was slow to catch on.

"And beyond that?" Julia asked, feeling a point of clarity may have slid by her unnoticed.

"To rule the world, of course," Jen said, winking.

Of course, Julia thought, following Jen to a large building that had once been a barn.

Julia didn't think she wanted to be queen of that.

Or queen of anything.

CHAPTER 27

CYNTHIA

*C*yn stepped off the plane into the well of people flowing from one destination to another and felt instantly lost. A bottle in the ocean, the current traveling in whatever direction it pleased, she its captive.

Get a grip, Cynthia, she told herself. Her eyes were clenched, her breathing finally getting under control. She looked around, someone jostling by her. Cynthia's backpack swung and she moved alongside one of the great, cylindrical concrete columns, pressing her backpack and herself against it.

There, she was out of everyone's way. For the moment.

She'd left everything behind. The backpack weighed about a thousand pounds with the things she couldn't part with.

The wedding photo. Cynthia gulped back the lump in her throat. Tears running down her face. She wasn't aware of it. The people staring at her didn't register either.

She missed Jules so much it hurt to breathe. She couldn't even think about Kev and Jason. She felt like a limb had been amputated without them.

Cyn swiped her face, surprised at the wetness she found there. She tore off in the direction the sign pointed.

Bus Depot.

She arrived at the fork in the great corridor, people flowing past her on either side and chose the town that sounded the simplest.

Actually, she remembered vaguely that it was a city.

Kent.

* * *

Truman

KARL TRUMAN WENT through the studio apartment in the seediest part of Homer, kicking the thrown drawers and papers as he went through. The whole fucking place had been tossed by someone. Or many someones. He turned to the beat cop on his ass. "Daugherty!"

He jumped like he'd been goosed. "Yeah, Detective!" His eyes were bulging fish bowls in his face.

Truman frowned. Good kid, not too bright. "Is our team here yet?" He frowned at Daugherty.

Shit, his boss was kind of a dickhead. He scratched his head. Truman got results though. He'd give him that. "Yeah, I called it in."

Truman was getting a head of steam and opened his mouth to let Daugherty have it when the forensic team came through, the first lifting the yellow tape, as he scooted under it. Turning, he lifted it for the others to pass underneath.

"Whatcha got, chief?"

Hell, Truman hated being called chief! He wasn't a damn Indian for cripe's sake! He neutralized his expression with an effort.

He gave the first specialist a look that clearly said, *follow me.*

He did, squatting down at the windowsill height. His eyes flowed over the deep gouges that ran the length of the sill. "Holy shit..." he breathed, his name badge, crooked. *Alexander.*

"Yeah," Truman leaned into him expectantly.

"I don't know what did this!" Alexander extolled.

"Bear, right?" Truman led.

Alexander snapped his plastic gloves on, the powder coating wafting up to Truman's nostrils. The familiar smell resonating from a thousand crime scenes, the memory trigger the same.

It was time to work.

Alexander put a fingertip across the groove. His eyes met Truman's and he shook his head no. "No way... this is something," his eyes went to the groove again and then lit with excitement. "Wait! He rummaged in his toolbox and took out a tool that looked like a dental instrument for cleaning teeth.

It wasn't.

He began carefully scooping the groove. Finally, Truman thought, watching the process as if it was an archeological dig. Alexander brought out the smallest sliver of something.

"What is it?" Truman asked as the two other members of the forensic team huddled around them like they were getting ready for a football play.

"Claw," Alexander said, his eyes meeting his team.

"From what?" Truman asked, eying the twice-the-size of a pinhead shard.

"Don't know," he paused. "But I've never seen anything like it." He met Truman's eyes. "Not a problem! We'll type this puppy and get the results back to ya," Alexander smiled.

One of the other forensics specialists said, "Nah, let's not type it. There's no blood or other fun here." He looked around at the trashed apartment, not a shred of evidence to support violence of the human variety. "Besides, what can it be anyway? Bigfoot?"

They all laughed at that.

Yeah, *effing hilarious*, Truman thought then said out loud, "That's horse shit. Any idiot knows there's no such thing as Sasquatch and that other happy crap!" Truman said.

The specialist laughed again, carefully collecting samples to type.

For DNA.

Truman sighed. He figured it was a long shot. Probably had some spoiling meat in here somewhere and it was as simple as a pack of wolves trying to get an easy meal. He gazed outside through glass so filthy it was gray. The forest mocked him, stretching into eternity. Hell, it could have been anything.

Truman knew animals tried to get in the apartment. But who had gone through every nook and cranny of this dump? What had they been searching for...

And, more importantly, where the hell had Cynthia Adams fled to?

Because she *had* fled. He was sure of it. Like she was escaping something. There was too much stuff just left behind. Abandoned.

Running.

But why?

Truman stared out the window, gnawing on the tip of his ballpoint.

Answers, he needed answers.

Like yesterday.

* * *

William

CLAIRE REPEATED HERSELF, "Hold your temper! I didn't say that I could locate her, only that it was possible."

William paced, he had returned empty-handed and Gabriel had not been surprised. Because Claire was a Precognitive, she had simply known that his quest was impossible. William had thought it was strange that Gabriel was not pressing other runners into service to assist him.

Gabriel laughed from his gut. "It is not as if you were prone to listen. I told you not to go. We knew the location of the dogs' stronghold. Yet, still, you would not listen. Your own cousin, a known precog..."

William strode to Gabriel and he straightened, knowing the tenor of the vampire he faced: volatile, fresh, angry. "No, she could give nothing of substance. It was all vague," he threw his arm out. "I would never be content with that as Julia's end. Ambiguity? No!"

"But William... I knew she would be safe," Claire reasoned.

William nodded. "Oh yes! She is quite safe... with the other Singers. How long do you think it will be before one of them recognizes Julia for who she is? What she is to them?"

There was no response from them. William faced Claire. "We have not one scrap of evidence as to where the Singers may be? It has always been our policy to not interfere in the balance. But now that scale has been tipped. And not in our favor, I may add." He lifted his brows in question and Gabriel sighed. "Alright," he lifted his palm up, "you've made your point. We will call in a Locator."

William was surprised. He did not think there was one in their kiss.

"We will have to..." he looked at Claire, "I have not been amongst their kind... my kind. What is the contemporary vernacular for asking to borrow...?"

Claire nodded her understanding. "Call in a favor."

He nodded. "Yes!" he snapped his fingers. "That's it. We will call in a favor to our sister kiss and borrow one of their Singers who locates. That will help us find the Rare One."

"And what will they ask in return?" William quizzed reasonably.

Gabriel sharpened his gaze on William. "I do not know. But rest assured, it will be something."

William nodded, knowing that the vampire did not solicit favors. They took what they wanted, needing no one. An autonomous group unlike any other.

Except the Were.

There was always them.

"Yes. It will be that," William agreed.

Claire nodded. "There is always recompense."

It was what and how much they would expect in payment.

Not a pound of flesh, no, not that.

But payment by blood would suffice very well.

* * *

Julia

JULIA HAD SPENT a lot of time that morning with her mouth hanging open while the boys (as she thought of the brothers), Brendan and Michael, and their spunky sister, Jen, gave her a tour of her newest home.

The barn looked like a red stop sign in a field of green. Fresh and iconic, it stood like a stoic anchor about ninety yards from the Victorian. It seemed so innocuous standing there, but when they went through the small doorway she entered another world. It was as if they remained hidden in plain sight. The floor was white, the walls, the desks... it was weird.

Then Jen spoke, "Weird huh?"

Julia nodded without speaking. Then she couldn't help herself and asked, "What's with the monochromatic thing...?"

"Helps us batten down the mental hatches, girlie!"

Girlie? Julia laughed despite herself. "Really?"

Brendan joined in, "Yeah. Keep everything one color, no distractions, helps with training." Michael nodded in agreement.

There were partitions that separated the "rooms." But one room wasn't quiet and the mats weren't white. They were blue and red. Blue in color.

Red with blood.

Julia stopped. There were three guys fighting and they were really going at it. One man had an open cut above his eyebrow like a second mouth and it was dropping blood splatter everywhere. "Wait a sec!" Julia began.

Brendan interrupted, "Training."

Julia's face turned sharply to his. "Is this what you do? I mean..." Julia hesitated, "to each other?" Just as she asked, the instructor, whose back had been facing her, turned. She was instantly sure he was one of the brothers. The missing one, because Jen had said she had three. He looked a little like Brendan but the hair wasn't red at all. It was black and he was clearly the eldest. He was tall, broad and built like an ox. He'd have fit right in with the wolves.

Julia assimilated these details in seconds.

Because in the next second, those thoughts were driven from her mind when he grinned at her and charged.

Fear surged through Julia's body, beginning at her gut and throwing a tingling shot of what felt like electricity into her extremities. They prickled uncomfortably when her tele-kinetic power flowed out of the hole that the fear had made, hitting the man as he advanced toward her at a dead run.

Julia felt the wall of her power slam into him while he

walked through it like it had been mist. Next thing she knew Brendan had barreled into her, smoothly rolling her out of the way of the locomotive relative.

"Knock it off, Scott!" Brendan yelled at him even as he came for them again. Julia didn't even think, she jerked them up into the air by fifteen feet. She wasn't sure which part was better, Brendan's face or his brother's.

"Well I'll be damned!" Scott said with a laugh. "Maybe she's not a useless figurehead after all!"

"Hey! Mannerless! Way to go on the introductions!" Jen said, smacking his beefy arm.

"What? It's my job to assess new talent," he said innocently.

"She's our Queen, asshat," Michael said in a droll way.

Scott paused, Julia and Brendan suspended. And it was taking its toll, Julia was shaking in Brendan's arms.

In Brendan's arms!

Julia was suddenly and acutely aware of being held by a guy she'd just met that was über-attractive. Julia lost the tenuous grip on her ability and her focus shattered. They fell and she yelped, bracing for impact.

Before they hit the hard concrete floor painted an obscenely bright white, their progress was halted in a sickeningly explosive lurch. Julia looked around her, as she was gently lowered the remaining half foot to the ground.

It was Jen.

But she had eyes only for Scott. "You stupe! Really? Look what almost happened? How would I have explained this to Marcus? That our queen's guts were strewn around the ground because you were 'assessing'!" She hit him again and folded her arms across her chest, stewing.

Jen huffed then noticed that Julia was there.

Listening.

"Sorry," she mumbled, then continued, "I mean... about the guts and brains part."

"It's okay," Julia said, scooting away from Brendan and standing. She gave a wary look at Scott and he looked back with steady eyes, so brown they looked black.

"Ya know," Julia said, "if there's any truth to this royalty thing, I'm demoting your ass first."

Scott threw back his head and howled laughter. Finally, when he could speak he said, "I think I like her."

"Not that it matters!" Jen said, still pissed.

Brendan and Michael looked at their brother. Michael asked, "Don't ya have someone's ass to kick or something? Stop stomping all over Julia and get over there and train!"

Scott walked over to Michael, getting up in his grill. "Whatcha gonna do about it if I don't?"

Suddenly, there was a ten foot stack of cow shit and Scott was in the middle of it, only his head peeking out of the top. "Michael!" he roared.

The siblings started to walk away, but Julia couldn't get past Scott howling and buried in a pile of manure that smelled so bad that Julia had to breathe through her mouth, her hand covering her nose. "Hey!" Julia called after them and all three turned. "Aren't you going to... you're going to leave him like that?" She didn't know whether to laugh or help him out of his predicament.

They nodded, grinning. "Yeah, he'll be free in about twenty seconds." Michael said.

"Too bad it couldn't last longer," Jen muttered to herself but Julia caught it perfectly.

"Let him sing in his own shit for a minute," Brendan said.

Julia followed as Scott bellowed, "Payback's a bitch!"

When they had walked to the end of the building, Julia turned. And there Scott stood, the manure gone. Not a speck of it remained. But the eyes that bored into her back had not been friendly.

They weren't friendly now.

Julia suppressed a shiver under their weight.

Turning her back, she followed the friendlier part of the family, leaving the discomfort of the encounter behind her.

For now.

* * *

introspection

JULIA WATCHED the swan paddle on a small lake, then shifted her eyes to the Olympic Mountains. They reminded her of home, a little. There were a few rocks that acted like small boulders that rimmed the shore, as it were. It was heavily pebbled with smaller rocks, not sand, per se. It was wonderful all the same. What was especially delicious was the time by herself. It had been overwhelming to see and learn all that she had. And... Julia got the distinct impression they had kept the walking tour short for her benefit.

There were so many classifications of abilities she had stopped trying to memorize them after the first ten. There were main abilities and all their sub-abilities. It was too much. Her head had buzzed with the sheer wealth of knowledge. One thing she did understand was Scott, the brother that didn't like her, was a Deflector and a highly skilled martial artist as well. He could cancel out another Singer's ability. But like his brother, Michael, it was powerfully effective, but only for a short time. Say... maybe a half minute. Then there was Jen. She was telekinetic like Julia, but different. Or maybe not different, just so much *better*. Then there was the post-puberty strength that came online.

Only for the males. But God was just and the female

Singer's abilities were usually stronger, or at the very least, longer-lasting. So, kinda a wash.

Julia skipped one of the flat stones and the swan startled, flying a few feet and craning its elegant neck to give her a disdainful look. Could swans be angry? She thought this one was. She sighed and sat down on the boulder again. Picking up a stick she twirled the water, her chin in her palm.

Then there was Michael. She felt her whole face break into a grin. That scene with the shit had been priceless. Beyond funny... even if Scott hadn't been laughing.

Payback's a bitch.

Julia threw the stick in the water, standing. She began to pace the shore thinking about Brendan. He'd been the one to carry her from the Were. How had he found her? He said simply, he was a "Tracker." It didn't fully explain things. He also said he had a crossover ability. Pyrokinetic. Julia was reminded of that Stephen King novel, *Firestarter.* She'd mentioned it to Brendan who'd laughed, "Nah, that's some trashy fiction story."

Right.

Hadn't seemed so implausible when the feet of ten were-wolves were on fire. Seemed pretty legit to her.

Her mind landed on William. He'd been trying to free her too. But the more Julia thought about it, the less "free" it felt. She cared for him... maybe more. But the reality was she'd be the bird in the gilded cage again. She would have... she almost was a bird in a cage of the Were as well. It wouldn't have been gilded though. Julia thought of Tony and shuddered. To think there was even a slim chance that she'd have been forced into a union with Tony. She understood instinctively that he'd been bad, evil maybe. And it hadn't just been Adriana's misgivings. Julia had plenty of her own, rather a confirmation. She sighed. She felt like she was shuffling a deck of cards, afraid to cut the deck.

Julia heard a noise and turned, her hand at her heart, startled. Julia smiled when she saw who it was.

Brendan.

He walked toward her, his bronze hair a low burning flame with the sun lighting it from behind, his eyes like onyx with the sun at his back. The mountains framed his silhouette as he approached and Julia felt heat rise to her face, seeing the evidence of his combative training on every square inch of his body.

He waved at her as he drew closer and she lifted her hand in return.

Julia already felt more at home with him than she had a right to.

CHAPTER 28

*T*he feral tracked the two beside the lake and could hardly contain his territorial urges over the female.

She was his and another was beside her. Putting his hands on her.

He would die.

The feral would enjoy tearing at the soft flesh of his neck, the hot spray from the blood coating his muzzle in a satisfying spray of fragrance.

With an effort that was almost painful, he retreated into the depths of the forest, his snout scenting their whereabouts. He would be cautious. The male that was with her had an advantage that the feral recognized and wished to cripple if he could.

He was not nose-blind. He was something other than human. The feral did not know how he knew this but when he had been near the male and the small female, their kinship was apparent, easy to scent. But his chest had tightened uncomfortably with a sensation he could not identify.

When he had the male in his grip, he would ascertain what that enigmatic detail was.

* * *

Brendan

BRENDAN HAD WATCHED Julia from a safe distance. She wore her discontent readily, he thought. Brendan sighed, he couldn't contain the Fam and knew not to even try. It was obvious Julia felt off-kilter, unsettled. Who wouldn't be? First the vamps took her, then the Were. He didn't know much about her past. They'd find out more later. There may be extenuating circumstances. After all, she was their Queen. Marcus had raised them on the legend, as his father had before him. He'd demand to know more.

He gazed at her a moment. She didn't look very queenly. She was slim, average height for a female. Her coloring was different, he slowed his pace, studying her. Julia had a unique, soft golden red hair color. But it was her eyes that took his breath away, they matched her hair, depending on the light. They were amber in indirect light but in the sun, they rivaled the orb's brightness.

He walked toward her and she jumped as if he startled her. He gave a short flick of his fingers, sort of an uncon-scious waving the white flag. She waved back and he smiled, walking the rest of the way toward her. He was puzzled by the expression on her face.

She looked for a moment there like she was assessing him. Taking his measure as a man.

Brendan's smile widened into a grin. Now that... he kinda liked.

When he reached her and she didn't seem resistant, he took Julia into his arms, giving her a brief hug then releasing her. She smelled like a ripe piece of fruit and he instantly wondered if it was the shampoo or her. Brendan stepped back, reluctantly letting her go, his fingers trailing lightly down her arms, causing goose flesh to rise where their contact had been.

Then it hit him. A smell so unique he couldn't name it. But it was familiar. Brendan swung his head in the direction of the woods that bordered the opposite side of the lake.

Julia leaned into the hug that Brendan had given her and sighed. She allowed herself that moment's peace then stepped away. Her chest tightened horribly. Her loneliness constricted her heart. She was desperately alone. At least it felt that way.

As a matter of fact, in only a few more days it will have been two years since Jason died. Tears threatened at the thought of it but were chased away by the sudden expression of wariness that washed over Brendan's features.

Julia looked around, frightened. They said she was safe! She whirled on Brendan just as he grabbed her.

"Let's get outta here!" he said, dragging her after him.

"What is it?" she asked on a half-jog. But he didn't answer until they had traveled the short distance to the house. When they bounded up the wide, wooden steps and were nearly at the front door he turned, taking her shoulders. "There's something in the woods!" His eyes searched hers, the grip cupping her shoulders almost painful.

"What?" she cried. Was it vampire? Were? What the hell... trolls? Could there be more mythological creatures springing to life to kidnap her away from the one group that she actually belonged to?

Jen stepped out the front door, letting the screen crack back against the wood frame. The noise of it reverberated everywhere. She took in Brendan's expression. Her eyebrows came together. "What's wrong?" Jen looked from Julia to Brendan.

Julia looked at Jen, "How did you know there was something wrong?"

Jen flicked her eyes at Julia, "It's a sib thing."

Julia waited. Finally Brendan said, "It's that Were from the compound."

Jen rolled her eyes. "Thanks for clearin' that up, bro! What, there's like... a hundred or something?"

They looked at each other and Julia watched their expressions. Jen spoke first, "You mean that giant red one?"

He nodded, "Yeah, that's him."

Julia remembered almost going to him, the connection was so strong. What could it mean?

Jen looked at her and huffed. "This is some of the awful crap that can happen..." she sighed and looked at Brendan. His eyes turned away from hers, trained on the woods beyond the lake.

At that moment Scott and Michael came walking from the big barn that acted as Training Facility for Singers. There wasn't a laugh or smile on their faces to be found. Not that she'd expected one from Scott. But Michael had been downright jovial in the two days since she'd been with them.

Julia looked at all of them. "Okay, I give up. What's lurking around in the woods that has everyone's collective underwear in a wad? You guys are scaring me!"

Finally, Brendan said, "We think..." Jen glared at him and he shook his head, resigned. "I think," he emphasized, "that we have a Singer who's been turned."

Julia stepped forward. "I don't get it... turned how?"

Michael shook his head to the negative. "Not how... what."

Julia sat there and let the idea take shape, blooming in her head like an ugly flower. Her eyes snapped to Brendan's. "Wait a second!" Her eyes pierced theirs. "You're telling me that we've got someone out there that was one of us... and now some Were or vamp has... changed them?"

Scott nodded. "Yeah, that's about it," folding his muscular arms across a barrel chest.

Jen turned to Brendan. "You're sure, Bren?"

"Werewolf," he said tersely. Julia watched her shoulders droop. "They're the worst."

"What's with all this? It can't be saved?" Julia asked to the group.

Brendan shook his head. "He."

It was a man. A Singer like herself, turned. Her gaze swung back to Brendan's. "Did... he *want* to be a werewolf?"

Scott answered, "Doubtful. The attacking Were would've known he was a Singer. Don't know why they'd do a Singer. After all, they need Singers to produce..." he lifted his fingers in sarcastic air quotes, "a Rare One." His eyes met hers, filled with loathing and derision. Somebody wasn't happy with her status. Like she could goddamned help it!

What the hell had she done to piss in his Wheaties? The putz. Julia felt her eyes narrow as heat suffused her face. In anger. He glared right back at her.

"What's your problem?" Julia asked.

Scott met the challenge in her words and stalked toward her as Brendan put her behind his back. "What are you doing, Scott?" Brendan ground out.

"It's her fault! He's after her!" His eyes found all of theirs and then went back to Julia. Well, she wasn't going to hide behind Brendan. She came from behind him and Brendan said in a low voice full of threat, "Don't you hurt her."

"Our queen?" he asked mockingly, putting his hand to his chest and looking at Julia like she was a piece of garbage on the bottom of his shoe. "Never! She is safe as a sleeping babe in the cradle of her mother's bosom!" he snarled, barely contained rage making his face more handsome, not less.

"Stop it, Scott!" Jen hissed.

"No!" he yelled back and she flinched.

Julia got right up in his personal space, defying logic as he was six foot three at least and built like a brick shit house, all brawn and anger. "I can't be that safe because I don't *have* a mother," she poked his solidly muscled chest with her finger for emphasis and he didn't move a centimeter. "I don't know what I did to get on the top of your shit list, but I assure you, it wasn't on purpose!" Julia was shaking with rage but continued, "I watched my husband die," their eyes widened while Scott's narrowed, "my best friend is gone forever, my parents dead. I was with the vampires, then the Were and now I'm with you. I have to be queen? of the Blood Singers? Maybe I don't want the job!" And with that last comment she pushed him in the chest, but it came out more like a slap, harder than she meant it to be, kinda like hitting a tree. Her anger overrode even the pretense of common sense.

He wrapped his huge hands around her small wrists and jerked her into his body. The siblings were too late to help, to stop it.

The moment he touched her the branding fire of his flesh on hers was complete. Neither expected it.

Neither welcomed it.

Julia's soul bound to Scott's in one earth shattering moment of clarity, as natural as the breath she took, she felt their beings knitting together and she gasped, it was almost painful.

He breathed out, "No." Even as he staggered back his hands went for her again, but Brendan was there. "What's wrong with you, Scott?! What are you doing?"

Jen and Michael looked at each other then at Julia. She was breathing shallowly, her body a throbbing mass of unquenched desire, longing and absolution.

Her eyes never left his.

Julia didn't even like Scott.

Then Marcus was there, their leader. He looked from one to the other of them, instant understanding riding his face with certainty, unity a thing that sizzled in the air all around them.

"Soulmates!" he extolled.

Julia looked from the leader and obvious father of the family who surrounded her as she leaned weakly against Brendan's chest, her back pressed against his warmth and comfort, her eyes fixed on Scott's.

His were filled with anger and hate.

Directed at her.

They couldn't be soul-anything. It was obvious Julia wasn't someone he wanted, respected... liked.

She tore herself out of Brendan's arms and ran inside the house. Taking the steps two at a time she rushed into the bedroom they'd given her and slammed the door, using the old-fashioned skeleton key to lock it. She backed away until her thighs pressed against the bed. Julia sunk down into the mattress, the firmness of it a temporary cradle to her sadness.

Could things get any more screwed up if she'd wished for it? She put her face in her hands and cried while off in the distance she heard a sound.

A howl.

* * *

Singers

"TELL ME," Marcus said, his eyes like slits on his grown children. "And it better be good."

Everyone began talking at once. Finally Michael took the conversational reins, "Brendan came back with news of a Singer turned Were..."

"What?!" Marcus roared, his eyes casting a wide net at the surrounding area.

Brendan shook his head. "It's in the woods for now. But... it will find its way here. Soon."

"Male?" Marcus queried.

They nodded. Marcus looked at Scott. "I understand your sentiments about the Queen. That you've never adjusted to the idea of it."

Jen rolled her eyes. "Adjusted, Dad? Try anarchy! That'd be more like it." She looked at her oldest brother. So sure of himself, nothing ever bothered him. He fought with a skill unmatched by any other Singer in their quadrant. He was the number one Deflector of their band of Singers, but one female Singer came to them, the queen and he'd lost his status of independence. That's what a soul-meld would do. The irony wasn't lost on Jen. She felt a little sorry for Scott. It would suck hating his soulmate but being bonded to her anyway. And Julia impressed Jen as independent. She felt a smile curl her lips.

"And now I'm bound to her!" Scott roared, his lip curling with distaste.

Above them, Julia listened from the window that was ajar. It was fine that Scott didn't want her. He was stubborn and... mean and ugh! Julia didn't even like him! She'd do better on her own. She felt confident enough with her telekinetic ability to get by.

Julia didn't want to be queen. And she didn't care if there was some "soul-meld" or whatever. She couldn't get out of being a Blood Singer. Or a Rare One. But she didn't have to be here. In this place, with someone that hated her.

She looked around her room. A profound melancholy slipped through her, her being still tingling from the encounter with Scott. Julia shoved away how painfully right it had felt to be in his arms for that one moment.

He hated her anyway so it didn't matter.

Julia grabbed the only coat in the room and slipped out

quietly, heading down the staircase that exited the back of the house. It had once been a little-used servant's staircase. She used it now in circumspection.

She utterly missed the most important part of the conversation.

If she had, she may have hesitated.

As it was, Julia was heading into the arms of danger.

Marcus looked at his eldest son and sighed. Scott had excelled at everything, his training, his ability, his... conquests. But his stubbornness was his biggest flaw. He had fought long and hard to let the legend of the Queen of the Blood Singers die a natural death. She did not exist, he'd argued, it was only legend. But Marcus remembered the reverent way that his father had discussed her Coming. He knew that Julia was the queen.

If her scent was not sufficient confirmation, she had the mark of the moon branded on her forehead, as foretold. The pearly crescent shone at her temple, a testimony to her position amongst them.

Scott could deny it until he was blue in the face. But Brendan was one of their finest Trackers.

His nose never lied.

Then there was the soul-meld. His eye's met his son's. Only Singers of royal blood could soul-meld. It was a double confirmation.

"Hate her if you will. But remember this," and he spoke to all of them but directed his words at Scott, "she has been through many traumas. We don't know what... or how many. What did she tell you?"

Jen told him what Julia had said to Scott.

Marcus threw up his hands. "So what we have here is a Singer who lost a husband..."

"Infant bride-much," Michael muttered and Marcus' brow cocked.

"Nothing," Michael expounded but was terrible at hiding a smile.

"And, she was held by both factions: Were and vampire?" When he looked for confirmation Brendan nodded.

"Then," he began to pace the wooden planks of the covered deck and some squeaked with age as he passed, "she is kidnapped by her own people, told she is queen, then treated abominably by my eldest son."

"Twice," Marcus said, looking at Scott who glowered back, the barest hint of shame creeping into his expression.

Scott folded his muscular arms across a chest that proved his time on the mat. "Okay, I guess I could have handled it better," Scott said, still trying to stop his guts from churning. His entire body yearning to get back to *her.* He hated it, the loss of his independence as he saw it.

"Ah... duh!" Jen said. He glanced at her and she continued. "Unless anyone objects, I suggest you get your dumbass up there and apologize!"

Marcus scowled at his daughter's use of language but let it go. From all accounts, Scott had behaved badly. And to a female Singer! The Queen, no less. It could hardly have been worse.

He nodded and Scott said, "I hate feeling trapped. She made me feel..."

"Complete?" Brendan asked with just a hint of envy. Why couldn't it have been him? He'd have been happier than a pig in shit to have Julia. Hello? The Queen of the Singers... his soulmate? Yeah, kind of a nice gig.

Scott thought about it. Yeah, he guessed she had; but she'd blind-sided him. He'd been totally, no... *completely* unprepared for a soul-meld. But dammit, he had reveled in his independence, refused to go on the wild goose chase of an acquisition for another Singer. Let his hot dog brothers and sister do it.

And look what the cat had dragged home.

He looked up at the window of her bedroom, feeling miserable. How could he fix it? Did he want to? He realized belatedly he may have misjudged her. Badly. Scott remembered those huge amber eyes looking up at him in anger... wounded by his careless words. He'd fallen right into them, as soon as she was inside the circle of his arms, he couldn't think of anything but her. And the protection of her. He sighed and began to walk toward the front door.

"Wait," Marcus said and Scott turned, a question on his face.

"She needs extra protection from this Were."

His children turned to him. When he had their full attention, he resumed, "You understand how dangerous a turned Singer is. The Queen will be like a homing beacon."

Brendan nodded, understanding. "He'll be a problem, alright."

Scott's heart began to speed, his intuition kicking online. Already his thoughts were on Julia. Where was she at this very moment? He was instantly pissed that he gave a rat's ass. He felt like his mind was tearing in two. His intellect rebelled against what his soul was compelled to execute... feel.

Julia, it screamed. *Where is Julia?* Scott shook his head to clear it from the fuzziness of the duality of his nature.

"Why?" Scott heard himself asking despite himself.

Michael hadn't paid attention to this part of his training and shrugged but Jen had been an apt pupil like Brendan and she said, "It breaks the mind of a Singer turned. His mind is gone. He'd want to belong with us, but wouldn't know how..."

"He'd hurt Julia if he got his hands on her," Brendan said. "Those Singers that have been turned are crazy-as-hell."

Marcus wanted to refute that but knew he couldn't. As descriptions go, it was a good one.

Scott's hand clenched the solid brass knob of the screen

door and it creaked in protest under his abusive grip. "So... let me get this straight, this... feral werewolf was once a Singer, got nailed by a Were attack and is now scenting after Julia."

"Yeah," Brendan said.

Scott scoffed, "Let it try. I'll rip its paws off and scratch his own ass with them!"

Michael laughed. He might be able to do it. Scott was the strongest male Singer in their group. He got a visual and Scott's eyes narrowed on him.

"What's so damn funny?" Scott asked.

"A couple of things, I'm guessing," Brendan said.

"Enlighten us, please," Marcus said in his droll way.

"First," Brendan held up a finger, "Scott didn't give two shits and an eff about Julia, hated her as a matter of fact." Brendan waited for a dissenting comment or grunt. When none came, he continued, "Second, the visual of you tearing off the Were's paw that we saw at the compound, and scratching its..." Brendan shook his head. "No pal, sorry. He's big-time feral in his pants."

"And just big time?!" Jen agreed, adding, "he's the biggest Were we've ever seen... red, different."

Scott frowned like, *so?*

"In other words, it may take more than your pissed off attitude to subdue this fella!" Michael agreed with his siblings.

"Ah!" Marcus began and they all looked at him. "That's where you're wrong..." he had them again and said slowly, "when a soulmate's partner is threatened, there may be more in the arsenal than what the Singer was bestowed with at birth."

Scott's hand dropped from the knob. "What do you mean, Dad?"

"I mean that it is your singular purpose to protect and

nurture her." Marcus' eyes speared Scott's. "She is in the gravest danger right now, the most vulnerable. Until this feral is caught and disposed of, he will not stop until he has her."

"Will he kill her?" Jen asked.

"I do not know. But, ask yourself this," they leaned forward to hear his last words, "does anyone want to find out?"

Hell no! A primal yell sounded from deep within Scott and against every intellectual imperative his feet strode through the doorway and flung him up the stairs toward her room.

Toward Julia.

Julia threw branches away as they scraped past her, crashing through the brush that threatened to stab her viciously. She was furious. The more she walked the angrier she became.

The emotion was useless, though. Being angry didn't matter, letting go of the Singers and what she was, did. Every step she took was a greater distance between she and Scott and in her mind she was happy.

But her heart grieved. She felt a little like she had after Jason died. But how could that be? She didn't even *know* Scott! In fact, he'd made a point of being an ass!

Julia rounded the bend of a stand of trees, having utterly forgotten the one that sought her when she stopped in her tracks. A massive Were stood in front of her, his green eyes pegging her intensely. She hauled in a lungful of air to scream and he was on her, his hand that had talons twice the length of her fingers wrapping her mouth and tickling her ears.

Julia's vision grew dim, her fear making her bladder burn for release. As her world faded to gray the last thing she saw were those emerald eyes staring at her.

Julia lost consciousness and the feral pressed her light body to his. He turned, covering more ground than she could have on her own, his half-wolf form perfectly suited to the dense conditions of the forest.

He ran, the burden of the female an abiding comfort. It was the only instance he had felt a sense of peace since he Became.

Whatever he was now.

CHAPTER 29

S cott put his hand on the multi-faceted knob, the crystal a solid weight under his palm and turned it. The five panel door swung inward, the momentum of it carried by its own weight. His eyes swept the sunlit room, missing nothing.

Julia was gone.

His heart thudded to a stop, the words he'd spoken crashing back with the weight of the ages into his mind. His eyes found the flaw in the room.

The window was open a crack, maybe two inches. The white curtains, like billowing fingers of smoke, fluttered with the breeze allowed in by the opening.

He walked to the window, his siblings entering Julia's room behind him. He stood at the window, the low sill pressing against his upper shins. Scott could clearly hear the voices of various people from a distance, the strange acoustics of the oddly formed bay accentuating the noises.

Amplifying them.

Julia would have heard everything he had to say about her down below.

His disinterest.

His hate and disrespect.

Scott hung his head, clenching his hands into tight fists. He understood now that she would have left before he had wrestled his emotions into some kind of basic order, prepared to right his wrong, give her some neutral deference.

Now she was gone. Possibly in danger.

Grave danger.

Scott turned, his back to the window. He spied something of hers and picked it up. It was a hoodie. He crushed it to his nose, inhaling the scent of Julia, his chest tightening with recognition.

Soul recognition.

His deep brown eyes flashed to those of his siblings and father.

"She's gone," he said. Guilt rode him mercilessly.

"Great," Jen said.

"You pushed her away," Brendan accused.

"Ya think?" Scott replied. His eyes were twin holes of burning fury. At himself. "I screwed up, I got that. But now's not the time for talk," he speared his brother with a look. "Can you find her?"

"Absolutely," Brendan said. Then paused for a heartbeat. "The better question is, has *he* found her?"

They were all quiet for a moment then with silent agreement, they turned and rushed out the door. Julia's hoodie was gripped in Scott's fist like a lifeline. He had never been so focused in his life. He needed to find her. All the bullshit legends of his childhood that he'd discounted, Singer Royalty, soul-melding, all of it... was no longer legend.

It was his new reality.

They ran down the back stairs, the very ones Julia had used but a mere hour before. Bursting out of the back door,

Brendan tracked Julia to the forest's edge. His grave stare focused on Scott.

"What?" he asked. For the first time, terror sunk its teeth into his psyche. Scott had never had need of fear; it was an alien emotion for him.

Until now.

"The feral's in these woods," Brendan said, using the very words that Scott had not wanted to hear.

"Does he... has he..." Scott asked, his grip on Julia's sweatshirt making his knuckles turn white.

Brendan nodded, once.

Scott yelled, his rage-filled bellow heard by the sensitive ears of the feral who swiftly widened the breach between the Singers and himself.

The feral picked up his pace, the girl in his arms unaware of who carried her.

Or who followed.

* * *

Were

ADRIANA FELT like her ass had been handed to her. As usual. She always felt that way when she got done "visiting" with Lawrence. She kicked a rock on the way out of his chamber. Which wasn't really accurate. His quarters, as she preferred to think of them, were huge, she'd never been in his actual bedroom. They always met in his cavernous library, his great desk a mighty wooden anchor in the center of a sea of books. She always felt like her ship was sinking.

Like now.

He'd reamed her up one side and down the other. Tony had come up smelling like a rose... like always. In fact, she wanted to kick his ass too, the list was growing. It really rubbed Adi the wrong way that she was every bit the fighter he was but when it came down to talon to talon, he'd best her. Her fists clenched. She had twice the heart that he had. But he was just that much bigger than she. If skill and training were equal, someone with all those pounds and muscle would be victor. It was the opposite of fair.

Sometimes she hated being female. Adi liked the one thing she had over him though.

Ironically, it was her gender.

He was destined to mate with a female Were. He was second to her brother, Joseph, the most powerful Alpha in their region. Because of his station within the werewolf hierarchy, she should have looked at Tony as top on the list of potentials. That's how he'd looked at her until she made it clear he was a Loser with a capital L. Now, his choices were limited. But Tony didn't really want a mate. No, he wanted a female Were trophy, squiring her about under the snouts of all the other male Were that couldn't be mated to a female Were. There were too few. She smiled.

Adi enjoyed bristling his fur with that every chance she got. He was so full of himself. Like today. He'd painted his role in the escape of the feral in such a way it made it sound like she'd been irresponsible. Not the truth. That he'd put off a difficult chore on a female at the worst point of the month? The feral had showed her a kind of mercy. Tearing her shoulder out of its socket yet not killing her. Not so crazy after all.

Then there was the other question about the feral.

Who was he? Really?

Why the interest in the Rare One? Because no one could convince Adi differently, if he'd wished for escape earlier he could have. No. He'd wanted Jules. She'd stake her life on it.

Tony followed her out with a smirk, whistling.

The asshole.

Then Joseph came, casting a look her way. She waited and he walked over to her. "You know, if you'd be a little..." he rolled his eyes skyward, searching for the perfect word, "*softer* with Tony, he'd cut you some slack." Her brother shrugged.

"No," she responded shortly. "He can kiss my ass!" Adriana said, folding her arms across her chest. "I'll never suck up to him. Besides," she looked at her brother again, "did ya see how he made me look in there to Lawrence? He never does or says the right thing. Every verbal angle he plays is uttered for his benefit, never anyone else but his own." Couldn't Joseph see that?

Joseph did. But Tony was his second, an excellent fighter. It didn't matter that his sister couldn't get along with him. They'd have to reach some kind of mutual understanding to co-exist. He told her as much.

"Whatever!" Adi responded in a loud voice. "I'll just avoid his obnoxious carcass and try for civility." She rolled her eyes then nailed Joseph with a solid stare. He raised his brows in question and she plowed forward, changing tactics. "Who is the feral?"

Joseph sucked in his breath. He had been sworn to secrecy. "I can't say, Adi. You know that. We've been over it and over it..."

She interrupted him, "it's for the safety of the pack... blah, blah. Yeah, whatever. I gotcha. But I want to know why we would even keep a feral?" Her eyes shifted to his, searching and a wild idea began to form. It couldn't be... she asked, "Does he have something to do with Jules?"

It was the barest flicker but Adi caught it, snapping her fingers. "Tell me!"

Joseph sighed, holding up a palm. "We thought that if the Rare One needed... encouragement, we could use the feral."

Adi scrunched her brows together. That didn't make

sense. Joseph saw her confusion. They stared at each other for several moments.

"How? How could... he coerce...?" she asked.

Joseph told her. It took almost a half hour and when he finished only the birds in the trees could be heard in the deafening silence that his revelation had left behind.

Her slap against his skin rang out, startling the birds which perched on high branches to exchange the safety of the trees for that of the sky.

"How could you?" her voice shook with contained rage.

Joseph felt the sting of her slap and knew he deserved ten times worse. There was no excuse, he should have fought harder against it. Now, there was no taking back the deceit.

Adi's eyes narrowed on him. "Whose idea was this?"

Joseph didn't answer, his eyes were answer enough.

Of-fucking-course.

Adrianna stalked off in search of Tony. Joseph tried to grab her arm to stop her and she tore it away from him, turning on him like the wolf she was. "Don't touch me! It was unforgivable." Her eyes locked onto him without mercy. "Ya know what? It's good that the Singers took Julia. Maybe somebody can treat her like a human being instead of something to be manipulated. We don't deserve her."

She strode off in search of Tony.

Joseph watched her go, his self-loathing a solid weight in his body.

In his soul.

* * *

William

WILLIAM WAS HOPEFUL. He clapped the Locator on his back as he left the kiss with a thank you and the blessing of their

284

lightwalker, Gabriel. A huge favor as future collateral. It would hang over the coven's head. But if he could regain Julia... it would not matter. Their kiss' prosperity and importance would be solidified forever.

The vampire turned, giving William his steady regard. "You have the map?"

William nodded and he gave the barest smile of acknowledgment. "I wish you the best fortune in locating your Singer."

They both knew that Julia wasn't just any Singer. But neither said it openly. They had put their competition aside for the moment but the possibility of a sister kiss trying for the Rare One was not beyond the scope of possibility. William was keen on not forgetting that basic fact.

He closed the door behind him and strode to where Claire and Gabriel waited. Gabriel looked up as William drew closer. His finger stabbed the map. "The Singers have powerful blocking in place from our location. But," his eyes met William's, "the Locator was quite sure that this is the general region." They all studied the area.

Mountainous and densely wooded.

Perfect cover for retrieval.

By vampire.

William assembled runners. They packed their gear and went out on their last mission. If they could not retrieve Julia this time, he knew that his window of opportunity would have closed to nothing.

Once she was in the womb of the Singers it would be an impossibility to get to her.

They afforded formidable protection. Something even his will and determination could not combat.

He imagined she would be important to them as well. Perhaps not labeled the same way she was with the vampire and werewolves. Maybe something else entirely?

Julia would be royal amongst their kind, William contemplated.

Like a queen.

* * *

the Feral

THE FERAL SWEPT *the hair that had fallen across the face of the female away from her eyes and studied her. It made a sweet longing like the finest blood rise unbidden within his wolf form. It was almost enough to make him slide back into his human shape. But not yet. His strange half-human form was the one he instinctively realized was best for the distance he needed. Even now he could feel his kind chasing after them.*

After the female. He clutched her tighter to his body. Soon, he would need to feed and would have to leave her unconscious and unprotected for a time. He scowled. An outsider would have noted how comical it made his facial expressions, that of the wolf, the echo of humanity etched about the edges.

He stood smoothly with the tiny female in his arms, a sense of rightness and purpose propelling him naturally. He searched until he was satisfied, finding the perfect den in which to hide her. He did, tucking her inside the small rock crevice. He backed away, his hunger a gnawing monster in his belly. Before he could compromise his strength further by lingering over her, he fled. In search of prey, which would keep him busy for a time.

More than he liked.

Julia woke up with darkness all around her and was chilled to the bone. She had a coat but the damp coolness of her environment had sunk into her bones and weighed her down. She put her hands out in an exploratory movement and hit something solid. All around her Julia could feel the solid weight of something, smell the earth surrounding her.

She felt like she was in a tomb. Julia panicked... scraping the confines of the dark space, whimpering in fear. Before she lost it totally something occurred to her. Julia's memory slid into place and she remembered what had happened.

The great red werewolf. Actually, his fur was like wine. Not that it mattered. She closed her eyes tightly. What was she doing here? Where was he? What had he put her in?

Calm thyself, Julia!

Her lips set in a determined line, Julia lifted her head as high as she could without hitting the ceiling of where she lay. Ambient light reached her eyes and she could just make out her toes like twin hills in the distance. Julia thought that she may have been stuffed in some kind of hole.

For safekeeping.

She gulped, trying not to think of what that meant. Maybe a tasty meal for later? Julia shuddered at the thought. She needed to get the hell out of here! She experimented, wiggling around and discovered that the only place of escape was where her feet were. Well... she couldn't move at all. Maybe she had six inches on all sides.

Didn't matter. She'd never been more scared since that night, *since Jason*, her mind spoke, but she wasn't going to give up yet.

She began to wiggle her butt like an inchworm, bunching her muscles then scooting forward, inch by inch. Julia knew when she made headway because she could see better. Finally, Julia's legs were free of the hold and she was able to bend her knees and drag her body further, stabbing her heels into the dirt at her feet and pulling herself out incrementally. In less than five minutes she was free. Even the dappled sunlight through the canopy of trees was bright and full of glare after the utter darkness of the hole she'd been in. Julia turned, squinting, and looked at where she'd been. It was a narrow slot at the base of a natural rock formation. Barely more that a crevice.

No one would have ever seen her unless they knew she was there.

Julia stood and the pins and needles of returning blood flow almost brought her to her knees. But she persevered, breathing slowly, in and out. She was tired of fainting, being kidnapped and told who she was and what she was going to be.

And do.

Julia was her. And she was going to be okay.

Julia turned and walked away, casting a glance behind her as she went. She didn't have the vaguest clue where she was but she was going. She headed west, where the sun rode above the mountains. At least she had a direction.

Julia hoped it was not the same one the Were had used.

* * *

Homer

THE PHONE BUZZED SHRILLY beside his ear and he snatched it up, his irritation rising like the tide beyond the window of the police station. "Truman," Karl answered in his gruff voice.

"It's Alexander," the chief forensic specialist said.

"Hello! Sing me the tune I like to hear."

"Okay... well, I don't know if it's what you *want* to hear but it's what I have."

Confusing but okay, Karl thought. "Alright, lay it on me."

"I've got the sample DNA typed but it's broad because I can't get a specific on it."

"Cut the cryptic shit and just give it to me straight."

"Canine genome."

Alright, just like he figured. No big surprise there. "Okay, wolves then..."

Silence. Karl could almost hear the static on the normally clear lines.

He cleared his throat.

"Listen... this is going to sound completely insane."

Karl waited.

"But the classification is not entirely accurate."

"What are you saying, Alexander?"

"I'm saying you've got yourself a new class of canine here."

"What... Bigfoot?" Karl gave a short bark of a laugh.

Alexander didn't laugh. "No. Not Bigfoot."

"Then what?" This was crazy!

"Something else. Something so different we don't know where to put it."

Karl leaned forward, his chair creaking under his weight. "Okay, give me what you know."

"Okay, more insanity. Ready?"

"Hell yeah." Karl tapped his ballpoint on the desk, listening. When Alexander was finished he whistled low in the back of his throat, leaning back in his chair and scrubbing his face. Finally he said, "A guy could lose his reputation over what you're postulating."

"Yeah, no shit."

"So... what's the plan?" Karl asked.

"Well, first off, I think the larger question is what are these things? Listen Truman, meet me back at the scene. Who knows, with some additional measurements I may have more answers."

"Like what?"

"Size, for starters."

"And?"

"Intelligence."

They were quiet for a full minute, the line buzzing between them.

"You're not suggesting these things are the same ones that tossed that dump are you?"

"I am," Alexander said.

"Holy shit," Truman breathed out.

"Yeah."

* * *

Cyn

THE BUS DRIVER looked as the forlorn girl entered his bus. When she told him where she wanted to go he was somehow reminded of that waif of a girl a few months back. The one with the whiskey eyes and phoney black hair dye. He wondered how she was doing now? His eyes met hers and she answered, "Kent."

He nodded. "I know just where to take ya."

"Good," she said. Turning away, she headed to the back of his bus. His eye followed her in the rear view mirror. When he looked at her feet he saw some funky boots. They looked like hard-core fisherman boots, reaching to her calves. Ugly suckers, shit-brown in color. Huh... they didn't really seem to go with the rest of her.

He shifted his eyes back to the road, putting the great bus into gear, it ground out of park and into first gear, a plume of exhaust hailing its departure.

Cynthia leaned back, pushing her knees against the seat in front of her. She let her legs dangle and right before she closed her eyes, she caught sight of Jules' boots on her feet. She smiled through her tears.

I'll never forget you, Julia.

After a few moments, Cynthia fell asleep, exhaustion

taking the reins for her, the tears drying on her cheeks as she slept.

The bus driver drove his route, twice. The same way he had before, giving the girl time to rest. When he was a couple blocks away from the women's shelter, he stopped.

This was as good a place as any, he thought. He jerked the lever and the bi-fold door opened with a burst of compressed air.

Cynthia's eyes snapped open and noted she was the sole person on the bus. Her eyes met those of the bus driver and she stood, her eyes flicking to his name embroidered on his uniform, *Alfred*.

When she came to the front she lowered her head and peeked out the bus door at a building she saw a couple of blocks away. She could just make out the sign, *Freedom Affirmed.*

She looked back at Alfred. "Where am I?"

His kind eyes remained steady on hers. "Kent," he said.

She nodded. "Right, okay." Cynthia began to descend the short bus steps as she heard the driver's voice behind her, "That place up there will give you a couple day's peace."

There was no peace for her, Cynthia thought. But she turned anyway and looked into his kind eyes. "Thanks, I'll check it out."

Alfred smiled and nodded, pushing the lever, the bus door closing with a snap and an air-driven hiss. Cynthia watched the bus glide away, the only proof it had ever been was the exhaust cloud in its wake.

Turning, she headed for the building.

It was as good a place as any, she thought. Her thoughts unconsciously echoing those of the driver.

Cynthia quickened her pace toward the building.

Toward a new life.

* * *

Julia

JULIA WALKED QUICKLY and made progress. However, she grew thirsty, her tongue swelling like a tumor in her mouth. She became so parched it was all she could think of. Shading her eyes, she looked up at the sun. Julia guessed it was well past noontime.

As she hiked the sun would move behind clouds, casting deep shadows in the forest. Julia's mind played tricks on her and she felt alone.

Scared... and foolish.

Mostly just scared, she decided. Finally, Julia thought she heard the tinkling sounds of moving water and when the forest floor grew greener and the topography of the ground at her feet began to slope away and downward, Julia figured she hit the jackpot. She grabbed branches to steady herself as she finessed her way down a short but steep ravine toward the sounds of a small stream. It was probably a river here in Washington, but by Alaska standards, it was a creek. She knelt by the crystal clear water and made a cup with both hands, letting the slow-moving water run over the top, then capturing the refreshing goodness in her already cold flesh. Ignoring her intellect she gulped greedy sips.

After she'd drunk her fill, Julia stood, wiping her hands off on her jeans. She turned and carefully made her way up the small ravine, refreshed and rejuvenated.

She abandoned the tree cover and entered an open meadow, stopping for a moment as the sun came from behind the clouds, beating its warmth into her as she stood in the open. Julia closed her eyes, lifting her face to the sun and reveled in the stolen moment of warmth. When the first pain began to pierce her guts she gasped, folding her arms across her belly protectively.

What was this? She groaned out loud, holding herself.

Julia felt the water she had drunk not thirty minutes before begin to churn in her stomach like curdled milk. A chill rolled over her skin and she began to shiver, goose flesh rose like chicken skin and she trembled again. Julia looked around, feeling ill. Maybe she drank too much at one time?

This was the worse possible time to get the flu or some other crap. No worries, just the big bad wolf after her.

She didn't think being Little Red Riding Hood was very funny.

Zero amusement.

Julia pressed forward, clutching her stomach as she walked. Her eyes searched the dim forest. She might have to find someplace to hide until her insides felt better.

She moved into the soothing coolness of the forest as the first cramp tore into her and pain rode her like a wave coming to shore.

* * *

William

WILLIAM and his five runners made haste. As soon as twilight had dropped its veil of protection over the city, they had left the shelter of the kiss.

The cattle parted like the Red Sea. Even in their ignorant stupor, there was some biological imperative that kicked in, a primal alert of sorts. When the vampire evacuated their lair, the steps leading to the street a yawning concrete hole of uncertainty and darkness, they moved aside unconsciously, giving the vampire a wide berth.

William moved quickly, Gabriel's words ringing in his

head, *Do not engage a large group of Singers.* His eyes had met his leader's and he had asked, *What is too many?* There had been a pregnant pause then Gabriel had responded with a question, *How many was too many at the Were stronghold?*

William understood. In that case, had it not been for the feral Were he might have stood a chance, even with the pair of Singers. He was not certain. He shrugged the thought away. Julia and he were connected, William had Singer ancestry. That accounted for some things. Alliance, Blood-share. However old it had been, it would cast weight to the positive for him.

He swiped the words away with a dismissive mental shrug. Gabriel did not fully understand battle reasoning. The Were, for all their flaws, did. In the heat of battle, decisions were made. Some lacking in any rational foundation. Nevertheless, they were deemed critical then, in that moment. There may be a moment which arose in just that way in the next few hours, and William would be reactive. It was the only thing he had not allowed himself in prior instances.

He had thought it a luxury. Now he recognized it for what it was. Necessary. If he wanted Julia, he would have to use his emotions as his barometer, not rationale. This was not the time for mental negotiations.

Now was the time for action.

Their noses were on keen alert as they made their way toward a remote spot on the Olympic Peninsula. William had chosen the runners for ancestry instead of warrior prowess.

They could all shift.

As they did now.

To the casual observer, it would look like black wings and bodies, flying against the backdrop of the night's sky.

Only the eyes would give an observer pause.

Crimson.

Like blood.

CHAPTER 30

CATALYST

*J*ulia rolled over onto her side, her body shuddering in response. She realized she'd made the gravest, most novice mistake in the world. She had drunk water from a creek. Untreated. Did her Alaskan upbringing teach her nothing?

Dumb!

She had Beaver Fever. Julia had consumed a ton of creek water and now it felt like someone was taking her insides out with a spoon. Worse, she wasn't throwing up or the other. Oh no. But a fine fever was there, securing a good foothold.

Climbing higher.

Julia remembered when she was young, her mother had said she was a "burner." One of those kids that got rid of being sick by jerking their core temperature up to an insanely dangerous level.

Like now.

Julia shivered, crawling back into the crevice of an old log. The wooden embrace was full of sodden leaves and God knows what else. She flung her arm out, bending it at the elbow to fit inside the tight space. She shuddered, as she put the bare skin of her forehead against the cold wetness of her jacket, dampened by her environment.

Julia fell into a fitful doze, her body intermittently shaking from exhaustion and sickness. She was completely vulnerable and alone.

The cougar knew that, having scented its prey in the meadow. It followed the female back to where she lay inside a downed log in the forest. The cougar slunk closer, knowing that the prey was weakened. And safely inside its territory.

The cougar prowled toward the log.

It scented danger too late.

The werewolves moved in with typical stealth, tearing the cat's large head off its shoulders even as it turned to swipe. They executed the maneuver with precision and accuracy. Wasting nothing, they feasted on the most delicate part of their kill, leaving the remainder for possible consumption later. They were wary. Many scents were all around them. The enemy... and others.

What lay within the folds of the log was too precious for dispatch from the dumb creature of the forest.

A lowly cat no less.

They moved to the log, peering inside.

* * *

vampire

THE RAVENS LIT upon the branches of the trees. They had not discovered the scent of the Singer, but that of the dogs. Circling the position, spying the group of four Were with the sharpness of their eyesight in raven form, they settled on the highest branches. William sent out an alert to the others, a single cawing tone of specific meaning. They fell to the ground as a well-oiled machine, from thirty of forty feet of height, their wings melting into deadened flesh and bone as they dropped. It was a beautiful symphony of purposeful landing which began with feathers and ended with feet which touched the earth with a thud-less hop, silent.

But not silent enough.

The Alpha amongst the Were snapped his head up, his senses on full alert. His snout swung toward the three he'd brought with him and turned to his first, giving a snort. The other Were scooped the girl out of the log. The Alpha scented her sickness and paused. She was very ill. He breathed deeper, maybe not permanent? It didn't matter, the time to move was now.

He moved in the opposite direction of the scent he'd caught that accompanied the noise.

Vampire.

They would not recapture his precious cargo.

They began to move away in battle formation, the Alpha at their back, his half-formed hands at the ready, the Rare One in the arms of his second.

* * *

the Feral

THE FERAL MOVED *from his discovery with precision and energy, the meal he'd consumed affording him the speed and agility that would be necessary to find the female.*

He knew he should never have left her. She had escaped him. Judging by the tracks in the rock cave he'd found, she had wiggled out. Her small frame had allowed maneuverability.

The feral ran hard, smoothly evading every obstacle, his form perfectly suited for the environment in which he traveled.

He hit upon her scent and stopped short. It had changed.

She was sickened by something. He scented deeper. She had

drunk water and had the sickness that humans were susceptible to. It was not possible for him to be affected. He moved forward, scenting the many nuanced odors which preceded him.

He welcomed the challenge of their presence. There would need to be many to keep him from the female.

Mine, his mind said.

Mine.

* * *

Scott

SCOTT STOPPED SUDDENLY. His hands went to the hard planes of his stomach. "What is it?" Jen asked, her breathing labored, they'd been near-running since they'd discovered Julia's disappearance.

Scott felt a dull pain in his guts, bowels and a burning in the back of his neck. He described it to Marcus and his father replied.

"She's sick and that's what you'd feel," his tone ominous, knowing.

Scott wanted to get moving but Marcus explained briefly, "A soul-meld is more than a pairing of Singers. It's an aware-ness of each other," he made his hands collide, the fingers lacing together. "She has encountered," he waffled his hand back and forth, "something and is ill."

Scott's teeth clenched together. This was just getting better and effing better.

"Well..." Brendan began. "She's sick alright and the Were have her again."

Scott's eyes locked with Brendan's, sweat running down between his shoulder blades, chilling as his skin dampened in the cool night air. Then Brendan said the thing that made Scott's blood run cold, "The feral is out there," he lifted his nose to the air, pushing a good amount of an invisible fragrance right underneath his nose with his palm, "vampire and werwolves."

"Wait! Flag on the play!" Jen yelled, throwing a flag on an imaginary football field.

They all turned to her. Jen planted her hands on her hips. "What... more werewolves? The feral and...?"

Brendan nodded. "Yeah, I'd recognize wet dog anywhere. And the red feral... he's his own tomato. The vampire, well... we know what they smell like."

"Shit," Scott responded definitively and began jogging in the direction they'd been heading, impatient to get to *her*.

"Scott!" Marcus yelled after his son.

Scott whirled around. "No! I'm not waiting another second. It's already been too many seconds."

The siblings all looked uneasily at each other, following Scott.

He couldn't think until he had Julia safe. His change of heart was breathtaking in its completeness.

* * *

Julia

JULIA MOANED, the constant rocking motion waking her. She wished she hadn't awoken. She looked up into a pair of eyes she hoped to never see again.

Tony. It didn't matter what form he was in, she'd recognize his stench anywhere.

She swore he grinned when he saw recognition dawn on her face.

Julia tried to struggle in his grasp but was too weak by far to do anything.

"Stay still," he said in a low growl, "you're sick."

Julia felt hot tears she couldn't afford to lose run down her face.

Helpless again. Grief crashed into her like an earthquake. It shook the very foundation of her soul and nothing but despondency remained.

Tony looked down at the flushed face of the Rare One. He could scent her displeasure at being held by him coming out of every pore of her body. Even if she'd been well, she couldn't have fought him. Except for her gifts she was helpless. Helplessly female and ill in an intoxicating mix that made his perverted heart speed. He could feel the presence of the Alpha at his back and didn't care.

Tony had never been one to follow rules.

He'd have her, squirming and fighting. It'd be amazing. He crushed her against himself and she made a pain sound, trying to beat at his chest weakly.

Scott felt a great hopelessness well up inside him that was so foreign to his nature he interpreted it for what it was.

Julia.

And on the top of it all, fear, discomfort and pain.

Someone was hurting her as she succumbed to illness. Scott's hands clenched into fists of rage. Fists which knew how to deliver punishment. And they would.

Soon.

Scott increased his pace to a sprint. His Singer strength, endurance and speed were on a par with the Were... and the vampire. His siblings and parent followed in a rainbow blur of colors, their hues mixing inexplicably as they drew closer to Julia. Their familial footprint as they advanced into battle was formidable.

Dangerous.

William and the others chased the trail laid by the Were as they ran, Julia's scent mingled with theirs. Her scent was off. Now that he had shifted back from raven form, his senses seemed almost dulled, even though he knew they were a hundred times more sensitive than those of humans.

He sped, every thought, every fiber of his being, trained to overtake them and rescue Julia.

The feral watched those of his kind take the female... sickened and unable to defend herself from the one Were which he hated most. The one who had taunted him. Given him hose showers that had bruised his skin with the force of the spray.

Given him prey that was spoiled or infirm.

Yes, he would know his foul odor anywhere.

A tingling rush of fighting adrenaline surged through him.

The feral charged from the left, crashing out of the brush, thinking two thoughts simultaneously:

They were nearly nose-blind to have not scented him this close. His step faltered for one half a second when he recognized the female Were he'd harmed in his pen, traveled with them. A moment's peace touched him as he realized she was whole and well again.

That peace fled as he barreled into the Were which led, his talons slicing the neck as he launched a counterstrike, one to four.

Joseph spun too late as the assault came at his third from the front and couldn't believe he hadn't scented another Were this close. It was completely unexpected. He growled at his sister, "Run!"

She would be crushed by the red, every protective instinct Joseph possessed punching to life, his reaction automatic.

Adi ignored her brother and ran toward where Tony held Julia, the feral having ripped three holes in the leading Were's vulnerable neck. As he dropped from the killing blow, his blood blanketing the forest like a carpet of crimson, Adriana leapt. As her arms were outstretched, Tony casually tossed Julia to the ground.

She landed in Adi's embrace and they fell together on the soft forest debris.

The feral met her eyes for one moment and she cringed backward, scooping Julia closer in her arms.

Her brother and Tony circled the red. His coat shone like fire burnt down to embers, and she knew they would kill him.

It made her chest tight to think it. Adi shook it off. What was wrong with her? He was feral.

He had hurt her.

But deep within, something stirred and responded to him, against every precept and instinct.

Adriana did not wish for his death.

She turned her attention to Jules. She was burning up, moaning and thrashing. Adrianna forced her human form to return, as difficult as it was to change to half-wolf, it hurt more to go back to human so quickly, a brutal energy siphon. But she didn't want Jules to see her and be afraid.

Adi held Jules in her arms as the feral and werewolves circled each other just as the vampire entered the glade and a troop of Singers broke out of the forest opposite them.

Oh shit! Adi thought... we'll never make it out of here alive.

Julia opened her eyes just then and her fevered stare latched onto Adriana. "Adi..." she said weakly.

"I'm here, Jules," she said, wiping sweaty strands of hair out of her face.

"Don't let them... hurt me..." Julia said.

Never, Adi thought, rolling the small bundle that was Julia into her embrace and standing without effort.

After all, she was a werewolf.

She faced off with the vampire and Singers, her grin looking like a wolf in sheep's clothing.

An apt comparison.

CHAPTER 31

RECKONING

Scott stared at the female werewolf that held Julia. Their queen. *His...* and growled. He didn't know where that primitive utterance had come from but he rolled with it instinctively. He saw the vamps at the same time the werewolves went after the big red guy.

Lots to do here. Scott was always game, his body practiced and ready for violence.

It moved forward of its own volition.

William saw the group of Singers and paused. His nostrils flared and he recognized something about the one which led, his scent was slightly different. William was a runner. He was bred to recognize the Rare Blood in Singers. Julia was pure. But this one, he had enough quantum for William to respond, every tracking instinct tingled inside him, even as Julia was in his sights.

Who was he?

William would soon find out as the one he stared at launched himself with the speed of a Singer who was trained, seasoned and in the prime of his life, his direction aimed for Julia.

Julia rose to consciousness as if swimming from the bottom of a pool but without the benefit of alertness. She was in a fog, the fever stealing her cognitive reasoning, making her slow and thick-feeling.

She watched the scene unfold from the cradle of Adi's arms.

Scott came toward Julia in a flash of brilliant color, the tailwind of colors behind him she intuited as the rest of his family. From Julia's left William and the vampire tore toward her, the feral howling in misery, the tone of it told her all she needed to know.

He drove to get to her, kept at bay by Tony and Joseph.

But maybe not for long.

Julia made the most difficult decision of her life but she knew it would solve the current problem instantly. Her mind sought what it needed and when she found it... the metal flashed in the gloom of the forest, making its way to her as if by invisible strings.

She grabbed the hilt of the stolen weapon, her telekinetic ability bringing it to her in a rush of surprise to all. The supernaturals in the forest stilled their movements.

The desired effect was instantaneous.

Marcus watched his utility knife, that he routinely wore at his hip, come unlatched and spin away from his body, lurching toward Julia.

Hilt first.

Julia caught it in her hand, flicked it open, held it to her own throat and screamed hoarsely, "Stop!"

Adi looked down at Julia. "No!"

"Let me down, Adi," her voice steady.

Adriana did, Julia sliding down the front of her body and swaying on her feet, her head swimming with pain and vertigo.

Julia looked at William, as still as a statue. "Do not," he

whispered. "None of us wish for this end, Julia. This is not the answer."

Scott stopped breathing when he saw the metal gleaming against the pale throat of the Queen of the Blood Singers. The fibers of his being pulled taut to the breaking point while his soul shrieked inside him. He made a move to step forward and Julia gaze shifted to his. "Don't even try it. I know you hate me," she hissed, her strength ebbing, her hand shaking from the strain of keeping it steady.

The fibers of his being cinched tighter in discomfort, her safety in jeopardy by her own hand. Scott stood poised to launch himself at her the moment her attention wavered, the pain of not touching her unbearable. It was unlike anything he'd ever known. Every bruise, every battle wound... nothing compared.

Julia backed away from all of them, her back touching the trunk of a tree. They stood, all eyes tracking her progress, knowing that a false move could end her life. Then what would they have? What would she be?

Dead is what.

As the tears began to flow, Julia realized that nothing good had happened to her since Jason's death. Her lower lip trembled and her hand shook as she determined that this was the best answer for her after all. She was tired.

So tired.

Joseph and Tony saw her expression first as they were the closest. But it was the feral who acted, his half-wolf form slipping off him like water sheeting off glass.

He sprang forward, human again for that moment.

The moment of truth.

Julia saw him and her heart stalled in her chest.

She dropped the knife, all thought of death forgotten.

It speared the earth at her feet and she staggered forward without thinking.

* * *

Kent

CYNTHIA THANKED the nice lady with the sad eyes for the room, nodding in all the right places when she told her it was but a transitional respite. Blah, blah, blah. Cynthia got it. A place to lay her head on a pillow, none of the creatures in sight. They couldn't have followed her all the way to the outskirts of Seattle. She breathed a sigh of relief for the first time in what felt like forever.

She opened the door to the dark room and saw a bunch of plaster repair and the evidence of damage all over the place. The lady turned to her, the chain that hung off her glasses catching the light. "Don't mind the mess, we're doing a touch of remodeling."

Cynthia looked around her. Looked like more than a touch. The window looked the worst. She walked over to it, seeing the remnants of hand-blown glass, wavy and warped, encased in a solid wood frame. Hairline fissures scattered about the center were taped so they couldn't splinter further. She turned her head and saw the old lady's face in profile. "What happened?"

The woman shrugged her shoulders, hauling the shawl she wore more firmly around her hunched shoulders. "We're not sure. But there was a young woman who stayed here a few months past..." she looked down at her sensible shoes, the pantyhose an unnatural tan color and suddenly looked up, guilt and a muted horror, contained like a stuffed sock riding her eyes. "She uh... we think she was taken."

Not much of a shelter! Cynthia thought, looking at the damage of the room more closely. She asked, "By who?"

The woman shrugged, backing carefully out of the room

and giving her a nod as she left, closing the door softly behind her. Conversation closed.

Cynthia looked at the windowsill more closely.

Her chest tightened in a gut clenching clutch of pain, her breath leaving her body.

She traced the marring left in the wood of the sill with a hand that shook so badly she grabbed it with its mate to steady it. She gave a shaky exhale.

It wasn't *who* took the girl.

But what.

Cynthia snatched her hand back. She looked outside, beyond the glass and the unkempt yard below to the forest. It was dark and quiet.

A perfect hiding place.

For *them*.

Cyn backed up until her legs hit the mattress and sat down. She stared at the window. It looked like she might have escaped one horror for another.

Breaking her stupor, she rummaged in her backpack until she found what she was looking for. She laid down on her back, her finger running over the one photo she had, a habit of comfort these almost two years past. She never missed a night without looking at them.

It was Vegas. Just the four of them: Jason and Jules, she and Kev.

Before.

She looked at Jules, dressed up for once, Jason's arm slung comfortably around her shoulders, like it belonged. Her eyes stung with unshed tears, hot and unwelcome as she looked at Kevin. When they ran down her face she didn't wipe them away, but pressed the photo against her chest.

Her heart.

She missed them so much, she felt like her heart would

never stop breaking. That's why her chest hurt so damned much all the time. A crack that wouldn't mend.

Her heart broken in shards inside her.

Cynthia covered the photo with both hands and put her head to the side of the pillow, stifling her sobbing from the other inhabitants of the women's shelter.

* * *

Truman

TRUMAN LOOKED AT ALEXANDER, their eyes meeting a final time. "I can't believe this. I know you're telling me all this but I can't..." Karl tapped his head.

"Wrap your head around it? Yeah, tell me about it!" Alexander responded, nodding.

Karl Truman fought the habit to take his small note pad out of its home in the upper pocket of his button down and clasped his hands together instead. "So they're..."

George Alexander nodded. "They're big suckers, standing on hind legs," he made his palm flat and put it a foot above his head, "that makes these guys about seven feet."

Truman whistled. "So, they're dexterous?"

"Very. They had no difficulty pawing through this apartment, turning knobs, unlatching windows. No," he paused, not a hint of humor in his voice, giving Truman the full weight of his eyes, "they used the doors and windows, they have higher reasoning, no doubt." George tapped his temple.

Truman paused, thinking about his words instead blurting just anything out. "How high?"

Alexander paused for a beat. "Maybe like us... maybe," he scratched his head and turned his back on Truman, pacing off to the window, gazing at the forest that stretched interminably beyond their position, "... they are something else."

"What are you saying George?" Truman walked up to him, getting right in his grill. He was going to spill this info if it killed him. His green eyes met Truman's.

"I'm saying we have real life werewolves."

Truman staggered back a step. "No," he denied, getting a physical reaction of heat climbing his body uncomfortably. His mind had spun around the possibility of it, eventually dismissing it as too unreal.

Alexander paced toward him, ticking off the facts on his hand, "Canine genome, DNA match, size, aggression, higher reasoning..." then after a pause, he let the final bomb drop, "the saliva tells us the final piece."

Real enough.

Truman leaned forward despite not wanting to, his heart in his throat, the evidence warring with his disbelief over anything that was not concrete, normal.

Sane.

"Human genome," George Alexander said quietly.

Truman stared at Alexander and he returned it, the moment swelled with portentous knowledge, belief solidifying.

Half human, half wolf.

Werewolf.

Alexander was reminded of one of the first precepts he had learned in med school, *when you hear hoofbeats behind you, don't expect to see a zebra.*

In this case, that's all he heard.

Zebras.

CHAPTER 32

*J*ason. Maybe her eyes deceived her but Julia's heart knew. She had watched as the feral melted away and a nearly naked Jason ran to her, staving off her killing blow.

She crashed into him, her arms snapping around him. His body felt at once shocking familiar and foreign in her embrace.

It was a moment before she knew something was wrong as pandemonium broke loose all around her. The different factions came together at once in a collision of claws, talons and speed.

Julia was prone on her back before she could move, breathe. Jason's now-human hands encircled her throat, her feverish skin burning against his cooler flesh. She frantically searched eyes that didn't know her, crazed and full of heat and hate.

Who was he now? Julia shrieked inside her head.

Her head swam and she began to grow dizzy, her stomach cramping as Jason... her husband from another life, another time... began to choke her to death.

Scott saw the feral return to his human state and launch himself at Julia. Scott bounded toward the feral werewolf just as he began to strangle Julia. The feral's mind was obviously broken.

William understood who it was the instant the red Were changed into human form. He had seen photos of Julia's former husband. But this was no longer the husband she knew, his mind was gone, the wolf in control even while human. Few Singers could overcome the transition to Were or vampire. It was never attempted, the results at this moment a confirmation of the dangerous consequence. The theory borne into fruition.

William charged Jason Caldwell at the precise moment as Joseph and Tony.

The vampire and Were collided and the forest grew still except for the sounds of flesh tearing and the battering of one against the other. Scott landed on the back of the Singer, aiming a blow to stun him, the vamps and Were fighting behind him, his siblings making a protective wall around him.

Jason felt the blow on the base of his neck, numbing in its accuracy and force, he began to slide away from the woman who he'd been strangling.

He recognized her too late.

Jason fell beside her, meeting her eyes.

Puzzle pieces of memories coming from a blizzard that twirled without pattern to a solid stream of consciousness.

This was not any female.

This was his wife.

Julia.

What had he done? He moved to get up and one of his kind leaped on his chest, knocking the wind out of him.

But not before her eyes had met his and Jason saw the one that had hit him pick Julia up as the Were and vampire beat each other into the forest floor, blood covering everything under five feet in a spinning tornado of gore.

Black and red ran together like a poisonous lake. He watched the blood of his kind and that of his enemy run together, his consciousness slipping away, the blow's accuracy successful in its intent.

Jason's last memory was Julia being taken from him in the arms of a large man, others like him surrounded them in a cocoon of protection, the vampire and Were dying and worse all around him.

He turned his head and looked at the female Were above him as his eyes closed, exhaustion from the Change and the revelation of what he'd done and who he was dropping him like a stone in a tumultuous sea of nothingness.

Jason fell away from her and Julia sucked in a lungful of precious air, a hitching sob the next sound that escaped, her abused throat on fire.

Jason had tried to kill her! It was worse than his death. He lived but wasn't him!

Two palms cradled her face and forced her to focus on the one who had saved her from certain death. First by her own hand, then the death that had been promised by a kiss of hands that had once loved her.

The electric shock of Scott's hands against Julia's skin instantly cooled the fever and stopped the internal turmoil of her stomach's roil. She felt him lift her from the ground, strong arms wrapped her against his body and he turned, a silent command which felt like intent rose from him like a sigh and the others gathered around him like soldiers.

Julia's head burrowed against his chest, her eyes just clearing his strong arm where they met the stare of Tony, dead vampire at his feet. William was nowhere to be seen.

Joseph was dead as well.

Tony was the new Alpha.

Fear rose in her instantly. Scott ran in the opposite direction and the group they left behind became smaller in her vision, Jason and Adi on the forest floor together. Jason unconscious and unaware, his head held by Adi.

Adriana's eyes were all for Tony, the victor over the vampire, his sights solely on Julia.

Tony threw his head back and howled into the still air of the forest, his rage filling Julia's ears, reverberating inside her soul like a discordant note of music.

Scott's arms pulsed around Julia once, tightening with protection.

Scott picked up his pace. The mongrel would never touch her again.

He'd stake his life on it.

THE END

But the adventure doesn't stop here! 🐭 [**Continue the journey with *Blood Song***] HERE. *If you loved Savage 1-3, you won't be able to put down the next chapter!*

⭐⭐⭐⭐⭐"**Wonderful Sequel!!**" ~*A Book Vacation*

. . .

👉 NEVER MISS A NEW RELEASE! Join TRB News for exclusive updates, early access, and special offers.

📚 YOUR WORDS ARE POWERFUL! If you enjoyed *Blood Singers*, please share your star rating and thoughts to help other readers discover their next favorite author. *Thank you!*

Continue your journey with more of TRB/Marata Eros' thrilling novels:

THE PEARL SAVAGE

⭐⭐⭐⭐⭐ "A real page-turner!"

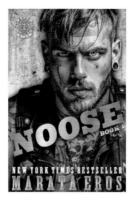

NOOSE

"Raw, edgy... graphically painted."

BLOOD SINGERS

"One hell of a ride!"

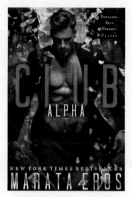

CLUB ALPHA

⭐⭐⭐⭐⭐"It's action-packed and so suspenseful....

THE FIFTH WIFE

⭐⭐⭐⭐⭐"Absolutely fantastic dark taboo toxic romance.
Loved it…"

THROUGH DARK GLASS

⭐⭐⭐⭐⭐"One of the best and I have read many!"

BROLACH

⭐⭐⭐⭐⭐"...oh hot hot **hot**..."

The Token 1 - Provocation

★★★★★ **Crazy good**. It draws you in..."

EMBER

★★★★★ "This story is... **explosive!**"

HER: A LOVE STORY

⭐⭐⭐⭐⭐"Emotively moving - gripping and *sensual*..."

THE REFLECTIVE

⭐⭐⭐⭐⭐"'...futuristic writing, hard characters, **powerful...**"

REAPERS

⭐⭐⭐⭐⭐"One of the **best**!"

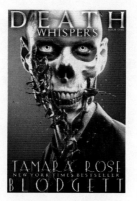

DEATH WHISPERS

⭐⭐⭐⭐⭐"HUNGER GAMES, 50 SHADES and DIVERGENT, anyone?"

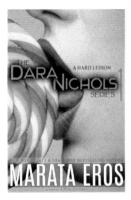

A HARD LESSON

" ... HOT! HOT! HOTTT...!

PUNISHED

"**Unputdownable from Start to Finish!**"

Enjoy a special treat! Read on for an **exclusive bonus chapter** from one of Tamara Rose Blodgett's unforgettable stories...

BONUS MATERIAL

BLOOD SONG
A BLOOD WORLD NOVEL
BOOK 2

NEW YORK TIMES BESTSELLER
TAMARA ROSE BLODGETT

WWW.TAMARAROSEBLODGETT.COM

* * *

*T*he pain was beyond what she could easily deal with, her guts twisting without mercy. Julia dry heaved into the commode for the twelfth time as Jen held her hair away from her face.

Jen stabbed a wet washcloth in front of her and Julia grabbed it, swabbing the inside of her mouth.

"You're gonna need some food and water..." Jen began to nag.

Julia held up her hand like a stop sign, "No water," she whispered, her hair falling forward again in limp strands.

Jen rolled her eyes. *Can we have some GD self-preservation already?* she wondered.

"Listen, Julia... we have regular tap water here, ya know, you're not gonna get the shats," Jen said, straightening.

Julia groaned, gripping her stomach with her hands. "Listen," Jen's voice softened, "let our Healer have a look."

"I'll be okay," Julia shuddered as someone began to pound on the door.

"Yeah... ya look *so good,*" Jen agreed sarcastically, noticing how pale Julia was, how her hands trembled as she pushed her hair behind her ears. Shock, dehydration and lack of food covered her like a well-worn coat.

"Hey!" Scott shouted from the other side of the door. "What's going on in there!" The door shuddered under the assault of his fist.

Julia rolled over on her back, the cool hexagon-shaped tile pressing against her feverish cheek as she threw her forearm over her eyes. "Tell him to take a hike!" Julia hissed.

Jen grinned. If it weren't for the circumstances this would be truly wonderful. She had never thought she'd live to see the day when her asshat brother would get all flustered and brought to heel with a soul-meld.

Bliss.

The door shuddered again from his pounding. "Julia!" Jen heard the frantic note in his deep voice and walked to the door.

"Quit it! She's okay," Jen said through the door, loving his discomfort in a way that was barely legal.

"Let me in, sister," Scott delivered with quiet menace.

Fine, she thought, sighing. Jen wrapped her hand around the glass knob and it rattled as she turned it.

Jen swung the door open and Scott roared past her into the bathroom where Julia lay on the floor.

Scott had sat on his hands all morning, worried about Julia, hating it. *Hating her.*

She'd irrevocably changed his life and it didn't matter that Julia was his, the whole thing had been thrust on him. But Scott couldn't stop thinking about her. He could feel an echo of her pain, her emotions.

It was kinda suffocating.

She was ill and his body moved to where she was like a satellite come to orbit. Where Julia was Scott needed to be. His emotions didn't really matter.

The loss of choice is what got on Scott's last nerve.

Though that riot of emotion began to slip away when he saw the Queen of the Blood Singers on the floor, looking pale and fragile, her warm blond hair acting as a silken rug around her. Julia was so weak she didn't even acknowledge his presence, her face in profile, one cheek pressed against the bathroom floor.

Scott could feel her indifference, as Julia could feel his contrary emotions.

Soul-meld stuff.

But it was her plight that spurred Scott to move to her side, his big frame folding beside her.

Julia looked up at Scott and fought the soul-meld, even as

their insides came together in a perfectly synchronized mesh of relief. Their parting was not a natural situation.

Their unity was.

She watched his hand move to brush a hair away from her face and Julia said, "Don't," in a low voice.

"Why?" Scott asked, frustration creeping into his tone.

"Because I know you don't want to," she replied, still lying on her back.

"Julia... don't look at me like that." His eyes bore down on hers with care, concern and anger.

Julia hiked herself up, glaring at him when he moved to help her, his hand falling away. When she was upright she said, "I'll look at you any way I want. After all," she cocked her head and pegged him with her bourbon eyes, smoldering with heat, hatred, "soulmates, right?" she spat with derision.

Jen sucked in the oxygen that remained in the room.

It wasn't much.

"Actually, it's soul-meld," Jen stated unhelpfully.

Julia gave her a withering look.

"Feeling better, pet?" Jen asked with sarcasm.

"No!" Julia said. Then glared at Scott harder. Just having him close to her had regulated her body. The illness from her creek episode was there but his nearness eased her physically.

She effing hated it.

Scott's eyes narrowed on her, Julia's body language clear and resolute. How could he be bound to her? He was definitely not the committing type.

He didn't choose this path.

Julia read his expression. "Don't worry about it Scott. You were the Big Ass Protector. You've done your Boy Scout Duty, you can dump my ass now."

"Julia," Jen threw up her hands, feeling sorry for her brother against her will.

No... nothing was stopping him, Scott thought, his eyes roving her angry features, those golden eyes flashing at him inside her pale face. He could feel how sick she was but more than sickness, Julia was stubborn.

His body ached to make hers right, Scott's hands clenched at his sides in the effort not to touch her.

It wasn't about choice. Fate had chosen for them. Through blood. Through destiny.

They were blood chosen.

And Julia was his.

His to protect, his to take care of.

Eventually, his to love.

It was a mandate from deep in the fiber of his being, inexplicable... irrefutable. As Scott looked at the thunderous expression on Julia's face... *so* obviously against her will.

"She won't see the healer," Jen told Scott.

"The hell she won't," he stared at Julia and she glared back.

"You can't make me!" she yelled, two feet away from his face.

"Well, sweetheart," Scott said, placing his palms on either side of her hips and leaning into her personal bubble, he loomed over her, "we're not in Kindergarten anymore and You. Will. Be. Healed," he roared at her, the fine hairs by her temple moving with the power behind his voice. Shame washed over him when he felt her response as a hiccup of fear.

Julia was scared of him.

Scott backed away as she continued to stare at him.

"Argh!" Scott grunted in frustration to her anxiety, raking his hand through his hair, her eyes holding something more than her irritation.

Fear. Fear of him.

Scott stalked off, slamming the door behind him and Julia

collapsed on the cold tile again, the hot tears she shed warming the coolness beneath her, the small energy she'd received from Scott's presence departing like smoke through a crack, and with it, her vitality.

Julia fell asleep where she lay, in a small heap on the bathroom floor, tears sticking to fevered flesh. Her dreams played like a sick nightmare she couldn't escape from.

* * *

Scott

SCOTT PACED in front of his father, Marcus, the leader of Region One of Blood Singers.

He threw up his hand, the energy from his anger racing around the office inside the Learning Compound and pinging back to the pair like a blazing boomerang of emotion.

Marcus stood, his coal black hair so like the son's. Scott charged back and forth in the small space like a bull with a red cape waved in front of him.

"Calm down!" Marcus roared in a voice full of command, authority. Marcus did not need to yell to be heard. As a point of fact, he knew that authority was not about control gained through violence and shouts, but respect through experience.

Scott stopped, his chest heaving, his hands buried in the front of his jean's pockets, his jet-black brows dropped like a brick over eyes that were so dark a brown they were like chocolate ink.

"Why?!" Scott shouted. "I was fucking fine without this," he ripped his hands out of his jeans and flung one toward the house where Julia was.

Still ill. Her sickness pressed on him like a weight he couldn't bear. It was all he could do to not be next to her.

Taking care of her.

"Language, Scott," Marcus said.

"Dad... come on."

"You are twenty-five years old and can use whatever colorful metaphors that come to mind. But bear in mind there are many here now who look to you as an example." Marcus spread his hands away from his body, imploring his eldest to see reason.

It would be the plow against a tough field. Of all his offspring, Scott was the most stubborn.

"They're not here now and I don't stand as an example before you."

"Good habits begin now, Scott," Marcus stated.

Scott bowed his head, reining his anger in. When a full two minutes had passed he locked gazes with his father.

"Did you know?" Scott looked at him with a dumbstruck expression. "Did you know this was real? That I would be a part of this dumbass destiny equation?"

Marcus stared at him. He deliberated, but in the end he decided the time had come to tell Scott the truth.

Scott watched his dad fold his hands behind his back and many things happened at once: Julia took a turn for the worse, he could feel his sister coming for him and his father had a look that said that there was a grave secret.

Scott literally felt like a fist was clenching in his guts. *Julia*, his soul whispered.

He was helpless; Scott did the only thing he could.

He went to her.

* * *

William

WILLIAM FELT his jaw flutter from clenching it so tightly and slammed his fist down on the table that had stood in the same position for the hundred years he had been part of this coven. It shook beneath his rage, rattling.

"How can you just..." he waffled his hand from side to side, Gabriel's glower telling him of his apathy, "let her go," William finished in a low voice.

Gabriel stood, as tall as William at six foot one and as their noses nearly kissed, Gabriel turned the tables on William with, "How many must perish for one?"

Damn, he's got me there, William thought.

William shoved the black hair from his gray eyes, his gaze darkening to pewter. "She is a Rare One. We must sacrifice much for her," William argued logically, his eyes searching Gabriel's, praying for a break, a flicker of anything that might advance him toward another rescue attempt.

"William, I *do* know how you feel about Julia," Gabriel began but William interrupted him.

"You do not," William warned in a voice warmed by raw emotion. As if the hundreds of years he had lived as vampire without emotion had suddenly caught up and come crashing down on him at once.

Gabriel sighed in frustration. He did not wish to give her up any more than William. But her presence within the coven had already cost them over thirty vampires. Soon, there would not be enough left for her prophesied abilities and traits to help their species. Julia Caldwell had become a liability.

Claire came forward and touched her cousin's arm. William stared at her; he found the intrusion unwelcome.

As Claire began to speak the males listened, William the most reluctantly. When she was done William's head hung.

"I refuse it." William looked from one to the other of them. "She is part of me." He put a fist to his heart. "Do you not see it?" he asked, looking at Claire who had tried to reason him out of going after Julia again. Loving her.

He could not be reasoned with.

William would not.

"Do you not feel it?" he asked, his vampiric voice reverberating in the enclosed space, stone walls all around them, the sound beating Gabriel and Claire's eardrums like a subtle weapon. Claire covered her ears, wincing and William inclined his head in apology. "I am sorry, but I cannot be governed by numbers. Julia is not a number to me." His gaze pierced them like lasers beams that tore the skin aside, seeking marrow. "Her blood is a chorus of voices that sing to my soul." William locked gazes with the leader of his kiss.

"I will never be in harmony as long as she is not with me."

William stalked out of the room, banging the solid wood door behind him with a resounding shudder.

"It is the blood-share," Claire said mournfully. "He is lost because of her blood."

"It is much more than that," Gabriel said as he slipped a most modern device out of the pocket of the black slacks he wore.

Claire gave him a quizzical look and he shushed her with a look.

Gabriel had a plan.

William would eventually forgive him.

Someday.

* * *

Northwestern Pack

LAWRENCE WAS AT A COMPLETE LOSS. His primary Alpha, Joseph, had been killed during the failed acquisition of the

330

Rare One, his sister was out of her mind with grief, and he had the Feral and Anthony at each other's throats.

Literally.

Sometimes, he wished for any job other than the one he held.

Instead, he showed up and executed his position as Packmaster of the Northwestern den. Even if it killed him.

Which it almost certainly would someday.

His morbid joke notwithstanding, it was time to establish order in the pack once again.

He looked at Adrianna, the most Alpha female he had ever met and felt a pang of sympathy. Normally, her abrasive nature was so punishing on his senses he was fine with his brusque treatment of her in return. But two things stood in the way of his usual tactics with her.

One, she was the most eligible female wolf in the den. Two, her brother had just died before her eyes. Murdered by their most grievous enemies.

Brutally.

Then, as females went, she had lost the Rare One and now had a double loss to contend with there. Moonless abilities aside, the Rare One had almost been more trouble than she was worth.

Almost.

Lawrence's gaze flicked to the Feral.

Right, he self-corrected, *Jason,* his mind restated. Yes, the Singer's husband.

Unconsummated. He and Tony had an intimate discussion on *smells.* And as the case may be, now that Tony had a firm grasp on both the Feral's scent and that of the Blood Singer, Julia, he was beyond certain they did not co-mingle.

Lawrence was not privy to the intricacies of their relationship. Only that they had not allowed the circle of their vows to close. This was a crucial detail to the Were.

Lawrence thought, not for the first time, how terrible it had been that Julia had been taken on the eve of the Ritual of Luna. If they could have just....

Ah! He shook his head, his thoughts turning to the mess at hand. The arguing before him a sure distraction.

It was Tony and the spry Alpha female (as usual), Adrianna- *Adi*. Lawrence sighed, flicking another glance at the Fer... *Jason*. His body was stock-still and his deep hazel eyes were hooded. They were distant and... contemplative.

Lawrence shouted above the two, "Enough!"

Adi turned, "I will not be under Tony!" she huffed, folding her arms underneath her breasts.

"Yes you will," Tony said in a voice so low she could barely make it out. Lawrence did not hear the softly spoken dark promise he made. Jason did, his eyes shifting to Tony, still Jason kept his own counsel.

He wasn't talking about hierarchy, the dick hole, Adi knew. He was talking about putting it to her.

"You'll never touch me, with your dick or anything else!" Adi yelled at him, frustrated. She knew that Lawrence hadn't heard the sexual threat. But she had. It had been meant for her.

"Adi!" Lawrence roared, pegging her with his gaze. "Stop this behavior. He is your dominant. You must understand that now that Joseph is... gone," he swallowed over the awkward wording, "that there must be another to replace him. It is the way of it. As it has been for millennia." Lawrence's gaze softened and Adi responded, switching tactics for once and trying to be a female instead of an Alpha.

It wasn't a simple transition.

"Please... Packmaster," her eyes flicked to Tony's, "he means me harm."

Lawrence scoffed, *foolish female*, he thought, but he schooled his expression for her benefit. Adi saw the flicker of the emotion on his face and knew she'd lost before he uttered his next words, "He would never harm a female Were, Adi. Think on it." Lawrence searched her face, waiting. Finally, when she didn't reply out of sheer disbelief and stubbornness, Lawrence added, "There are too few of you to ever trifle with your safety or protection. As it was, your brother did not show good judgment when he took you along on the raid for the Singer." Lawrence met Tony's eyes. "It is a mark in Anthony's favor that you were returned unharmed."

Adi seethed in frustration, her wolf roiling dangerously close beneath her skin, stretched taut to bursting. Tony would be *him* and Lawrence would allow it with Joseph no longer serving as a buffer. Adi turned to the Feral and his nostrils flared, picking up her scent change. And she suddenly remembered when he had awoken in her arms only to be knocked into Timbuktu by Tony, who was only too happy to do it.

They couldn't have him popping her arm off like his favorite drumstick again.

Although, Adi didn't have the sense of that anymore. *His desperation to escape and be feral had slid away*, she thought. Adi studied Jason Caldwell in human form with his borrowed jeans and a T-shirt that read, *When there's no more room in Hell, the dead will walk the earth.* It didn't nail her funny bone in the slightest: A) there were no such thing as zombies and it was the lamest thing on the planet to consider it B) she was spoiling for a fight. Her good humor had deserted her. He stared blankly back. Jason made no effort to speak, having ignored everyone and everything. Including her. He was almost robotic.

Where the hell was he in there? she thought, searching those brooding eyes.

Why did he go after Julia? Wasn't he in love with her? Adi

would never forget the look on her face when she told Adi about their romance, their secret marriage.

That horrible night when he was attacked and apparently killed by the Were.

Presumed dead.

But not. No, now he was a rare red Were. One of very few. Of course, it wasn't every damn day when Singers got turned into *other*. Whether it be drinker or claw.

Adi would never forget the look on Julia's face when he decided to choke her to death either.

Where was she now? And who in the blue fuck were those crazy-ass Singers that had shown up, kicked ass and taken names?

What was their fairy tale story?

Lots of questions, not enough answers.

Story of her damn life.

Read more

ACKNOWLEDGMENTS

I published both **The Druid** *and* **Death Series**, in 2011 with the encouragement of my husband, and continued because of you, my Reader. Your faithfulness through comments, suggestions, spreading the word and ultimately purchasing my work with your hard-earned money gave me the incentive, means and inspiration to continue.

There are no words that are sufficiently adequate to express my thankfulness for your support.

I truly feel connected to my readers. It is obvious to me, but I'll say the words anyway for clarity: a written work is just words on pages if they are not read by my readers. As I write this I get a lump in my throat; your enjoyment of my work affects me that deeply.

You guys are the greatest, each and every one of ya~

Tamara xoxo

Special thanks:
You, my reader.
My husband, who is my biggest fan.
"*Bird*," without who, there would be no books.

Special mention:
Jackie
Dawn
Susan

Erica
Liz
Cherri-Anne
Theresa
Bev
Phyllis
Eric

ABOUT THE AUTHOR

www.tamararoseblodgett.com

<u>**Tamara Rose Blodgett**</u>: happily married mother of four sons. Dark thriller writer. Reader. Dreamer. Beachcombing slave. Tie dye zealot. Digs music.

She is also the ***New York Times*** bestselling author of <u>***A Terrible Love***</u>, written under the pen name, Marata Eros, and

75+ other novels. Other bestseller accolades include her #1 bestselling **TOKEN** (dark romance), **DRUID** (dark PNR erotica), **ROAD KILL MC** (thriller/top 100) **DEATH** (sci-fi dark fantasy) series. Tamara writes a variety of dark fiction in the genres: erotica, fantasy, horror, romance, sci-fi, suspense and thriller. She splits her time between the Pacific NW and Mazatlán Mexico, spending time with family, friends and a pair of disrespectful dogs.

To be the first to hear about new releases and bargains—from Tamara Rose Blodgett/Marata Eros—sign up below to be on my VIP List. (I swear I won't spam or share your email with anyone!)

SIGN UP TO BE ON THE **TAMARA ROSE BLODGETT** VIP LIST

HERE

Connect with Tamara:

Clapper (*a TicTok alternative*) 31K followers

Rumble (*Free audiobooks/ Tin Foil Crown thoughts*)

Website

YouTube

Follow Marata Eros on Bookbub

Follow Tamara Rose Blodgett on Bookbub

ALSO BY TAMARA ROSE BLODGETT

 **Read more titles from this author**

A Terrible Love (NYT & USA Today bestseller)

The Reflective – REFLECTION

Punished– ALPHA CLAIM

Death Whispers – DEATH

The Pearl Savage - SAVAGE

Blood Singers– BLOOD

Noose – ROAD KILL MC

Provocation – TOKEN

Ember – SIREN

Brolach – DEMON

Reapers - DRUID

Club Alpha – BILLIONAIRE'S GAME TRILOGY

Dara Nichols Volume 1 – DARA NICHOLS (18+)

Her

BLOOD GLOSSARY

Blood Singers/Talents:
- **Julia:** Queen of the Singers; Telekinetic/telepath.
- **Jason:** Singer; Talent undisclosed.
- **Scott:** Royal Singer Blood; Deflector/Combatant.
- **Brendan:** Tracker/pyrokinetic.
- **Michael:** Illusionist.
- **Jen:** Telekinetic.
- **Cyrus:** Healer.
- **Paul:** Negator/amplifier.
- **Angela:** Feeler (empath).
- **Marcus:** Region One Leader.
- **Jacqueline:** Royal Singer Blood; Region Two Leader.
- **Victor:** Region Two; Combatant; Boiler/Flame of Blood.
- **Lucius:** Combatant.
- **Cynthia "Cyn" Adams:** Rogue; Healer.
- **Heidi:** Reader (clairvoyant).
- **Trevor:** Deflector.

Northwestern Were Pack:
- **Lawrence:** Packmaster.

- **Emmanuel "Manny":** Beta to Lawrence.
- **Anthony "Tony" Daniel Laurent:** Second to Lawrence.
- **Adrianna "Adi":** Alpha female.

Southeastern Were Pack:

- **David:** Packmaster.
- **Alan Greene:** Alpha male.
- **Lacey Greene:** Sister and female Were to Alan.
- **Buck "Slash":** Alpha male.
- **Karl Truman:** Former Homer detective.
- **Ford:** Alpha male; FBI agent.

Southeastern Vampire Kiss:

- **Merlin:** Coven Leader (now deceased).
- **William:** New Coven Leader.

Northwestern Vampire Kiss:

- **Gabriel:** Coven Leader.
- **Claire:** Cousin to William.

Unseelie Fey:

- **Queen Darcel:** Sidhe.
- **Tharell:** Mixed Sidhe Warrior.
- **Cormack:** Sidhe Warrior.
- **Domi:** Sidhe Warrior.
- **Rex:** Sidhe.
- **Kiel (key-ale):** Dragon-shifting Sidhe.
- **Celesta:** Sidhe Warrior.

FEDS:

- **Tom Harriet:** Agent.
- **Tai (Tie) Simon:** Agent.

BLOOD SINGERS

A Blood World Novel

Book 1

New York Times BESTSELLER

TAMARA ROSE BLODGETT

Paperback Edition

ISBN: 9781469970332

Made in United States
Cleveland, OH
18 January 2025

13517729R00206